The
Treehouse
on
Dog River Road

The
Treehouse
on
Dog River Road

A Novel

CATHERINE DRAKE

SHE WRITES PRESS

Published 2022
Printed in the United States of America
Print ISBN: 978-1-64742-351-3
E-ISBN: 978-1-64742-352-0
Library of Congress Control Number: 2021921737

For information, address:
She Writes Press
1569 Solano Ave #546
Berkeley, CA 94707

She Writes Press is a division of SparkPoint Studio, LLC.

Treehouse sketch drawn by Bridget Phillips
Book design by Stacey Aaronson

For Diane

JUNE

One

I'm against it, but I'm not above it. Hannah walked to her car, parked in a handicap spot at the crowded service area, and considered how often those words came to her. It was at little times, like this, or when she obsessively checked her likes on social media or threw apple cores out the car window. And more significant times. Calling in sick when she was hungover. One-night stands. Her career choice.

Clutching a chocolate croissant, she set her coffee on the car's roof and rifled through her purse for her car keys. The car was jammed tight with boxes and bags, loose items wedged between them. She was unable to use her rearview mirror or see out the windows, and it was a miracle she had been able to navigate the crowded downtown streets. It was a beautiful morning, though, clear skies and crisp air.

Hannah entered her car, slammed the door shut, and put the key into the ignition. As she silently sipped her coffee, a tiny wave of anxiety prevented her from starting the vehicle. How could she leave Boston? This was her home. This was where she grew up, where her friends were, her life, her future opportunities. She took another bite of the croissant. Her going-away party at work had been fun—cake in the break room, followed by drinks at the bar in the lobby of their building, the small group of well-dressed, energetic, mostly under forty-five investment bankers and analysts toasting her. But it had also been a repeat of every farewell for every laid-off employee since the merger was announced. She drank way too much and said some things she regretted about the lack of humanity in their work. And why —*why*—did she make out with Daniel?

She took a deep breath and looked at the sticky note on the dashboard: IF YOU WILL IT, IT IS NO DREAM. The wisdom of *The Big Lebowski* always calmed her down. And besides, now she had a plan. Okay, not so much a plan, but a plan to consolidate all her other plans. That was the plan. Realizing she was still parked illegally, she started the engine. *I'll be fine, and it'll all work out.* That's what her momma always said.

A few minutes later, she was out of rush-hour traffic and settled onto the interstate, heading north and ready to commence her "car dreams." Car dreams always made a long trip bearable. On long car trips, she and her older sister Molly would listen to their parents talk about things as if children were not in the back seat. Home improvements were debated, future vacations imagined, and new hobbies envisioned. "Alaska," her mother, Elizabeth, said on one such drive. "We should go there before the girls get too old." Most car dreams, such as the idea to build a wine cellar in their basement after a trip to wineries in Napa, never materialized. Thus, Hannah couldn't believe it when she found herself squeezed into a helicopter, landing on a glacier in Alaska the following summer. Hannah told her family that she figured Alaska was just a "car dream," and a family saying was coined.

However, on this car trip, Hannah's dreams were not about fantasy vacations but of the unknown chasm that was her future. The past few weeks felt a little foggy at this point; it all happened so fast. How exactly had she ended up here?

It started with her sister Molly, of course, and Molly's husband, Ted. Three weeks ago, Hannah had been with her best friend and roommate Sara watching *The Bachelor* when her sister called with the news. Molly and Ted lived in Waterbury, Vermont, and were both biologists who taught at different colleges. Ted, an evolutionary biologist, had received a long-desired grant to do research on invasive species in Patagonia. Ted would be going to South America for nearly the whole summer, living in remote locations, backpacking, ice-hiking, and doing challenging field research. It would be winter in South America, so there was also hope for some challenging skiing. Molly wanted to go with him and spend time working on *her* research—worldwide deforestation and climate change. As avid scientists and outdoors people, it would be a dream come true for both to go. As parents of two small children, it left them completely conflicted. There was no way the children could come along.

In a stunning display of impulsiveness, Hannah volunteered to take care of the kids for the summer. Following the announcement of a merger and buyout, layoffs at the Lyman Group, where she had worked for the last three years, had been rumored for weeks. She had no idea what she would do if she were to be let go. Taking care of the kids for the summer could offer her the chance to plot out her next step. She figured her expenses over the summer would be minimal and hoped that her six months of savings could tide her over until she got a job. Her biggest expense would be the payments on her student loan. Still, since making the decision, she regularly felt waves of apprehension crest over her. A change could be scary, but it also made her feel gutsy. *I can do this. I don't know exactly what* this *is, but I can do it.*

Her most recent visit with Molly's family had been a ski trip in February. She had enjoyed every moment with Nora and

Owen. Nora, at six, possessed an exceptional imagination and a flair for the dramatic. "Aunt Hannah. Your hair is so beautiful. You're like a real princess, and you'll find your prince, like Prince Eric, and you'll get married and live in a castle, and I'll be your princess friend, and we'll eat feasts, and all the forest creatures will live in our castle rooms and help us with our fashions." Hannah had to laugh; this, coming out of the mouth of Molly's daughter! Molly was feminine enough but practical in her attire. Busy with a full-time career and two kids, she wasn't modeling the princess of her daughter's fantasies. It was shocking that a little girl raised by down to earth, organic-if-at-all-possible-split-your-own-firewood kinda parents could spew forth such indictments as "Our house is ugly. Why isn't it beautiful like Lady Lovely Locks's castle? We need a kingdom!" Nora was particularly fascinated with the prospect of princesses getting married. Many of her princess dramatizations involved elaborate weddings, and she owned several bride costumes.

Owen, just-turned four, was eat-'em-up cute, with a charming personality and a penchant for silky things. Never a dull moment with him. It was as if he got wound up in the morning, activated at full tilt until his batteries slowly died and you found him, thumb in mouth, passed out on the couch holding a pair of Molly's Victoria's Secret undies. Attempting to take away the undies could produce a catastrophic result if executed at the wrong moment. *Mental note for the summer.*

The thought of being fully responsible for the lives of the children she loved more than anything was daunting. *How hard can it be?* It wasn't like they were in diapers. It wasn't like they were even going to be together twenty-four seven, as Molly had registered them for summer day camp. This arrangement would, theoretically, allow Hannah to enjoy the summer and get reenergized before the fall and the perfect career move. Maybe there would be time to do something creative. She had always wanted to make time for a creative pursuit. Not since high school had she painted, written poetry, or done any kind of crafty project. Or cooking. Maybe she would give that a go.

Hannah pulled into Molly and Ted's by midafternoon and looked at the house with fresh eyes. The white clapboard house, set on a large lot a mile out of town, had stunning views of the mountains. She loved the quiet road with its mix of meadows and trees. *My home for the summer.* Another wave of apprehension. *What the hell have I gotten myself into?*

Before Hannah could open the car door or fully engage in a panic attack, Nora burst out of the house dressed in a long pink tulle skirt, cowboy boots, and a golden crown, carrying a foam sword. "Your Majesty is here. Your Majesty is here," she cried out. Hannah pulled out her phone. She had promised to text Sara, her now-former roommate, when she arrived safely in Vermont. *I'm here. My kingdom awaits,* she texted.

Molly and Owen followed Nora out the door, and Ted appeared from the back yard. Hugs and squeals all around.

"Let's get you unpacked," Ted said, pulling the suitcases out of the car. "Soon it'll be time for the briefing in the Situation Room. Your sister has a three-ring binder."

In the afternoon sun, the Green Mountains off in the distance, and her niece and nephew holding her hands and chattering nonstop, Hannah's erratic emotions receded, and she allowed the kids to lead her to the house.

TED WASN'T EXAGGERATING. After a delicious dinner of a Moroccan tagine, the kids settled in for their weekly screening of a

Lady Lovely Locks episode. Ted, Molly, and Hannah positioned themselves at the kitchen table with the three-ring binder.

"Please humor me," Molly began. "You have no idea how hard this is for me . . . for us."

"Bring it on," Hannah said. "I want to know everything." Although they'd been talking about the details for weeks, she knew that enthusiasm for the three-ring binder and a detailed discussion was what Molly needed in order to surrender her children to Hannah's care for the summer.

"First and foremost, I . . .we . . . we need you to keep them alive and uninjured," said Molly. "Everything else is the icing on the cake, although, ideally, it'd be great if you could try to keep them on the path we've set in motion. Just for their sakes—so they're not too confused. You know our values, Hannah. We want them to eat good food, play outside, not watch screens excessively, sleep in their own beds, be kind."

They spent the next hour and a half reviewing emergency contacts, the kids' schedules, Molly and Ted's itineraries in both Chile and Argentina, household maintenance information, and a list of Nora's and Owen's idiosyncrasies, including but not limited to:

- Nora's milk aversion ("which is a power play and not lactose intolerance")
- Sleeping habits ("never let them sleep with you in your bed—they're both thrashers")
- Medication philosophy ("try not to give unnecessarily")
- Owen's thumb sucking ("get him to stop this summer and we'll buy you a new pair of skis")
- Nora's desire to watch the 1980s classic *Lady Lovely Locks and the Pixietails* daily ("she can watch *one* episode on weekends")

Hannah paid close attention but was secretly relieved that the information was all in the three-ring binder, well-organized for future reference as needed. And while she *was* thrilled that Ted had hired someone to mow the lawn, as it wasn't something she enjoyed, they both were awfully intent on Hannah's sole focus being on the kids. Did they think she was inept? As if on cue, Molly said, "We don't think you're inept. We just know this can be hard, and we don't want you to be overwhelmed."

"If I could handle working for Steven, I can handle this," said Hannah. Hannah's managing director Steven had been the subject of many family discussions. Although not her direct boss, he took micromanagement to a new level. She particularly loathed how he would summon her, and all the women analysts, to his office, sit behind his desk, and give them detailed feedback on their reports just to hear himself speak. There were few instances of any substantive changes in the reports required.

"Steven's no match for Nora's willpower, but you'll be okay," said Molly.

As soon as the credits on the movie began to roll, Nora and Owen appeared in the kitchen.

"Time for bed, you guys," said Ted.

"Big day tomorrow," Molly mumbled under her breath.

Two

"What's going on next door?" Hannah sipped her coffee and peered out the kitchen window. "Looks like somebody's moving in." A U-Haul sat in the driveway of the house next door, and about five twenty-somethings were making a lot of noise for nine o'clock on a Sunday morning. They were unloading furniture, boxes, and a great deal of sporting equipment—bikes, a couple of kayaks, a canoe, skis, and what appeared to be a full-size stuffed deer.

"The Hendersons just moved to Burlington to be near their daughter," said Molly, "but I never found out who bought the place. It's a great house, needs a little work, but it's got potential." Molly rose from her chair at the kitchen table and joined her sister at the window.

"It looks like it's going to be some kind of Wilderness Society clubhouse," said Hannah. "Are we supposed to bring them wine or a ham or something? What do you Vermonters do in a situation like this?"

"Don't worry about it; the other neighbors will be on it. Just introduce yourself and wave and smile at them for the summer. I'm going to finish packing." Molly headed upstairs, and Hannah washed the breakfast dishes while continuing to spy out the window at the new neighbors. A couple, about her parents' age, pulled into the driveway and exited their car. Many of the twenty-somethings greeted them with big hugs, and the whole lot of them went into the house. Hannah did not know anyone in Vermont and hoped she would meet some people her age this summer. She could always connect with her friends on social media or by text or video chat, but some actual humans to hang out with would also be nice. The idea of using a dating app floated in and out of her mind.

Fifteen minutes later, Molly returned with Owen and Nora at her heels. "Lea's coming over soon. I'll make some lunch, and we can sit out back. Ted's going to take the kids on a picnic." Molly and Nora went off to the kitchen, leaving Hannah with a thumb-sucking, silky slip-toting Owen.

"Aunt Hannah, will you pway twucks wif me," he asked. He looked up at her, his blond hair tousled, thumb in his mouth but with the most beguiling eyes.

"I'd love to play trucks with you, but no thumb sucking, okay?"

Hannah sat on the family room floor with Owen and his crate full of cars and trucks. She had no idea how to play trucks. She took one of the vehicles and scooted it across the room, making a "vroom" sound. "No, that's not right," said Owen. "You has to line them up first."

"Take your thumb out and show me how to, please," said Hannah. She found the truck-playing lesson that followed confusing. Her mind wandered while going through the motions of playing with Owen, but she found if she made occasional interested comments, he was content to have her simply sit beside him while he played.

Molly came into the room and looked in disbelief at Hannah and Owen on the floor. "Oh my god, what are you doing?"

"I'm playing trucks with Owen."

Molly stomped over, grabbed Hannah's arm, pulling her

from the floor, and whispered in her ear. "Han, be careful about playing trucks with Owen on the floor. If you start, it'll never end. It's best to stay nearby and let him play by himself and act interested from afar and kind of keep a dialogue about trucks going. I'm warning you; it's a bad precedent to sit down. He gets extremely upset if you quit on him once you sit down."

Hannah scowled at her sister, questioning what was so wrong with sitting on the floor with her nephew when Owen screamed, "Aunt Hannah, come back and pway wif meeee!"

"Just a minute, Owen," Hannah responded.

"Come now—come now—come now," wailed Owen as Molly tilted her head and gave Hannah a sympathetic but I-told-you-so look.

"Okay, Owen, I'll come play for a few more minutes, but then I have to do something."

Hannah stood over the boy as he shuffled a giant Tonka truck over the floor toward the fireplace, mumbling to himself in an incomprehensible babble. As soon as she started backing up, he said, "Da red truck goes wif da big wewwow twuck to da dump and den it gows to da stweet . . . get da red twuck, Aunt Hanwah."

Oh, boy. It's impossible to get into a four-year-old's imagination, which appears to have a set agenda for what the trucks do and do not do. She grabbed the red truck from the crate, and as she did, her phone rang. Owen thankfully appeared to accept the phone interruption and continued to play as Hannah left the room.

"Mom! Hi," said Hannah as she walked outside to the back deck to update her mom on recent events. Hannah and Molly's parents lived in Massachusetts. Both were adoring grandparents but, with demanding careers, were unable to take on the entire summer as caregivers for Nora and Owen. Thankfully, they planned a couple of long weekends to visit and relieve her.

Hannah ended the call as Ted was preparing Nora and Owen for their outing. The kids had on child-sized backpacks, lunches and drinks stowed inside. "We're going to the reservoir," said Nora, skipping out the door. "It's beeyooootiful there. There's an enchanted forest, and we're going to have a picnic feast."

"And you're going to have a great time." Hannah followed them into the driveway as a 1980s red pickup truck approached the house.

"Hey, Lea," Hannah called out, walking to the truck to greet Molly's best friend. Lea and her husband, Chris, lived about a half mile away with their three young children, two of whom were paired nicely in age with Owen and Nora, the third a tow-headed two-year-old girl.

Owen went wild with delight when he saw the truck. He flew down the driveway as Lea exited and flung himself on her. "Lea, can we go for a wide in yow twuck?"

Lea simultaneously hugged Owen and tossed the keys to Ted, saying, "Sure, Owen, your daddy can take you guys in it to the reservoir."

"Thanks, Lea." Ted pulled the kids' booster seats out of his car and installed them in the back seat of Lea's truck. With wide smiles, they drove off as Lea, Hannah, and Molly retreated to the house.

"Claire has an ear infection, so Chris is staying at home with all of them. In other words, movie day," Lea said.

"Poor little Clairebear," said Molly. "If it ain't one thing, it's a mother fuckin' other."

"Shit yeah," said Lea.

Molly turned to Hannah. "Just so you know, Lea and I curse

all the time when the little fuckers aren't around. It's our therapy."

"Okay, bitches, I'll play," said Hannah.

The three women took their iced teas and plates of chicken salad out to the deck in the unseasonably warm sunshine of early June. Lea eased off her shoes, placed her legs on an empty chair, and looked out over the yard to the mountains beyond. "I never get tired of this view," she said.

"It's pretty fabulous," said Molly.

"I guess no garden this year?" Lea pointed to the neglected raised beds on the side of the yard.

"We abandoned it when Ted got the grant approved. We didn't want to add one more thing for Hannah to have to take care of this summer."

"A garden would have been nice. I could have managed," said Hannah.

"I think I want you to keep it simple. Keeping these kids alive might be more effort than you think."

True. They were adorable, loud, funny, whiny, needy, non-stop. Since arriving, it had occurred to Hannah that she may have idealized her summertime role as a caregiver. She had never spent more than a week with the whole family and never more than a few hours alone with the kids.

Between mouthfuls of chicken salad, Lea recounted her understanding of how the summer would unfold. She would be the round-the-clock backup for Hannah and insisted Hannah put her number on her phone's speed dial. Lea would be responsible for driving Nora and Owen to and from day camp. Her all-wheel-drive minivan was fully outfitted with Molly's second set of car seats, making the pickup and delivery easy. "It's no problem; I drive right by," she insisted.

"Thanks, Lea. I've been wondering why camp is necessary

when I'm here with nothing else to do, but Molly says she'd have it no other way. She says I'll understand why this is a good idea after about two days alone with the kids," said Hannah.

"Wait, sister, just wait." Molly laughed. "I love you, but you've got no freaking clue how exhausting kids can be."

"I'm grateful my mom lives nearby and pitches in so much," said Lea. "She's even taken to doing some of my grocery shopping now and then. It's such a godsend not to have to take the kids. She likes it too because she loves finding deals and spends a ridiculous amount of time each week figuring out which store has the best prices on stuff. Last week she showed up with four little bottles of personal lube and just put them in my cupboard like it was tomato paste."

"Mom and Dad being here last week helping me get organized and ready was so helpful." Molly raised her glass, grinning. "To family and girlfriends. What would we do without them?" They clinked their glasses.

Lea turned to Hannah. "I've been curious to know what made you do this. What made you leave Boston and come here this summer? You could have stayed and gotten another job there. I've heard Molly's take on it but wanted to hear from you. Was it a guy?" She leaned forward, raising an eyebrow.

"No, nothing like that." Hannah had not yet articulated a complete answer to this question. To her friends, she had been glib about moving. Now she searched for the right words to explain herself. "I guess . . . I guess it's been building for a while. I went to Boston after I got back from volunteering in Kenya, basically because I didn't know what else to do. I want to give myself time this summer to figure out what I want to do with my life. My job sucked. I made good money, I liked my coworkers, but it was soulless." Hannah rocked back and forth in her chair and gulped a mouthful of her drink. "I can't believe I stayed there for three years. I feel like such a sell-out."

"Wow, I didn't realize you were there so long," said Lea.

"Yeah, I got in through my friend Sara's brother, and it seemed like a good idea at the time. I needed a job; it just materialized. And Boston was fun. But then my company merged with a bigger fish, and they started doing layoffs, but with decent severance packages. Then Molly called with this opportunity." Hannah formed air quotes at the word "opportunity." "The next day, I hinted to my boss that I'd be cool with getting laid off. If you get laid off, they help you get another job, let you keep your insurance for a while, and give you a good reference if you leave on good terms. So, I got laid off that afternoon. I know my boss was so relieved that she wouldn't have another person crying in her office. So now I have a little nest egg to get me through for a while till I sort things out."

"That's brave," said Lea. "You're brave for putting yourself on the chopping block like that."

"Or stupid. It hurt that she was so fine with letting me go. I mean, she handed me my layoff paperwork that afternoon. Didn't even talk to me about it. It made me feel undervalued. I worked hard there even though I hated it."

"Yeah, I get that," said Lea. "But now you've given yourself this opportunity to start something new. You're young and single and smart."

"Oh, that sounds good, but I have no idea what I'm doing. I'm so confused about what I want to be when I grow up. I don't want to sound like a cliché millennial. It's not like I'm *expecting* to have a job that I'm completely passionate about. I don't believe that what our parents told us is true—that we can be anything we want. And I don't want to live out my unemployment back home with Mom and Dad in my old bedroom staring at my everyone's-a-winner soccer trophies." Lea and Molly both laughed.

"You don't have that many trophies, but I get your point," said Molly. "I'm so lucky to love what I do. I want that for you, but geez, Hannah, you've been all over the map with your choices, and you're only twenty-eight. I want joyful Kenya-Hannah back. That was a great experience for you."

"I forgot about Kenya," said Lea. "What exactly were you doing that made you happy?"

"Happy is not quite the right word, but I was in my element. I felt very much in control of my life." Hannah leaned back in her chair and rested her elbows on the armrests. "So basically, right after graduation, I went to work as a volunteer for Habitat for Humanity with the idea that I'd do it as a gap year before going to grad school. I lived in a small village with a core group of long-term volunteers who worked with us to build desperately needed houses."

"Again, brave," said Lea.

"Kinda. Definitely not boring. I learned so much about construction! I could probably build my own house now as long as it was simple and had a corrugated tin sheet roof. I lived in the Kisli region. It was really pretty."

"Was there lots of wildlife?" asked Lea.

"There was this tree full of giant bats in the town, but no, there weren't, like, elephants walking by all day. The community was pretty heavily populated. I met so many cool people, and I'm still in touch with some of my Kenyan friends. My days there were peaceful. You got up, you made your meals on coal or kerosene stoves, you worked hard, you socialized, you read, you went to the occasional village soccer game, and you slept."

"Sounds like your bliss," said Lea.

"You know, Mom was pretty happy that you left your job in Boston," said Molly. "She said she never thought it was a good fit for you. I mean, she gets that you might not easily find another position given the job market, and of course, what she really wants is more grandchildren, so she's also wondering when you're going to get a real boyfriend."

Hannah rolled her eyes and laughed. "Mom, stop worrying. But yeah, I'm concerned about the job thing too. I know so many people who are gig workers, and I don't want to do that. But I'm going to use this summer to figure it out. I haven't exactly been living a very purposeful life, and that's my plan—to get a plan!"

"But what about a partner? A family?" asked Lea. "Any plan for that?"

"I'll get on it, no worries. I've thought about it a lot. I figure if I stay laser-focused on getting the right job in the right place over the next few years, then when I'm thirty-two, I'll get married and then spit out a kid before I'm thirty-five. Bada bing, bada boom."

"Hannah thinks that finding a guy hasn't changed since high school," said Molly. "She was a riot when it came to boys. She once told me, 'Why would I want a boyfriend? You have six minutes between classes, and if you have a boyfriend, you have to go to your locker and get your stuff for your next class, then meet them in the hall and make out, and then try to get to your class on time. It's stupid. Then after school, you have to go watch them play video games. Also, stupid,'" Molly said, mimicking a younger Hannah's voice.

Lea broke into laughter and looked at Hannah, who sat with a bemused look on her face. "So, no high school boyfriend?"

"Oh, they all wanted her," said Molly. "She loved going to the dances. When it came time, she'd just point to one of the guys in her group and announce what dance they'd be taking her to." Molly jumped up from her chair on the deck. "You, Nate Goldman, homecoming," she said, pointing to an imaginary figure to her right. She swiftly turned and pointed into the air, "Zach Powers, winter formal, get a suit." Spinning around and pointing again, "Andy, I can't remember his last name, prom."

Molly plopped back down on her chair, and all three women roared with laughter.

"Yeah, that's pretty much an accurate depiction of my high school dating life," said Hannah.

"So, what do you think is going to happen?" asked Molly. "You think you're going to meet some guy, point to him, and shout, "You, yeah you, the good one, in the corner, you're husband material. Get a ring."

"That's a great idea. That sounds like the way to do it," said Hannah. "Going to wait, though. I'll get my life on track with something I can be proud of, and I'll send you a Save the Date."

"Geez, who's that?" Lea pointed over the hedge line to the yard next door. In the back yard of the neighbor's property, a shirtless man was hammering away on a small storage shed. The three women simultaneously rose, glasses in hand, from their respective chairs to get a better view.

"New neighbors," Molly said. "We spied on them this morning. I think it's an older couple with some grown kids helping them move in." The women stood shoulder to shoulder silently and watched as he moved about the shed measuring, bending over, and writing in a notebook. He appeared quite young, was lean and tall, but the baseball cap and sunglasses hid his face and eyes.

"This view just got even better. But if he's still living with mommy and daddy . . ." Lea stopped speaking as he abruptly turned and looked in their direction. The three of them squealed and scattered, embarrassed they were caught standing like schoolgirls watching him.

"Shit, do you think he saw us," said Molly. She grabbed Lea's arm firmly.

"Oh yeah, we're busted," said Lea, and the trio continued giggling as they sat back down.

"He's probably seventeen and thinks we're a bunch of creepy old ladies," said Hannah.

"Or MILFs," said Lea.

"Ew," said Molly. "Hate to break up the party, but I've gotta get my ass in gear. Jake's coming to take us to the airport in a few hours, and I still have a lot to do."

Molly and Lea hugged and began their goodbyes.

"I'll miss you, girl," said Lea. "But don't worry—everything will be fine." She held out her arms and patted Molly's shoulders. "Just don't get eaten by snakes or head-hunters or anything."

Molly exhaled sharply. "It's remote, but I assure you there are no head-hunters. We'll be fine. Just watch over Hannah and make sure she keeps my kids alive and doesn't sleep with any teenage neighbors."

AN HOUR LATER, Ted arrived home with a tired Owen, who slept most of the late afternoon on the couch while Molly and Ted made their final flight preparations. Nora and Hannah sat at the dining room table, doing a puzzle and talking about their upcoming adventures.

Nora watched as Ted carried the suitcases downstairs. "You're going now?" she cried out in panic. She jumped out of her chair and ran to her parents. "Don't leave, Mommy. I don't want you to go." She wrapped her arms around Molly's legs.

"Norabean, sweetie." Molly, ashen-faced, turned and gathered her daughter into her arms. "You are going to have so much fun this summer with Aunt Hannah while we do our work project." Hannah could now see tears welling up in Molly's eyes. "We're gonna call you all the time and talk to you on the computer, and before you know it, we'll be home again. We'll bring you lots of presents, and you get to go to the summer camp with Ava. You're going to have a great time."

Nora flung herself on the couch, wailing uncontrollably, genuinely heartbroken. Owen, still lying on the sofa, flashed open his eyes and immediately started crying as well, for no other reason than it seemed to be the thing to do. The noise was deafening. Hannah stood speechless in the middle of the living room. Molly and Ted attempted to console their children without much luck. Finally, the wails subsided, and Molly and Ted looked as beaten as the children. Calm restored, the kids got special consolation treats of lollipops, and the family cuddled on the couch.

Moments later, Ted's grad assistant Jake suddenly appeared in the house with a cheerful "Taxi's here!" The screaming resumed.

LATER THAT EVENING, Hannah collapsed into bed and scrolled through her phone. She read a missed text message from Sara.

Today 10:17 PM

Sara: Hey what's up?
me: kill me now. Owen woke up and was crying and peed the bed, and I had to change the sheets and calm him down. Molly and ted left. The kids are freaking out.

Sara: geez

me: I'm freaking out too. They're crying so much I don't know how to make them stop. I'm exhausted already and they've only been gone 4 hours

Sara: ambien? Valium?

me: you can't give that to kids

Sara: for you dummy

me: I wish - hang on a sec

me: I'm back

Sara: whats up

me: I was checking out the neighbors. trying to figure out who lives next door. somebody moved in today and now a bunch of cars are pulling out

Sara: and . . .

me: there's a bunch of people like young - our age - and an older couple but all the young people left so I think it's the parents house

Sara: god . . . youre like the nosey neighbor Gladys Kravitz on Bewitched

me: just trying to get the lay of the land

Sara: lay haha call me tmrw

me: when?

Sara: lunchtime

me: k bye

Sara: bye

Three

Hannah turned in her bed the next morning, slowly waking up from a delightful dream starring a Goldendoodle puppy. Her eyes opened, and there was Owen, silently standing next to her bed staring at her. He was holding her favorite pair of satin boyshorts in hand, thumb in mouth. "Hi, Aunt Hannah." Had he gone through her drawers without her hearing him? A jolt of shock tore through her. Owen could have been up for a while wandering around the house, wandering outside, anywhere.

Hannah pulled him into the bed beside her, glancing at the bedside clock. 7:11. His sweet face gazed at hers, drool flowing from his thumb-plugged mouth onto her pillowcase. Before she could suggest that he might unplug, Nora came bounding into the room and flopped between Hannah and Owen. The two started giggling immediately and commenced tickling Hannah until she got up to make them breakfast. Even though it was summer, the mornings were still chilly, and the house had yet to warm. She flipped on the furnace, and the kids climbed onto their chairs in the kitchen.

Hannah stood at the kitchen counter slicing bananas into oatmeal-laden bowls. "Let's think about what we're going to do today. We can do whatever we want. How about the farmers market in Stowe?"

"Yay," said Nora. "I love the farmers market. Can we get cookies and cheese?"

"Ithe cream," said Owen through his thumb. "I want maple creemee at da fawmas maket."

"Sure," Hannah said. "We can do that, and how about we go to the library after and get some books?"

Hannah readied herself and the kids and, by midmorning, finally loaded them into her car. Ted had secured the children's boosters in her car, and she learned yet another new thing about children—getting into the car takes about ten times longer with kids. Once settled, Hannah started the engine and began the K-turn necessary to exit the driveway and point herself in the right direction to head onto the main road. When she was a couple of yards from the street, a sudden roar came from the back seat.

"WHEAS MY SILKY? WHEAS MY SILKY?" Owen screamed. Hannah flashed her eyes to the rearview mirror to see a shrieking, red-faced Owen. Her gaze returned to the road. To her horror, a cyclist was coming right at them. She slammed on the brakes. Too late. She had pulled too far out, and the cyclist had to swerve into the middle of the road to avoid her car. *Shit.* There was nothing she could do to apologize. Thank God she hadn't hit them.

Reversing the car back down the driveway, Hannah took several deep breaths to slow down her racing heart. She had never almost hit a human being, even in the traffic of Boston. She ran back into the house to fetch Owen's "travel silky"—a scrap from an old satin nightgown. Once again, on their way, the kids happily maintained a pleasant chatter about a book Nora was reading to Owen. She kept a lookout for the cyclist but didn't see them again along the route.

Hannah quickly found parking at the farmers market, and they walked the short distance to the entrance. Stalls of vendors lined the perimeter of a grassy field, the center filled with picnic tables, a bluegrass band, and families on blankets. Quintessential New England. They made their way along the stalls. Hannah discovered there was no means of containing Nora and Owen while she looked at the array of goods ranging from the ubiquitous maple syrup to organic non-genetically-modified vegetable seeds and, was it possible, Vermont vodka? She asked Nora to hang on to her brother but recognized that putting a six-year-old in charge of a four-year-old was a child abduction movie in the making. She squatted down to speak to them to determine how best she could navigate the market, and Nora offered, "Mommy brings the running stroller with the big wheels." Of course, that would be the way to do it. The stroller was back at the house.

Determined to get the goods, Hannah requested that they not let go of her hands, and while it was challenging to shop this way, she didn't lose them. They secured the desired cookies and cheese, as well as the vodka (who could resist?), early lettuces, jam, honeybee soap, and free-range chicken eggs. Hannah would have bought more, but Nora and Owen could only carry so much. "Mommy usually puts the stuff under the stroller and hangs the bags on the handle," Nora helpfully informed Hannah.

After wandering through the stalls, Hannah bought panini sandwiches, and they sat at a picnic table to listen to the band. An older couple joined them at the table and kept an eye on the kids while Hannah acquired the promised maple creemees. For close to twenty minutes, Hannah enjoyed the children quietly licking their cones and relaxed for the first time all day. When Owen began getting squirmy and was ready to bolt, Hannah asked them, "Ready to go to the library?"

The Waterbury Library, located south of the Village, had surprisingly ample parking on a beautiful Sunday afternoon when everyone was out and about. The threesome marched toward the library steps, holding hands and singing, "We all live in a magic flying house, a magic flying house, a magic flying house," to the tune of "Yellow Submarine." Hannah's phone buzzed. Sara.

"You're not going to believe this—Derek and Kaitlyn broke up!" Sara said before Hannah even had time to say hello.

Hannah gasped. "What? What happened?"

"It's so fucked up. Derek slept with some woman after an office party, and the skank posted a picture of them together and *tagged* Derek, and when Kaitlyn saw it, the shit hit the fan."

"What an asshole!" Hannah blurted loudly. Nora threw her hand over her mouth, eyes wide with a disapproving glare.

"Oh god. Listen, I can't talk now. I've got the kids. I'll call you back tonight, okay?"

"There's more to tell. Call me later."

"I will, I promise." Hannah hit the end-call button.

Derek and Kaitlyn were friends from Sara and Hannah's undergraduate days and had been together since senior year. This was unexpected, sad news. She would call Kaitlyn as soon as she had a moment. She reached for the library door and was surprised it wouldn't open. The sign adjacent to the door read CLOSED. Sighing, yet trying to keep an upbeat attitude, Hannah remembered Bridgeside Books in town and told the kids of the change in plans.

"Can we go to the park to read the books?" Nora asked as they were completing the purchase of three paperback easy-reading books at the cash register.

"Sure, but it's a bit of a walk."

Marching to the park, once again to the tune of "Yellow Submarine," Hannah felt smugly satisfied that the afternoon had been mostly pleasant. The trick to this "parenting" thing appeared to be staying in the moment and not wishing you could be doing something else, like talking to your best friend.

At the park, Nora and Owen arranged themselves on the bench on either side of Hannah while she read them a story. The plot centered on the letter X trying to alter alphabetical order, which was quite clever as children's literature goes. Halfway through the book, a guy walked by with a large brown dog, and Owen catapulted off the bench toward them. Hannah sprang from the seat after him. "Hang on, Owen, don't touch the dog." Too late, Owen was petting and hugging the dog before Hannah reached them. The owner stood patiently while Owen cooed at the obviously gentle canine.

"He's good with kids, no worries," the man said. Hannah gave him a quick look: thirtyish, light brown hair, tall with hip-yet-nerdy glasses.

Owen continued petting the dog, and soon Nora was beside him, doing the same. Hannah stood there somewhat perplexed about the proper protocol in such a situation. Should she suggest they not touch him, or would that be uncool? He was cute—the guy as well as the dog.

The man squatted down to eye level with Owen and tapped his Boston Red Sox baseball cap. "I like your hat." He smiled.

"What an asshole!" Owen said, loudly and clear as a bell. He continued petting the dog.

"Owen!" Hannah screeched. "That's not a good word."

"That's what you said." Owen frowned at Hannah.

"I'm so sorry, I'm really sorry," Hannah said. She did not look at the man. She was turning a deep, sweaty shade of crimson. "Let's go, guys." She grabbed them both by the hands and began to scurry away.

"It's okay," said the man. But Hannah, Nora, and Owen were already trotting down the sidewalk.

"You said a bad word, Owen," said Nora to her brother on their way to the car.

"Wat word?" asked Owen.

"Asshole is a bad word—don't say it again," said Hannah. "And I won't either." She was so embarrassed. *That poor guy.*

Owen looked up at her, cocking his head and shrugging. "Okay."

Later that evening, after dinner and baths and jammies and stories, Hannah sat on her bed, talking to Sara about the details of the Derek-Kaitlyn split. They were both feeling depressed that a guy they'd admired for so long could be such a dick. Hannah recounted the "asshole" story to Sara.

"That's hilarious. A good way to meet guys . . . call 'em assholes, get it over with right away!" said Sara.

"It was mortifying. And it all happened so fast. He was, like, the first guy I've run into here. I didn't even have a chance to meet him, and I'll probably never see him again."

Four

The alarm clock, as well as Hannah's head, began buzzing at seven sharp the next morning. She had sipped too much red wine while talking with Sara last night. But Molly had warned her to be awake by seven in the morning at the latest to get the kids ready for Lea's pickup at eight thirty sharp during this last week of school, so she threw her legs over the side of the bed and stumbled in to wake the kids. An hour and a half seemed too long for dressing and eating breakfast. But Hannah was sure, after only thirty-six hours in this new world of hers, that her sister didn't exaggerate the emotional and physical effort required to care for Nora and Owen. Ted and Molly had called the previous evening and spoken with the kids for a long while. When Hannah closed the door after putting Owen to bed, he'd been teary. He began a sad, repetitive refrain Hannah could hear outside his door: "I wanna see my daddy, I wanna see my daddy, I wanna see my daddy, I wanna see my daddy . . ." But he never full-out cried, and, for that, Hannah was grateful.

Cereal and yogurt eaten, shorts and T-shirts donned, lunches packed, teeth brushed, Nora's hair styled in pigtails, everyone was ready ten minutes before Lea arrived. Hannah was smug with satisfaction—she had passed her first morning readiness test. Lea met them in the driveway and, after a brief inspection, said, "Looking good, kids, jump in. Nora, you in the way-way back, and, Owen, you sit in the middle row with Tyler."

Lea told Hannah she would have them back by three thirty that afternoon. "I'll be here," said Hannah as she waved goodbye.

Entering the house, Hannah experienced the sweet relief of liberation also known as getting the children off to school. She was now free from their perpetual motion for the next few hours. It was time to recharge her patience batteries.

Hannah had not devoted much thought to precisely what she would do with her free time when the kids were gone. Molly had been clear that school and camp time was her "off-time" and that her "work time" was *all* the other time. Hannah had imagined her summer as a time of reflection and a period to consider her next move. All she wanted was to enjoy this bit of peace, so she grabbed a magazine and a fresh cup of coffee and flopped on the couch. Reflection could come later; now was the time to see what *In Style* had to say about summer sandals.

When she exhausted her interest in the magazine, she turned her attention to tidying the house and kitchen cleanup. All accomplished within an hour. *Now what?*

A perennial list maker, Hannah sat at the kitchen table and wrote a list of all the things she could do this summer:

1. Think about a new career
2. Think about where to do a new career
3. Get haircut
4. Get crafty
5. Work on cooking
6. Apply for jobs (see number one above) in the new city (see number two above)

This was basically the same vague list she had developed weeks ago when she first agreed to mind the children for the summer. Zero-point-zero progress made since, as most of her time and energy had been spent packing and moving and saying goodbye to friends in Boston. She needed to get serious about her future, but every time she thought about it, her brain seemed to freeze. She was mentally paralyzed when it came to imagining her best life.

The grinding of wheels roused her from her reflections, and she rose to see who was there. Lea was back. Hannah opened the front door to let her in.

"I wanted to give you this." Lea handed Hannah a plastic bag. "It's all of Owen's extra clothes and things from daycare. They like to empty the cubbies before the end of the year. Did Molly remember to tell you about Nora's end-of-the-year school party and Owen's graduation?"

"She gave the teachers gifts already, and I know I have to go to graduation on Thursday, but she didn't mention a party. Hey, do you have time to have some tea or coffee?"

"I can only stay for a while. I have a dentist's appointment, ugh."

Hannah took mugs from the cabinet and placed them on the kitchen table, motioning to Lea to take a seat.

"The party's no big deal," Lea said. "There was a sign-up sheet outside the classroom, so I put you down for apple juice. A gallon should do."

"I'm immensely qualified to bring juice."

"What's this?" asked Lea, looking at the legal pad headed "Things to Do This Summer."

"Ha." Hannah slid the pad toward Lea. "Just me and the same damn list I made three weeks ago. Feel free to provide me with counsel. Besides making lists, I'm not sure where to begin in figuring out my life."

"I love giving advice. It's my superpower. Go," said Lea.

"I forgot you are an actual therapist." Hannah poured the coffee into the mugs. "Okay, so I gave you the general background about my plight the other day. And now I'm ready to tackle looking for a job, but the problem is, I don't know where to begin. I know for sure what I don't want to do. I don't want to work for a big corporation, and I don't want to stare at a computer all day." She grimaced. "I want to work on something that positively contributes to society. I want a new environment—maybe a small or midsize city, but not a huge city."

"What was your major? Let's start there. Money, right?"

"Economics. Interesting to learn about, but it prepared me for jobs that don't give me any joy. I don't like talking about money all the time. It was a huge mistake. But in college, I knew everything, and no one could tell me otherwise." Hannah threw her arms on the table and sunk her head onto them.

"That sounds like everyone's college experience. But you've been out in the real world for a few years now. What kind of work looks good to you?"

Hannah raised her head but left her arms splayed on the table. "I don't know for certain. I have high expectations for my life. I want to do meaningful work, make a good living, have amazing colleagues, get good benefits. I don't want regrets. Whatever I do has to check these boxes. It's overwhelming. Some days, I secretly want some guy to whisk me off my feet and make all my decisions for me like in a Disney princess movie. But that's usually after drinking a bottle of wine at night alone with my roommate's cat. Then I wake up in the morning, ashamed of myself for even having those thoughts and remembering my mom telling me, 'Dreams first, boys later.'"

"I agree with Lizzy. Dreams first." Lea paused to take a sip of her coffee. "It's good that you want to take control of your own life. I was super happy doing counseling before I took this break to stay home with the kids, and I can't wait to get back to it. What were the things you liked best about your life and job in Boston?"

"Definitely knowing Mom and Dad were close by. Just in case. Also, I liked my colleagues. They were smart and engaged and challenged me. The work itself also challenged me. It wasn't boring, but the subject matter made me nauseous."

"What do you mean?"

"I was a financial analyst . . . did the sell side stuff, which meant I looked at industries and wrote research reports and made recommendations to buy, sell, hold. Tracked stocks in a portfolio, made lots of charts and graphs; crap like that, you know?" Hannah grabbed the neck of her T-shirt with both hands and tugged it down a couple of inches.

"I don't really," said Lea. "But I kind of get it."

"Sometimes, it was like a puzzle, and when I was doing the work, it was fun." She let go of the T-shirt. "I was immersed. But after I was done with a project and sat back and examined my work, I was disgusted with the lack of humanity involved. Most of the time, employees were considered cogs in the machine and only evaluated by their efficiency and the bottom line. It was depressing."

"Yeah, sounds it. But I don't know anything about finance. What other kinds of work is there for economics majors?"

Hannah sighed and slumped back in her chair. "I don't know. I've never looked! I should check out what my college friends who were econ majors are doing. I'm at such a crossroads." She waved her hands in the air and dropped them on her thighs. "But I am determined to get this right. Don't laugh, but I was thinking of making a vision board and googling 'creating the life you want.' I'll take a page out of Oprah's book. Did you know she makes vision boards? It looks like her life is working out pretty well—maybe it'll work for me. Plus, it'll fulfill number four on my list: Get Crafty." Hannah slammed her finger on the pad of paper.

"Do it. It's as good a place as any to start. And hey, sorry to cut this short, but I gotta get going. I have a ton of errands." Lea stood up and placed both of her palms on her lower back and stretched. "When you make your vision board, don't forget to think about work-life balance—not just the work part. I'll think about what you've told me, and we can talk more."

"Thanks so much for listening." Hannah walked Lea to the door and gave her a warm hug. "You're the best. Send the bill to my sister."

"Glad to do it. I love hearing about other people's problems. See you when I drop the kids off." She waved her hand at Hannah without looking back as she headed to her minivan. Hannah watched her from the doorway and envied Lea's self-possession. She was confident and took ownership of her life choices. Hannah wanted some of that.

Hannah returned to the couch and opened her laptop. Heading straight for Pinterest, she typed "Vision Board" in the search box. Pinterest was great with its collage of photos on every possible subject, all connected to the source link. Seconds after hitting the "search" button, voila. Hundreds of pictures appeared. She clicked on the first photo entitled "How to Create a Vision Board."

"Bingo." She didn't need to look any further. This was just the tool she needed to get started on her job hunt. After perusing the website and getting the gist of what was involved, Hannah searched around the house for the suggested items to create the board: magazines, photos, markers, pens, glue, tape. She found an only mildly beat-up poster board tucked behind the file cabinet in the office area outside Molly and Ted's bedroom.

Hannah set up her supplies on the kitchen table and returned to the computer.

Questions to ask yourself to start the visioning process:

What is it that brings value, meaning, and purpose to your life?
Where are you right now?
Where would you like to be?
Who are your role models, and what draws you to them?
How can you own these qualities in yourself?
How can you create more balance in your life?
What are your short-, medium- and long-term goals?
How might you sabotage your goals?
How will you put your visions into action?
What are your next steps?

"I think I'm going to need a bigger board," Hannah mumbled to herself.

Five

Nathan Wild hit the send button, slid the computer mouse away, and stretched back in his chair. He'd been working since early morning with few breaks, and the sun was now low in the sky. "Hey, bud," he said, reaching down to scratch the chin of his dog, Cooper, who'd been lying at his feet for hours. "Let's go for a walk." The dog leaped with enthusiasm and bounded toward the mudroom.

Nathan grabbed the dog's leash and his phone and headed outside. It felt great to breathe in the fresh, crisp evening air. They walked along the driveway; his mind was still spinning from the intensity of his workday. Before he even reached the road, his phone buzzed.

"Kendall. What's up?"

"I'm checking in to see how my big brother is doing. Are you good? You eating? You sleeping?"

"I'm fine. Finally finished. So glad I'm done and happy that I have a light schedule for the next two weeks. I'm going to put the last piece of Mom's lasagna into the microwave and have a beer and watch some TV and pass out early."

"Sounds thrilling. Why don't you go out, do something? Call Dylan, hit a bar."

"I'm exhausted. I'm staying in. I'll tell you what though; I'll have more than one beer."

"Okay, old man. Want some company tomorrow? I could come over."

"That'd be great. You could go food shopping with me and help me organize my office."

"Yeah, no," she quipped. "Why don't we go for a bike ride or hike or something?"

"We should do that, too. We could take Cooper for a good hike. I've been neglecting him. What time?" He paused along the quiet road to allow Cooper to do his business.

"I'll come by around noon. Would you mind if I brought my laptop so you could work your magic on it? It's been running slow. I hate to ask you, but I'm kind of desperate."

"Ahh, ulterior motive. Sure, no problem."

"You're the best. And I do want to spend some time with you—it's not just about the computer. I'm happy you're back home."

"Me too. It'll be good to have some just-us time. See ya tomorrow." Nathan clicked off his phone and stashed it in his pocket. Kendall was the last in a long line of "Wild Children," as they had been known in the small town where his parents still lived. At twenty-one, Kendall, a recent college graduate, was living at home with their parents, helping their other sister, Grace, with her wedding preparations and working part-time at a garden center.

Gracey is getting married. Nathan still could not quite believe it. The wedding was in one month, and she was trying hard to get everything done. The affair would take place in Waitsfield in a barn on a hill with an unbelievable 360-degree view of the mountains. She had enlisted the entire family to create her fantasy wedding of "rustic-elegant chic," whatever the hell that was. His responsibility was to build the wedding arbor and carve small birds that would serve as table numbers. He was handy with woodworking, and this would not be particularly challenging, but he'd better get on it soon. The arbor was to be made of stripped cedar; the debarking of the cedar would be the most labor-intensive part. The logs were stacked on the side of his house. The wooden birds were simple enough, cut from pine boards to be painted by Kendall. Kendall and their mother, meanwhile, were recruited to do all kinds of other arts and crafts projects, the purpose of which he could not fully understand.

He was happy Grace had found Nick, who fit seamlessly into the Wild clan. Grace was a small-animal veterinarian in a large practice in Burlington, and the couple had recently bought a small farm in Richmond, not far from their parents. Having a vet in the family was very appealing to the Wilds, whose collective menagerie included several dogs, a half-dozen cats, a donkey, llamas, sheep, a flock of chickens, and a bunny.

As Nathan turned back home, his thoughts of Grace and Nick reminded him that Cooper was due for a check-up soon. Nathan had rescued him the year before in Chicago, and Cooper was the most grateful dog Nathan ever encountered. His every look and action exuded faithfulness and appreciation for his good fortune.

"You poor dog," Nathan said to Cooper, entering his house after the brief outing. "You haven't had any good exercise all week." Cooper was an athletic dog, a trait that Nathan valued. He loved running alongside Nathan and was an excellent ball-catcher. Between the move and work demands, the dog's needs had been put on the back burner over the last month.

Nathan reheated the lasagna, grabbed a beer, and headed outside to eat dinner on his back patio. This was the first time he had sat outside of his new home. Looking out upon the moonlit sky and taking a long gulp of his beer, he finally felt the stresses of the day beginning to wane.

An outdoor light illuminated the back of the house next door. A lone figure sat in a chair on the deck. He knew a woman with two children lived there. Was that her or perhaps her husband sitting outside in the shadows? The two times he had seen her, once when she nearly hit him when he was cycling and the other time at the park, she seemed far too young to have kids that age, and he figured she must have been unusually young when she started a family. She was pretty. Nathan had found it hilarious when the boy called him an asshole. Although taken aback initially, he later concluded that the woman must have called him an asshole in front of the kids when she pulled out of the driveway and failed to see him pedaling down the road. Except she didn't look like a road rage type of person. She looked nice.

Nathan placed his empty plate on the ground beside his chair and stretched out his legs, poking his toes into Cooper's belly as the dog lay sleeping. The dog opened one eye and shot his owner a monocular glare. "Tomorrow—a hike, you, me, and Kendall," he said to the dog. "I promise." Cooper's eye closed as if he understood.

Nathan stared out into the darkness, content with his new status as homeowner as well as with the satisfaction of having completed his latest work project. He sat for a while in an almost trancelike state until he heard the scraping of a chair on the deck next door. He turned to see the figure, a woman, walk into the house and the back yard light go out.

"C'mon, Coop. Time for bed," he said.

Six

Hannah pulled her car into the last available parking spot of the Moziozagan Elementary School on Friday afternoon. As she entered the school, she spotted Lea and a little squad of children, including Owen and Nora, huddled in the hallway.

"Aunt Hannah!" Owen called out, waving his arms frenetically. "Aunt Hannah!"

"Hi, everyone." Hannah pulled Owen into her arms and squeezed him. "Are you all excited about the party?"

"Yes!" said Nora, with a pirouette for emphasis. "Did you bring the apple juice?"

"Right here." Hannah tapped the tote bag she was holding. "I hope they have some treats."

"Yes. So many treats. Let's go." Nora grabbed Hannah's hand and dragged her toward the multipurpose room, packed with children and adults. Hannah headed to the tables set up along the back wall to deposit her contribution to the feast. Nora and Owen and the other children scampered away to join their friends in attacking the tables filled with cookies, cake, chips, pretzels, and a yet untouched vegetable platter. Hannah stood, staring into the mayhem of the party.

"Your first week completed, and you're still standing." Lea's voice snapped Hannah to attention.

"Yup." Hannah raised her hand to give Lea a high five. "If you told me three months ago that this is how I'd be spending a

Friday afternoon in June, I'd have never believed you. Do you think if I can get them to eat a couple of carrots and celery from that platter, we can call that dinner tonight?"

"Throw in some cheese, and I think you're done." Lea spun around to grab Claire, who was making a beeline for an enormous plate of brownies.

"Check out Nora and Ava over there." Lea nodded over to the two girls, who were dancing with complete abandon as other children watched in amazement. Ava danced over to a classmate and pulled him into their circle. At first, he was hesitant, but then the three of them continued their spazzy jumpy dancing as the other kids watched. They were clearly enjoying being the center of attention.

"Looks like they're going to be the cool girls," said Hannah.

"It's horrifying," said Lea, shaking her head.

An hour and a half later, they were headed back to the car. "Hey, when we get home, you guys can watch a movie. Special occasion because it's the last day of school," Hannah said to Nora and Owen.

After the movie, dinner, baths, and a video chat with Molly and Ted, Hannah was thankful they fell right to sleep. Tomorrow they would go to the aquarium, and Hannah made a mental note not to forget the backpack and other supplies for the trip. She couldn't just grab her purse and head out the door. Not anymore.

Exhausted, Hannah poured a glass of wine and went out to the back deck to watch the sunset. It was a beautiful evening, and the clouds and sun rays created brilliant colors over the mountains. Tomorrow, she knew, there would be rain all day.

She considered the week and how she not only survived it but managed the kids well—she had only lost her temper with them about a dozen times. There had been neither catastrophes nor career revelations, but she had completed a kick-ass vision board that fulfilled its purpose of clarifying her intentions. The board included both pictures (images of people and landscapes) and words (inspiring, get-going directives). She had hung it in her bathroom with the hope that it would provide daily inspiration.

She looked over at the new neighbor's house. Nothing had been going on over there all week. One day a car entered the garage, but she could not see who was driving. Otherwise, it had been completely quiet. Maybe they had not fully moved in yet.

Staring into space alone on the deck, she admitted to herself that she was bored. The kids were gone all day, and she had no friends except Lea, and Lea was extremely busy. When Nora and Owen were home, it felt like nonstop action. If the first week was any indication, the day times were going to be painfully tedious. In addition to planning her next move and surfing the internet for inspiration for her vision board and job options, she needed a project.

The days were long now, and although the sun had set, it was still light out as Hannah sipped her wine and surveyed Molly and Ted's back yard. Nora and Owen were the proud owners of a sandbox and two swings hanging from trees. The kids usually loved to play outside, Nora, with her constant search-and-rescue-themed doll and pony play and Owen with his trucks. The trees did not obstruct the view but were off to the sides to provide a little privacy from the neighbors.

Hannah studied one maple tree off to the right adjoining the new neighbor's yard. With its broad and sturdy branches, it would make an excellent climbing tree. Growing up, she and Molly and some friends from their old neighborhood spent hours up a tree just like it in the Wilson's yard. They had loved their leafy hideaway, but what they had really wanted was a treehouse.

As Hannah stared at the tree, she envisioned a treehouse in the maple. A platform would easily fit in front of the two largest branches sprawling from the trunk. A couple of poles would be needed to hold it up and, of course, a ladder. It would be so much fun for the kids. She envisioned Nora playing Tarzana with her imaginary monkey friends. Owen, as he grew older, could play—what did little boys play these days? Cowboys and Indians? Surely not. Dungeons and Dragons? House? Hannah had no idea. She mulled over the thought, weighing the challenges of such a grand project until it grew dark.

Settling into bed with her laptop and phone later that evening, Hannah sent Sara a text.

Today 11:06 PM

me: Hey

Sara: hewo. What's up in the green mountain state?

me: got me an idea for a project

Sara: utoh—a project? 2 kids 24/7 not enough?

me: I want to build something

Sara: what????????

me: a treehouse!

Sara: u cray cray

me: I'm an experienced home builder

Sara: true . . . but that sounds tricky what with it being IN A TREE!

me: not a problem. now that I have put it in writing to you I'm committed.

41

Sara: total challenge to do by yourself

me: don't be a dream killer. I can get help with the heavy lifts

Sara: true. how fun will it be for them! playing make believe and having picnics. then when they get older it can be where they go to have sex

 me: shut up that's so disturbing!!!! Go to bed I'll call you soon.

Sara: ❤

Seven

The Echo Center at Lake Champlain in Burlington was more of an environmental education center than a typical tourist-attraction aquarium. The website claimed a typical visit would take one and a half hours, and so Hannah was thrilled when she was able to drag it out for two. After lunch and a short stroll along the waterfront, they were headed back home by midafternoon. Both kids slept in the car on the way home, and when Hannah stopped for a coffee in town, she left them in the car, windows rolled down, in front of the shop's big glass window. They were sound asleep with their little heads turned and their mouths agape. She snapped a picture and texted it to Molly with a note: *"Had a blast and wore them out."*

Hannah could see the kids out the window as she stood at the counter ordering her coffee. She glanced around the sparsely populated café and was startled to see "the Asshole." She immediately looked away so that he would not catch her eye. Looking at the mirror behind the counter, she saw him sitting with a woman, looking at a computer and talking. His arm was around the back of the woman's chair, and they seemed awfully familiar.

Hannah left the coffee shop with her head averted and hurriedly got in her car. She sat for a moment out of the viewshed of the couple. She had a strong reaction to seeing him—perhaps because he had been on her mind since the incident in the park. He was attractive in that geeky-glasses self-possessed calm way that always intrigued her. She had been wondering what would happen if they ran into each other again and what she would say. Then, when the moment came, she froze. Damn. But he was with a woman, and they were very cozy. *Oh well, who needs men?* She backed out of the parking space. She had her darlings in the back seat, dinner to make, and Candy Land to play.

Eight

"Don't turn around," said Nathan. He and Kendall sat in the town coffee shop after their hike, sipping from blue Dream Bean Café mugs, coffee with cream for him, maple latte for her. He was now attempting to fix her computer. "There's a woman at the register who has a little boy who called me an asshole the other day, and I'm also pretty sure she's my next-door neighbor."

"Poor Nathan. Still getting bullied by kids." Nathan could see that Kendall was having a hard time not turning her head to stare. "What did you do to deserve that?"

"I don't know. I just said hello to the kid."

"Great start in the new town. Okay, I'm going to turn around and look at her now." Kendall turned slightly in her chair and, without moving her head, turned her eyes to glance at the woman. "She looks pretty young to have kids who curse out old men. Are you sure that's her?"

"Yeah, I'm sure. I don't think she knows I'm her neighbor. She has two kids who were petting Cooper, and the boy just blurts out, 'You're an asshole' to me when I told him I liked his hat." Nathan looked out the window as the woman walked out of the café and entered her car.

"He probably had been warned about pedophiles with dogs." Kendall shrugged. "Cooper seemed good today. How's he doing with the move? Any issues?"

"He's good, loves the new place. Already acts like he's lived here forever."

"And what's the update on work, are you happy with the new gig?"

Nathan did not usually like to talk about his work. He was in IT, and he presumed everyone who was not into technology would find it boring. He was a project manager at a consulting firm doing web software application development, work he loved and was good at, but when he described his work to friends or family, he could see their eyes glaze over. When his company offered him an opportunity to work remotely as they expanded, Nathan jumped at the chance to move back home, especially now that his grandfather was ailing. He could travel to Chicago when needed and have occasional meetings with clients across the country.

"Job's going well," he told Kendall now. "I finished my first project, and so far, the feedback's been excellent. I'll know for sure when we meet in Chicago the first week of August. I have a break now before I start working on something for a health-care network. The workday goes by fast, and I like that. Plus, if it's nice out, I can go for a hike with one of my favorite sisters."

"You don't need to use the 'one of.' I know I'm your favorite."

"Grace *is* being pretty type A about the wedding," said Nathan.

"Tell me about it." Kendall rolled her eyes. "I guess all brides get obsessed. But thankfully, she's not bitchy. We did have a blast at her bachelorette weekend in Montreal. She was relaxed, and it was a lot of fun. Oh, and by the way, Lindsey didn't show up, but she's definitely coming to the wedding."

"Grace told me. I got to say I'm not thrilled about that. It'd be different if I had a date to bring."

"She's not bringing a date if that makes you feel any better."

"That's what I'm worried about. You've seen her when she's had a few drinks."

Kendall laughed. In unison, they said, "Jenny Gordon's wedding."

"I don't want a repeat of that," said Nathan.

"Oh, I want a front-row seat. But seriously, you need to get back out there, bro. Have you gone on one date? Have you met anyone?"

"I'm open to it. I've just been busy. Actually, Dylan said he has someone he wants to set me up with. A friend of Kim's from work. I have to go to Chicago on Monday for a couple of days, but then I'll arrange it."

"That's a start. You need to meet some nice Vermont girl and stay put. I like having you around, and not just because you're a genius and fixed my computer." Kendall picked up her computer bag and rose from the chair. "Next time I see you, I want to hear about your date with Kim's friend. You better go. Promise?"

"I will." He followed his sister to the door. "I'm psyched about it."

Nine

On Monday morning, after getting the kids off to their first day of camp, Hannah made her way back to the library, intent on gathering some books on back yard construction projects. Not surprisingly, she found nothing at the library devoted explicitly to treehouse building but was able to get some promising titles on interlibrary loan. They would be available in two days. Impatient for a quicker start on her project, she headed west on the interstate toward Burlington with the plan to check out the big box home improvement store where she had previously noticed a display of construction and decorating books. Her extensive internet research and YouTube video viewing were helpful, but she always preferred a book in hand, especially one with lots of diagrams.

At Home Depot, she found what she needed, *The Complete Guide—Build Your Kids a Treehouse*, courtesy of Black and Decker. Skimming the book at the checkout line, she optimistically concluded the project was not beyond her skill set. She could measure, saw, hammer, and drill as needed. Her only concern would be the more significant lift requirements, for instance, actually getting the stuff up in the tree.

Driving back to Waterbury, Hannah's thoughts turned from treehouse to regular house, and she stopped to do some grocery shopping and get some badly needed toilet paper. Nora and Owen wouldn't be home for another few hours, and if she hurried, she could spend some time doing a preliminary schematic and figure out how much this grand plan of hers would cost.

She pondered about when precisely she should tell the kids. She recalled Molly's advice that she should never tell the children about any plans until they were definite and you were in the car, going to "fill in the blank." They would never stop nagging, especially Owen, who lacked any understanding of time frame. It reminded her of the family vacation to Alaska when her parents employed the same policy. She would figure it all out, determine if it was feasible both financially and physically, and then spring it on them. The idea had only been incubating for a short time, but her excitement was building, and she was confident she could make it happen. Of course, there was the small detail about asking Molly and Ted for permission to do the project as well. She could never tell the kids before they approved it.

But she would not bring it up yet, and when Ted and Molly video called that evening, she did not mention her grand plan. Nora and Owen were in the bath, and Hannah brought the laptop into the bathroom, but it was an unrewarding conversation, as the kids were involved in one of Nora's kidnapping adventures with bath toys and did not want to change gears to speak to their parents. Molly was concerned that the children were not appropriately dismayed at her absence. Hannah reassured her that nearly every evening, at least one of the kids would become distressed over the fact that Mommy and Daddy were not there to tuck them in.

Hannah was playing child psychologist frequently in this new job of hers. It was a balancing act to try and keep the kids secure in the knowledge their parents loved them, missed them, and would be coming back, while not talking about them too much. All in all, they were managing well.

For the next few rainy days, while the kids enjoyed "Around the World Week" at camp, Hannah read the construction books and searched the internet for treehouse designs. She found everything from simple platform designs to actual homes and hotels built in trees. She needed to find a design both aesthetically pleasing and within her abilities. It had to be simple enough to complete before Ted and Molly returned. She thought long and hard about how to ask them for permission to construct what could potentially be a disaster in their back yard. She did not want to upset or worry them. It would be great fun to surprise them, but that could backfire. What if Ted had always longed to build a treehouse with his children, and she stole this from him? And, really, a surprise was out of the question because there was no way that Nora and Owen would be able to keep that kind of secret from them.

In the end, she decided the best approach would be to write them an email and describe what she wanted to do, where in the yard it would be, and how she would implement her ideas. She would send along pictures of the tree and a rough sketch of her design. That way, they could understand the full scope, mull it over, and get back to her. Midweek, she pushed send on the email:

Dear Molly and Ted,

You'll notice at first glance that this is a very long email complete with attachments. DON'T WORRY— everything is fine, kids are great, everything is okay. I just want to write and ask you something important. Before I continue, I want to, first of all, say that a) I'm genuinely excited about this and b) I'll completely understand if you are not.

Here is the situation. I adore spending time with the kids, and after a week and a half, I'm happy to have this time with them. The thing is, while I'm grateful they're busy all day, I do find the hours without them kind of boring. The other night I had a great idea that I'd love to do but am writing to ask your permission since it involves your home. I'd like to build Nora and Owen a treehouse in the back yard. (oooohh, would love to see your reaction right now)

I'd like to think your first thought would be "that's so cool." But maybe it's "what the hell is she thinking?" But in either case, I'd like to continue to tell you about my idea.

You know I can build. You've seen my work, pictures of it anyway, from Kenya. I know that I can do this on my own in terms of general construction. I may need help with the raising of the platform onto the tree and plan to hire a handyman if need be. I have already found a simple plan and am attaching a picture of a finished project. Because the kids are young, the plan doesn't call for the house to be too far off the ground, just about six feet. And the structure will not actually be attached to the tree, just built around it, giving it room to grow.

This will, of course, all be at my expense. Oh, and I'll check out the permitting requirements, setbacks, etc. I want this to be legit and not cause you any problems. I'll buy from the local stores and lumber yards, etc.

So that's my idea. I know that I can do it in my "spare time" without taking away any of my energy or time with the kids. I have not told them, so if you think this isn't a good idea, no harm done there.

So, what do you say? Let me know if you have any

questions or want more details. I promise it's going to be awesome.

Please say YES!

Love you. Hannah

P.S. Remember how we always wanted a treehouse, Molly?????

Ten

"Larry, do we have any ordinances regarding treehouses?" shouted the clerk to her coworker at the town hall the next morning. Hannah had promised Molly and Ted that she would get permits, and she wanted to investigate the regulations immediately in case they presented a problem.

"Just the same setbacks as other ancillary buildings without foundations," Larry shouted back, without looking up from his desk.

"Could you tell me what the setbacks are for ancillary buildings?" asked Hannah.

Larry looked up at the sound of Hannah's voice and raised an eyebrow as he rose and walked to the clerk's desk.

"You going to build a treehouse?"

"That's my plan."

"A playhouse, right? Not a structure that you plan to live in?" he asked.

"Nope, just a playhouse for kids."

"I always wanted a treehouse when I was a kid. That's cool," Larry said. "Do you have plans? Who's going to do the work—your husband . . . a contractor?"

Hannah pulled a file folder from her handbag and laid it on the desk. "No husband. I'm going to build it." Hannah pulled out the sketch of the treehouse. She had a lot of experience with people, particularly men, questioning her ability to use a hammer. Sometimes they were intrigued, sometimes they laughed and said something sexist, but always they were surprised. Larry did not disappoint.

The municipal worker took the picture and studied it with both eyebrows raised this time.

"That's some treehouse! Are you serious? Are you going to do this by yourself?"

"I plan to get some help with the heavy lifting, but yes, I plan to build it."

"Impressive. Good for you. Okay, just make sure you keep ten feet from the side property line and ten feet from the back. Give me your address, and I can look up the property line on the tax map, and we can also look at the satellite image on the internet."

"It's 293 Dog River Road," said Hannah.

Larry disappeared and returned, setting a big book on the counter. After finding Molly and Ted's block and lot, he showed Hannah where the survey markers could be found on the property and instructed her how to keep a proper distance from the sideline. They looked at the satellite image, and it was clear the tree was a safe distance from the property line. She was grateful she did not need a permit and happy she had stopped in to verify the rules.

"You may want to let your neighbor on this side know what your plans are," said Larry. "Sometimes, people get bent out of shape and complain if their neighbors build structures they can see from their houses or decks. It's nice to let them know that it's a permissible structure."

"That's a great idea. I'll let them know."

Hannah drove home and went directly to the house next door to introduce herself and tell them about her treehouse plans. She marched up the steps of the front porch and rapped on the door. No answer. After a moment, she knocked again. Still, no response. Disappointed, she peered cautiously into the front window. If there was someone in there deliberately ignoring her, and they saw her, that would be both embarrassing and discouraging, but it did not appear that anyone was home. She took a moment to look around. She liked the open floor plan of the house. Some living room furniture was in place, but artwork and a dozen unpacked boxes lined the walls. There was a dog bed near the fireplace. It did not look as if the homeowners were progressing much in their unpacking.

Anxious to move things along on the planning front, Hannah walked back home and wrote a note to the neighbors explaining her project.

Welcome to the neighborhood! We've yet to meet, but I live next door in the yellow house, and I hope you're getting settled and enjoying your new place.

I've stopped by a couple of times, but you were not in. I look forward to meeting you soon, and I'd like to also talk to you about a project I'm planning for our back yard. Please drop by and say hello when you have a chance. I'm home if you see the blue car in the driveway.

Hannah Spencer

Hannah tied the note to a bottle of Pinot Noir and returned to the neighbor's home, taking a short cut this time across the yards. The exterior of the neighbor's house was nice too, gray clapboard with a fieldstone path to the front door. The yard, as was typical in the area, was large, and there was an attached garage, which was a real bonus for the snowy winters. The lawn needed mowing. On the porch lay a box from Amazon, which had not been there before. She leaned in to examine the address label. Nathan Wild.

By noon, she had yet to hear back from her sister and brother-in-law and did not know if they had even received her email yet. She lay on the couch, laptop open on her stomach, and stared at the ceiling. Molly and Ted typically responded promptly to her messages, but sometimes they were delayed. She might have to be patient for a couple of days. Patience was not her virtue.

Hannah opened the Monster.com tab on her browser to see if there were any new postings in her saved job search. To her surprise, there were two. One in Portland, Oregon, and one in Boise, Idaho, two of the cities she had included in her search criteria. Reviewing the details, she considered the possibility of putting together an application for the position in Boise. Both applications were due in mid-July, and she wondered if they would want to fill the jobs right away. She would not be able to do any in-person interviews until mid-August. Her HR person had said summers were slow for hiring, so maybe they would wait for her availability or do everything by video conference.

The frustrating part of her job search was that she was not clear what exactly she was searching for in terms of work. She knew she needed a change, and she had taken the first step when she walked out the door of her office in Boston. The problem was, she had no idea where to begin after she closed the door behind her. The vision board was a start, but only a start.

Hannah abruptly sat up. *The treehouse isn't on my vision board.* Launching herself off the couch, she went to the bathroom and removed the poster board from its place on the wall. She brought it to the table and took a good look at her creation. It was intended to inform not just the summer but also her post-

Boston/post-Vermont life. She had created the project quickly and organically, almost through a stream of consciousness sprouting onto the board. Despite that, it was specific. The words she had chosen were deliberately placed over the pictures.

There was a picture of young professionals strolling down a city sidewalk, conducting a "walking meeting" dressed in business wear and clutching their phones. The words "Be the energy you want to attract" were pasted on one side and "Good things come to those who hustle" on the other. A woman at a computer with a spreadsheet was labeled "Use your Gifts." A woman with a briefcase in hand getting off a bus was captioned "Boldly Going." Men and women with perfect bodies lying on lounge chairs staring at an idyllic beach with fruity cocktails on little tables beside them had a caption that read, "Happiness is not a goal—it's a byproduct."

She had printed a photo from the internet of *Buffy the Vampire Slayer*, who, when she was thirteen, had been one of her first feminist role models. A quote from the show accompanied the photo: "And what are we if not women up to a challenge?" The treehouse could go with that quote, but she did not want to cover up Buffy.

There it was. The *Big Lebowski* quote: "If you will it, it is no dream." It was placed over a picture of a woman on a stage with an award. She carefully peeled off the photo of the woman with her fancy dress and cut the quote off the paper. She used Nora's markers and drew a colorful representation of her treehouse and glued the new picture and quote back on the board. "Perfect."

Plopping back on the couch, Hannah rechecked her email, to no avail. She hoped her sister would not be pissed at her for even suggesting she build a treehouse. Molly liked to keep things simple. She and Molly were getting along so well in recent years.

They had been quite close as young children, but during Hannah's teenage years, while Molly was away at college, Hannah had felt like an only child. Molly had left home and was enjoying the freedom of university right as their parents' marriage started deteriorating. Molly's departure left Hannah alone to navigate the difficulties of middle school as well as a cheerless home life.

Hannah had resented her sister for leaving her alone. Molly never did realize the impact of their parents' troubles on Hannah, and the few times Hannah had attempted to discuss the issue with her back in the day, Molly had been dismissive. Hannah's parents had even briefly separated just after Molly returned to school for her sophomore year (although the revisionist history story was that their dad was on an intense work project that required him to live in a hotel near his office). By the time Molly came back for Thanksgiving, their dad was back home, and Bob and Elizabeth were acting as if nothing had ever happened. Hannah never knew precisely what had gone wrong in her parents' marriage—typical midlife crap, she figured, whatever midlife crap was—and she never asked. She was glad they worked it out, as she loved and admired them both. She and Molly had discussed their parents' relationship a few years ago and agreed they were happy they didn't know the details of their difficult time. But a lasting result was that Molly and Hannah experienced two different upbringings, and Hannah felt that Molly did not have enough appreciation for how hard it had been on Hannah. Now, as adults, the gap in their ages had contracted, and Hannah was grateful they were once again close.

The sudden shrill ring of her phone pierced the silence and startled Hannah.

"Molly?" Hannah asked, seeing her sister's number on her phone as she came to attention on the couch.

"Hannah?"

"Moll, how's it going? Did you get my email?" Hannah could not contain herself. She stood and began pacing the living room, phone to her ear.

"Yup, we did. You're crazy, you know. Don't you have enough to do? You want to start a construction project?"

"I knew you'd say that!" Hannah laughed a fake laugh. "But here's the thing. I've been practicing this speech, so please listen. It's weird being in someone else's world. I don't have much of my stuff here, and I can't spend all day cleaning and reading and making dinner. I need a project. You know how I love building things."

"But a treehouse, Hannah? That sounds like a car dream that oughta stay in the car. I'm a little worried it'll consume you, and you won't have enough energy for the kids."

"It's not going to be a problem, I promise. The plans say it should take six weeks, and that isn't working on it all day long but a schedule for weekend warriors. I know that I can do it in our time frame. You know me, I've totally researched this. They'll love it—it'll keep them outside. Pleasssse say yes."

"Ted is jealous, but he knows he'll never get to it. He's more of a play-in-a-treehouse kinda dad rather than a build-a-tree-house kinda dad. He thinks it's a great idea."

"Does that mean yes?" asked Hannah, breathlessly.

"You must promise to abandon it if you get in over your head. And you gotta swear you won't get hurt building it, and *don't* let them help." Hannah knew Molly was smiling.

"I promise, I promise, I promise. I'll be careful. Did you notice the design has safety steps? I added those myself—rails and everything. Above all, it's going to be hard to get hurt in this thing. That's my number-one priority."

Ted took the phone and gave Hannah a long-distance tour of his workshop and let her know where she could find his tools. "You're an ambitious woman, Hannah Spencer."

Hannah and Molly continued chatting for a while longer. Molly reported that they were doing a lot of backpacking with heavy gear on long hikes and that Ted had lost three toenails already from hiking. In between tales of high adventures, they would sprinkle the conversation with "but we miss the kids so much." Hannah slightly envied their freedom and ability to see and experience the raw beauty of the land. Hannah updated her sister on recent adventures at camp. "Around the World Week" was a big hit, and the kids were doing all kinds of crafts and games from various countries. "I'm saving every single one of their craft projects for you. Next, I'm going to have to build an addition to your house to display them."

They hung up, and Hannah danced alone in the kitchen, singing, "I'm gonna build a treehouse, I'm gonna be a builder, it's gonna be fantastic, I must be crazy."

Eleven

Nathan coasted up the driveway with Cooper by his side, just back from riding on the mountain bike trails close to his house. He was tired, having just returned from Chicago, but at the same time, energized by the ride. Cooper, on the other hand, was just plain tired. Nathan noticed some items on his front porch, so he parked his bike in the garage and went to see what had been delivered. Next to a midsized package from Amazon was a bottle of wine with a note. He was expecting the box, a special cable for his computer, but the wine was a surprise. The note attached to the bottle was written in a neat and precise hand.

He read it once and then reread it. He observed that throughout, the note said "I," not "we," but then it said "our." *Wouldn't a person typically write "we" if they were married?* She was, he suspected, a single mother of two. He wanted to get to know more about her. She was attractive, but he didn't have anything to go on personality-wise other than their one brief encounter at the park. If she was a single mom, getting to know her better could be complicated. If she was a married mom, well, no way. What was it she wanted to discuss about the back yard?

Nathan looked at the house next door, where a blue Honda Civic stood in the driveway. He needed a shower, had a conference call soon, and was going to meet some high school friends in Burlington for dinner. Tomorrow, Grace would be coming for the day to direct him on bird carving and arbor details. He would go to the neighbor's sometime over the weekend and find out what "Hannah Spencer" was cooking up for the back yard.

Nathan loved his new house and first-time homeownership. One of the things he liked best about his home was the unobstructed views and big yard. When he had asked the realtor who lived in the house next door, she had only said it was "a very nice family."

"I guess we'll see about that," he said to Cooper, who followed him up the stairs.

Twelve

Hannah pulled the materials list from the computer printer and reviewed it for the third time, comparing it with the detailed plans she had bought off the internet. She loved the idea of constructing the treehouse out of used materials and knew it would appeal to Molly and Ted as well. She found a nonprofit group in Burlington devoted to deconstructing houses and selling the salvaged lumber, windows, doors, and hardware. It was Friday, and she hoped that the materials could be delivered on Monday, but she hadn't a clue whether this was a reasonable request. In Kenya, gathering the materials for building the houses was the most challenging part of the job—that and making sure they were not stolen once they were received.

Craving a run, she put on her running clothes and drove to the park along the river, which had recently become her favorite running spot. The area was growing on her. Not only was it beautiful around every corner, but the people, overall, were friendly, and there weren't too many of them. Boston was so crowded she had felt claustrophobic and tense much of the time. She could run this whole route and see maybe only a dozen other people. Running in Boston Common or along the Charles River was like running an obstacle course dodging skaters, strollers, skateboarders, and other runners and walkers.

Her four-mile scenic run was on a half pavement, half dirt road along the Winooski River, and afterward, she felt exhilarated. Following a shower and change, she was soon back in her car headed to Burlington.

Hannah found the warehouse without any problem and parked her car. She headed to the large brick building and the doorway painted with an ENTER sign above.

"Can I help you?" A man approached her as she walked through the surprisingly big warehouse.

"Hi, I need some lumber and other stuff and wanted to see what you all have available." Hannah handed him her detailed list.

"Let's see what you've got there." He scanned the paper. "I'll get somebody to help you." He reached for an intercom, and before too long "Walt" appeared and whisked Hannah away to the back of the building, which housed massive piles of lumber.

"I think we have a lot of what you need here. What are you building?"

"A treehouse. It's for my niece and nephew. But I don't have a truck or any way to transport it. Do you deliver? I live out in Waterbury."

"A treehouse. I always wanted a treehouse when I was a kid. But delivery, that's not something we do," said Walt. "There is a guy who you can hire to deliver it, though. I can give him a call and see if he is available. We'll load his truck, and to Waterbury, it'll be around $75.00 for the delivery."

"That'd be great. I'd appreciate that."

Hannah and Walt examined the lumber, and he explained to her their various qualities. There was a lot to consider, but she had done her research. She did not want the wood to be too heavy, as it was going to be challenging enough to do this job by herself. The reclaimed timber was already weathered and dried, so it was denser and sturdier than fresh wood. She inspected each piece to check for previously applied hazardous finishes.

Hannah was able to get most of the lumber she needed with Walt's help and was pleased with the quality of the material. He called the delivery guy, and Hannah was thrilled when she learned he could have it to the house on Monday.

Walt pointed Hannah in the direction of the hardware department to select the screws, bolts, and other miscellaneous hardware. She chose three small windows, an old pulley, and a mermaid door knocker, which Nora would love. She left the warehouse feeling satisfied with her purchases.

Hannah drove to the Waterbury hardware store, intending to pick up the remaining items not found at the reuse warehouse. As she made her way to the nuts-and-bolts section, the "Asshole" walked through the door. *Geez, this is a small town.* She ducked behind a stack of paint cans as he moved by her. He was with the same woman she had seen him with at the coffee shop, Hannah was certain. She could see she was pretty, and she had her arm locked in his as they walked down the aisle. Hannah stealthily followed them, keeping her head down, at a safe distance from the couple.

"How many of these things do I need to make?" asked the Asshole.

"We need twenty, but if you could make a few extras, that'd be good," the girl said. "Wow, this place is amazing. We should have registered here for the wedding. A lot of useful stuff." She stopped to pick up a cordless drill and examined it.

The couple walked toward the lumber department, and Hannah peeked around the corner to get a better look. They were a great-looking couple and were now laughing at something he said that Hannah could not hear. She could, however, see a diamond ring on the woman's finger.

Hannah gathered the remaining items on her list and

brought them to the checkout, keeping a close eye on the couple, hoping they would not see her. She wanted to somehow explain to this guy why Owen called him an asshole at the park and clarify that it was not directed at him personally. She did not think it would be a good idea to bring this up in front of the woman who wasn't present at the incident. It was a "you had to be there" moment.

Hannah managed to get out of the store and into her car with her goods without being seen. Donning her sunglasses, she slid down on her front seat and waited until the couple exited the store. He was carrying a large piece of wood, and she carried a small can of paint. They walked right in front of her car but did not glance in her direction. Hannah wondered what they were making and when they were getting married. She also thought that he didn't look like an asshole at all.

Thirteen

On Sunday, the weather report called for a ninety-degree afternoon, a rare occurrence for a June day in Vermont. Hannah and the children finished breakfast and were lounging around the living room doing their own things. Hannah was on her computer, Nora was playing with her dolls at the table, and Owen was on the floor, taking his trucks through an imaginary carwash.

"Hey, do you guys want to play in the pool in the back yard today? asked Hannah. "It's going to be super hot."

"Yes, yes, yes," cried Nora, jumping up and down. "That will be so much fun. I'm going to put on my bathing suit and pretend I am a mermaid."

"Of course you are." Hannah smiled at her niece. "How about you, Owen? Do you want to splash around in the pool?"

"Yes, I do." He did not look up from his trucks on the floor. It occurred to Hannah that Owen was not sucking his thumb as much this week. She did not want to ask him about it, so instead, she asked Nora if she had noticed the same.

"Someone called him a baby at camp. I told him it was because of his thumb sucking, and I think he's trying to stop."

"That's sad, but it'd be great if he could stop." Getting Owen to stop thumb sucking would be another accomplishment for the summer.

Hannah arranged the blow-up pool in a sunny part of the

yard and filled it so it would warm up enough for the kids to enjoy. While it filled, she gazed at the tree where, beginning the next day, she would erect a treehouse. The maple was beautiful, and Hannah would make sure the treehouse did not distract too much from its grandeur. Shel Silverstein's *The Giving Tree* was one of the most influential books of her childhood, and Hannah recalled the sacrifice the tree gave to the little boy to bring him joy. "I won't let that happen to you," Hannah whispered to the tree. She made a silent promise to herself to make sure, above all else, no trees would be harmed in the fulfillment of her passion project.

"Okay, let's go!" she said after the threesome finished their lunch and were slathered with sunscreen. She did not think a two-foot-high pool would require the customary half-hour wait before swimming.

Owen and Nora belly-flopped into the pool as Hannah, in her bikini and an oversized T-shirt, pulled a chair beside them.

"Aren't you coming in?" asked Nora.

"I think I'll just watch you for a while and warm up first."

She opened an old copy of *What Color Is Your Parachute?* found on Molly's bookshelf.

Owen and Nora ran through the yard, jumping in and out of the pool for a full half hour before they started begging her to come in with them. She considered this a huge victory, so she obliged, taking off her T-shirt and glasses and stepping into the pool. It was cold to her, even on the hot day. But she took the plunge and lay down in the grass-clipping-filled pool with the kids, who had great fun splashing her. No sooner had she fully immersed herself than Owen stood up, pointing to the house.

"Who's that?"

Hannah turned to see a man near the back door. Without her glasses or contacts, she couldn't see him clearly.

"Hello," he called out, staying put where he was, several yards away from the pool. "Sorry to bother. I knocked but heard you in the back. I'm your neighbor. You left me a note."

"Hi. Yes, I did," said Hannah. She was still sitting in the pool, feeling ridiculous. Owen and Nora were uncharacteristically quiet as they sat transfixed by the scene playing out before them.

"I can come back later," the man said.

"No, now's good," said Hannah, thinking the opposite. "Lemme just get outta here."

Bikini-clad Hannah exited the pool in full view of her neighbor. Fortunately, there was a pile of towels on the chair, and she quickly wrapped herself, put on her glasses, and headed toward the visitor.

Hannah looked back at the kids. "You guys stay in the pool, please." She didn't want them to hear about the treehouse just yet. The children thankfully obliged and commenced with their splashing.

As Hannah approached her neighbor, her stomach lurched. It was the Asshole. *What is he doing here? Is he my neighbor?*

The man put out his hand and said, "Hi, Nathan Wild."

Hannah stared at him and was momentarily speechless. Hannah was never speechless.

"Hi," she mumbled, shaking his hand. She did not know what else to say. Words were not coming.

"IT'S PRINCE CHARMING!" Nora yelled from the pool. She stood and raised her arms into the air, twirling. "IT'S PRINCE CHARMING!"

Hannah sunk her head and threw her hand to her forehead,

embarrassed. "Don't mind her; she lives in Fantasyland. That's Nora and Owen. I'm Hannah."

Nathan smiled and looked at the children. "Thanks for the wine."

"Yeah, sure, ah . . . welcome to the neighborhood."

A big brown dog suddenly appeared, tearing through the back yard toward them, and bounded toward Nathan.

"Hey, buddy, how'd you get out?"

The dog breezed right by Nathan and headed toward the kids. He circled the pool good-naturedly, wagging his tail, begging for attention. Owen and Nora jumped out of the pool to pet the dog. Hannah turned abruptly, heading for the children.

"Don't worry, Cooper's gentle."

"You mentioned that last time we met." The dog did seem friendly and was sitting patiently, letting the kids pet him. She turned back to Nathan. "I'm sorry Owen called you an asshole. He didn't realize what he was saying. He heard me talking to a friend and just repeated it."

"You call your friends assholes?" Nathan asked.

Wow, great smile. Hannah laughed. "No, I didn't call her an asshole. I was talking about someone else, and he's definitely an asshole." Hannah pointed her thumb in the direction of Nora and Owen chasing Cooper around the yard. "I think we should probably stop talking about assholes now."

"Yeah, probably." Nathan chuckled as he looked at the dog and children. "What is it you wanted to tell me about? You mentioned a project in your yard." Cooper bounded toward them, and Nathan picked up a stick and threw it toward the pool.

"Hey, you guys, come here and meet our neighbor," said Hannah. Nora and Owen ran back with Cooper to the spot where Nathan and Hannah stood.

"This is Nathan. He just moved in next door," said Hannah. "This is Nora and Owen."

"Hi," said Nathan.

"Hey, I know you," said Nora. Hannah could see Nora processing their previous meeting at the park.

"That's the man you called a bad word," Nora whispered to her brother, although all could hear. Owen looked at him, and his face went blank. He then took a couple of steps toward Hannah and leaned into her, turning his face into her thigh. Hannah's arm went around the boy, and she squatted down to his eye level.

"It's okay, honey," she said, comforting him. "Nathan wanted to meet us so we could all be friends. Just say hi."

"Hi," mumbled Owen, without making eye contact with Nathan.

The boy suddenly darted away to resume playing with the dog, and Nora ran after him.

"He's embarrassed," said Hannah. She adjusted her towel, tightening it around her chest. "I haven't told them yet, but I'm going to build a treehouse in that maple over there." Hannah pointed to the designated tree in the side yard.

"Wow! That's ambitious," Nathan said, eyebrows raised.

"I wanted to tell you so you were prepared for all the banging and stuff that'll be happening. I went to the town hall, and they said I don't need any permits, but since it's on the border, I wanted to be a good neighbor and all." She smiled nervously. "Because of the way the tree line is, I don't think it will impact your view. The treehouse will be oriented so it'll face our yard and the kids won't be able to spy on you or anything."

"We had a treehouse growing up, but it's kind of a deer stand now," said Nathan. "It'll be fun for them."

Suddenly Hannah's phone began an untimely buzzing.

"Just a sec." She turned away to pick up the phone, resting on the chair. *Molly*. She had to answer. Molly had told her she was planning to call that afternoon.

"I have to take this. It's from South America," she said by way of explanation. She hoped her look portrayed her disappointment in having to end their conversation.

"Hi," she said into the phone to her sister. "Hang on a second."

"No worries," Nathan said, seeming to take the hint. "Good luck with . . ." He pointed at the tree, smiled, and winked. "C'mon, Coop," he called, and the dog bounded for him. They turned and left the yard.

Hannah waved sheepishly and said, "Bye."

The moment Hannah was off the phone and the kids reengaged with the pool, Hannah texted Sara.

Today 1:43 PM

me: OMG my new neighbor is the ASSHOLE.

Sara: What????

me: He came over today and introduced himself and he's the guy owen called an asshole. I could barely speak to him. and I was in a bikini

Sara: Is he cute

me: That would be a yes

Sara: What happened

me: I told him about the treehouse and we talked for a few minutes and then Molly called and I had to take the call so he left

Sara: How old is he what does he look like

me: Our age . . . brown hair glasses tall, John Krasinski-ish didn't study him cuz I was so freaking nervous what with me being in a bikini and a towel and Nora's calling him prince Charming and all. I don't know what his story is - like does he live with his parents there or what? He's got a dog.

Sara: Prince charming, huh? . . . what'd he say about the treehouse?

me: He was cool with it oh ya . . . and he winked at me

Sara: Ewwwwwwwwwwwwwwwwwwwww

me: I know but it was about keeping it secret from the kids so it wasn't that weird

me: Whats up with you?

Sara: Good weekend went to Cleves last night drank too much and Aaron had to put me to bed like back in college . . . going to the cape next weekend

me: Who's going?

Sara: Amanda, Holly, Matt, Seth, Kevin we rented a house.

me: Seth???

Sara: Amanda invited him. she knows what he did to you. she's so stupid

me: He's such a douche. Did I tell you right before I left he texted me a "what's up" . . . after ghosting me?

Sara: That tracks

me: But the Cape sounds fun - I might go to see my folks for the fourth - but you'll be in Maine. I'm not going to see you at all this summer

Sara: I know. we'll figure something out

me: I gotta go

Sara: ❤

me: ❤

Fourteen

"Please sit still and let me finish." Hannah pleaded with Nora as she attempted in vain to attach an elastic band around the girl's gathered locks.

"But I want to go play before Lea gets here, and I'm running out of time." Nora's whine was irritating. Hannah could not wait to get them out of the house.

"Hold still, and then you can go." Hannah struggled with the elastic band and brushed the ponytail. "*Do not* take off your shoes."

Owen walked up to them. "I don't want to go to camp today." He said it with a confidence that indicated a new battle ahead.

Hannah sighed. "Seriously? It's 'Safari Week' at camp. That's going to be so much fun. You'd hate to miss that."

"I want to go in the pool and pway wit the bwown dog today," he said, thumb in mouth.

"I don't know if the dog can play today, and I have to go somewhere, so I really need you to go to camp."

"Can we pway wit the dog afta camp?"

"I don't know if the dog can play, but maybe." She knew this was a bad tactic to take with him (don't make promises you can't keep), but she was getting desperate; Lea would arrive soon, and they were going to be late today.

"Okay, you two—get your bags, and let's go wait for Lea,"

Hannah said as she released Nora and went to put on her own shoes.

Lea pulled up with her three kids in the minivan and waved cheerily as Hannah and the children approached the car. She always made the whole parent thing look so damn easy, but Hannah knew it couldn't be with three of them. Hannah buckled Nora and Owen into their seats and kissed them goodbye.

"Have fun, everyone. Can't wait to hear all about Safari Week. Thanks again, Lea," she said, waving. As the van pulled away, Hannah turned and glanced at the neighbor's house. Nathan was in his yard under a tree, stacking a pile of big logs. He certainly was up bright and early. She watched him rip the bark off one of the logs with a tool. He wore a baseball cap and a T-shirt, and it occurred to Hannah that it must have been shirtless Nathan they had seen that day eating lunch on the deck. Hannah was dying to know what was up with him and the house next door. Who else lived there? His parents? His fiancée?

She wanted to strike up another conversation with him without looking too obvious. Now, however, was not the time. She had on thin cotton pajama bottoms and an old T-shirt that read *I Did It. I Let the Dogs Out* leftover from her college days. Hannah headed back into the house, wanting to get dressed before the lumber truck showed up. Nathan reconnaissance would have to wait.

FOLLOWING HIS USUAL morning walk with Cooper along the embankment toward the creek at the back of his property, Nathan resolved to begin working on the arbor for Grace's wedding. He assembled a log-stripping station under the shade of the trees in his side yard near the driveway, strategically arranged to watch the action at Hannah's house surreptitiously. Slipping on his earphones, he commenced the stripping of the bark. The "log guy" had explained that the most efficient method of stripping would be to soak the logs first. The previous evening, he had laid them on a tarp and wet them, and sure enough, the bark was coming off easier than he expected. He planned to set four good-sized posts into the ground, and he needed four others, two short and two long, for the top. He had made sure the logs were similar in circumference as well as the proper lengths. Grace and Nick would be putting the arbor in their yard after the wedding, and Nathan was determined to build it to last.

A minivan pulled into the driveway of Hannah's house, and Nathan glanced across the yard to watch the morning routine. Ever since their all too brief meeting yesterday, he was more curious than ever about the woman with the kids and her plans to build a treehouse.

No sign of a husband or any other adult since he had been casually surveilling the house. As he had noticed on a couple of other mornings, the two children, Nora and Owen, came out of the house with Hannah and got into the minivan driven by another woman. One day the previous week, he had seen the minivan return the children later in the afternoon. This meant Hannah was by herself during the day a lot, as the blue car was frequently parked outside. There could be someone else in the house who never went out. *A bedridden relative? A TV-watching, computer-game-playing or work-at-home husband or boyfriend?*

Nathan was sweating from his labors by the time a flat-bed truck pulled into Hannah's driveway. He stopped his log stripping and made his way into his house. Water bottle in hand, he trotted upstairs to his office, where he could discreetly check out the activities next door from the second-floor window. He peered out the window, carefully pulling the shade to the side so he would not be observed spying. The back of the truck was full of lumber, and he concluded it must be for her treehouse project. He watched as the delivery man, assisted by Hannah, off-loaded the lumber. It was an enormous pile of wood. The truck driver stuck around to chat Hannah up following the unloading. She was dressed in faded jean overalls with a tank top underneath. She seemed to be enjoying the conversation with animated laughter.

They eventually shook hands, and the truck backed out of the driveway. Nathan bolted down the stairs and walked back into the yard. Careful not to glance her way, he returned to his logs.

AS THE TRUCK pulled away, Hannah surveyed the impressive pile of lumber now resting in the driveway of her sister's home. For a moment, she was struck with panic. *I must be out of my mind.* This was going to be a lot of work.

Her first chore would be to reorganize the lumber into stacks based on their future purpose. She dragged the boards and posts into several piles and categorized each, cross-checking them with her list. She was thankful that all items were present and accounted for but also knew there would be many more components to purchase. She sat on one of the wood stacks and opened a granola bar.

"Hey there, buddy," she said to the dog who suddenly appeared next to her. "You're Cooper, right?" The dog sat down, making himself at home at her feet, looking at her with his sweet brown eyes.

"He wants a handout," said a voice from behind. "Cooper, stop begging." Nathan walked toward Hannah, dog leash in hand.

"Hey . . . he's not bothering me, are you, Cooper?" Hannah said as she rubbed the dog's ears. Her pulse quickened as Nathan stopped in front of her, blocking her from the sun.

"He's a wanderer. Try as I might, unless I keep him tethered in the back yard, he loves to go off exploring. He's gotten himself lost a few times."

"That's no good. How old is he?"

"About three, but he still acts like an adolescent. Thinks he knows everything and can still use his charm to stay out of trouble. I see your project is underway," he said, gesturing toward the woodpile.

"Yup. I was sorting through everything and realizing I was out of my mind." Hannah considered mentioning that he, too, was working on some construction but stopped herself just in time. She did not want him to know she had been watching.

"Have you done this kind of thing before? Not being sexist," he said, holding up his palm. "It seems like a huge undertaking."

"I'll have you know that I've built entire houses before," stated Hannah, proudly raising her chin. "In Kenya, to be exact."

"Really?" said Nathan. "That's cool. Plus, I'm sure you'll have lots of help."

"Help?"

"I mean from your family. The kids, your husband?"

"Husband? I'm not married!" As she blurted out the words, Cooper sprang up and darted after a squirrel. He was gone in a flash. "Hey, come back here. Cooper!" Hannah jumped to her feet.

"COOPER," called Nathan. "COME."

Cooper was in the wind. He bolted into the back yard and ran toward the embankment and creek. The squirrel had escaped up a tree, but the dog kept going.

"Ahh, shit, I don't want to spend my day searching for him. I gotta go." Nathan jogged off after Cooper.

Hannah followed him. "There's a path down this way that he probably took."

The two clambered down the path toward the creek, repeatedly calling for the dog. Cooper was nowhere in sight. Hannah sensed Nathan's anxiety.

"Maybe we should call the police in case anyone reports finding him," she suggested.

"I only do that after a half hour. I can usually lure him back."

By the creek, Hannah noticed paw prints in the sand. "I think he was here," she said, pointing at the sand.

"Could be, or maybe those are coyote tracks." He looked at her with a charismatic smile.

Hannah felt her cheeks flush as she turned her head to look at him. Behind them came a rustling sound followed by Cooper flying toward them, jumping through the long grasses like a baby deer.

"Get over here, you bad boy," said Nathan. Cooper came immediately, and Nathan hugged the dog to him, petting him roughly. "You have got to stop running off. He's a rescue dog. I got him when he was a year old, and no one knew where he came from. He's the best except for this wandering part." Nathan attached the leash to Cooper's collar.

"Hmm, that's a problem." They headed for the path to the house. "I like that he came to visit me, though. I love dogs, and he's a sweetheart."

"I've been trying to train him. I was hoping my treat method would work, but he usually steals the treat and runs off again. This was no big deal—he was only gone a few minutes. Right before I moved here, he wandered off for about three hours before I got a call. It was a nightmare. I was crazy."

An opening. "That's horrible. Where were you living?"

"Chicago."

Unsatisfactory amount of information. Hannah was not sure how much she should press the personal questions.

After a moment, Nathan took over and asked, "What about you? Did you grow up here?"

"Massachusetts, actually," said Hannah. "My parents still live there, but my sister Molly moved to Vermont after college."

"Where does your sister live? Nearby?"

Hannah stole a glance at Nathan, who was looking at the ground as they walked along. "Yeah, you can say that. I'm staying in her house!"

"I haven't seen her around—just you and your kids."

"They're not my kids!" She sounded more horrified than she meant. "Nora and Owen are my niece and nephew. They're Molly and Ted's kids—my sister and her husband's. I'm taking care of them for the summer while they're in Chile. They're both college professors, and they're on sabbatical."

Nathan stopped in his tracks and looked at Hannah. "Ohhh," he said with open astonishment on his face. He then lit up with a wide grin.

Is he flirting with me? Talk about a dog. He had a fiancée! She was not satisfied with the amount of information she had obtained about Nathan on their short Cooper hunt, but she wasn't going to keep up the conversation *now*.

They walked the rest of the way back to the driveway in silence. Hannah was processing their conversation. He thought she was married and that Nora and Owen were her kids. How old did he think she was?

"Well, Hannah from Massachusetts, I'll let you get back to your work. Thanks for helping me find Cooper. See ya now. Come on, Coop." He turned and walked to his house.

"See you." She lifted a large two by four and pretended to get back to work in case he peeked back at her.

But in truth, she was puzzled by their interaction. Nathan was friendly, a bit awkward, but legit handsome. He had the best grin, authentic with white, perfectly aligned teeth. And squinty eyes, just the kind she liked. She had been hit on enough in her life to recognize a hit when she got one. It was perplexing. Well, he was a player, that's all. But if he was a player, the hint of awkward did not fit. Unless that was part of his game.

She put Nathan out of her mind and continued making the list of the additional items she would need for the treehouse. She would call Sara later to talk about Nathan. Sara had mad skills when it came to analyzing men and would dissect every word of their conversation and present her findings.

Sara was rarely wrong in her assessments.

HANNAH WAS CLEARING out one of the garage bays to create a weatherproof workstation when the minivan full of children arrived in the afternoon. Hannah rushed to the parked van and opened the sliding door. "Guess what, everyone? I have a big surprise!"

"I love surprises," crooned Nora. She clapped her hands rapidly and grinned at Ava.

Owen slapped his hands over his eyes and peeked through his fingers and said, "What surprise?"

"Come on, let's get you out of the car and I'll show you," said Hannah, unbuckling his straps.

The group walked to the garage, where much of the wood was now neatly stacked in several distinct piles.

"Hannah . . . ," Lea said. She stopped and waved her hand at the wood. "What's all this for?"

"Is this the surprise?" asked Ava. The tiny girl frowned and put her hand on her hip, shifting her weight to one leg.

"Yes," said Hannah. "I'm going to make something out of it. Ready? Here it is: I'm going to make a treehouse in the back for you kids to play in." Everyone started whooping and talking at once.

"Oh. My. God," said Lea, drawing her hand to her mouth. "You're kidding? You're not kidding. Are you out of your mind?"

"A treehouse. I want a treehouse. I want a treehouse," said Nora. She clutched Ava's arms and shook her as the two girls jumped up and down, grasping on to each other, circling and laughing.

Owen and Tyler, who were clueless, nonetheless started mimicking the girls, and they too were jumping and hollering. "Oh my gawd, oh my gawd."

"Here," said Hannah, picking up her clipboard. "Let me show you a picture of it. See?" Hannah held the picture out as everyone drew closer to look.

She beamed. She had waited to tell Nora and Owen about the treehouse until they could see something that would make it real for them. She knew they'd be wildly impatient for something they could immediately access.

"Is it going to have a door like this?" Nora asked. She pointed to the Dutch door with a peephole adorned with a turtle.

"Yup," said Hannah. "And look at this picture of the inside.

It's going to have these little bunk beds so you can sleep in it, and we can put a table and chairs inside, and you can play games and color."

"I want to sleep in it," said Owen. "Can we sleep in it tonight?"

"Just what I was afraid of." Hannah gave a sideways glance at Lea and then turned back to Owen. "This is going to take me a *long* time to build. It won't be ready for many weeks, but when it's done, we'll sleep in it, okay?"

"Okay," said Owen. He quickly lost interest in the picture and walked with Tyler toward the house, where he had left some trucks on the porch.

"Aunt Hannah, could you perhaps add a tower to the top of the treehouse so that I can look out upon my kingdom?" asked Nora. Hannah and Lea chuckled. Leave it to Nora to provide some unsolicited suggestions on how to improve the already ambitious design.

"We'll see. I'll build it this way first, and maybe we can add an addition later."

"Okay, that sounds good. Can we paint it blue? I think it'd look pretty if it was blue."

"We'll see," repeated Hannah. "I promised your parents that it'd blend in with the back yard, so I don't know if blue would be a good choice for the outside, but maybe the inside."

"Molly and Ted are good with this?" asked Lea. She raised her left eyebrow. "You told them?"

"Yeah, they're cool with it. I talked with them about it last week, and I've meant to tell you, but the kids were always around, so I didn't get a chance."

"I mean no offense, and I know you worked for Habitat, but isn't this sort of a ridiculously difficult thing for you to do? Like, how are you going to lift all this stuff? It looks heavy."

"I can do it. They're not individually heavy items, but I may ask Chris to help me a little bit when it comes time to hoisting the deck on to the support posts."

"I don't know what that means, but I'm sure he'll be happy to give you a hand," said Lea.

"I may need you too. We'll make a party out of it."

"Okay," said Lea. "I think you're one crazy woman, but it's such a cool idea. Hey, did you notice that kid next door is building something? Unfortunately, he has his shirt on."

"Turns out that he's no kid. I met him the other day. Believe it or not, he's the same guy that Owen called an asshole."

"No way." Lea laughed hard. "Oh my god. What's his story?"

"Not sure, but he's engaged. I saw him at the hardware store with his fiancée talking about their wedding registry, and she's got a big ole ring on. And he saw me in my bathing suit the other day. It was so embarrassing. He thought I was Nora and Owen's mother and he kinda flirted with me, which is super creepy."

"Geez . . . ," agreed Lea. "Hey, I gotta get. We'll talk some more later. C'mon, kids. Load up." Ava, Tyler, and Claire ran from the yard and scrambled into their respective seats. Ava and Tyler even buckled themselves. Hannah marveled again at how Lea made it all look so easy. Hannah, Nora, and Owen stood in the driveway, waving goodbye as they pulled away.

"Okay, guys, let's get dinner started, and by that, I mean go wash up 'cuz we're going out to eat." With all the excitement of the day, she had not given a thought to dinner.

Fifteen

By Wednesday morning, after three more trips to various lumber and hardware stores, Hannah had gathered everything she needed to begin her project. Nervous and procrastinating, she was hesitant to start the actual construction, fearful it would be beyond her capabilities.

But she knew it was time to begin. Many times, when she was at a crossroads in her life, Hannah would jump into a new (and usually physical) challenge: intensely learning how to play soccer one summer right before middle school so she'd have a team to join; training for a triathlon after her best friend in high school moved away; swimming every day for a month sophomore year of college after deciding she wanted to change her major; going to Kenya to build houses right after graduating college. These changeups came naturally to her and allowed her to plow through the transition.

These physical challenges sometimes resulted in clarity and a plan, not always the best plan, but a plan nonetheless. Hammering away in the beautiful countryside would be more helpful in informing her future path than a mind-numbing computer search on Monster.com.

And so, she began. The plans were sketchy, not as detailed as she would have liked, but she understood the general direction. Building the support framework would be the first task. She would do most of the cutting and drilling in the garage and driveway, where the wood was stacked. There were many benefits to this setup. She would have a convenient power source, and the lumber could be cut into smaller sizes before she had to haul it to the project site. A side benefit was that it afforded the best view of Nathan-next-door, who was sometimes out ripping bark from logs for god knows what reason or playing with his dog.

Hannah worked all morning, assembling the two spreading triangular braces that would support the front and back of the treehouse. Remembering to measure twice, cut once, she sawed, then drilled the leg and crossbar pieces together. It was noon before she knew it, and she found herself hungry. Absorbed in her effort, she had not paid any attention to what was happening next door. Nathan was now outside at his bark-stripping station, tearing away. Shirt on. She gave a little wave as he caught her eye and went into the house.

NATHAN WAS ON his eighth and final log when he noticed Hannah leave the driveway and head into the house. He had seen her when she wandered into his viewshed all morning. He was impressed with her concentration. Sure, there was the occasional "Shit!" and "Ah hell" that he could faintly hear, but all in all, she was making good progress. He had never seen a woman use a circular saw. She was cute with her short overalls, ponytail, and baseball cap, sawing the large pieces on the ground and smaller ones on top of sawhorses.

He wanted to figure out a way to speak with her again without infringing on her privacy. He could send Cooper over, but there was always the risk that the dog would run off, and he didn't want to face that again. He got two of his long climbing ropes and tied the dog up in a spot that would allow him to wander over to Hannah's but not take off. If Nathan had to "res-cue" Hannah from Cooper's intrusion, well, that was just the neighborly thing to do.

An hour later, plan successfully launched, Nathan walked to where Hannah was sitting on her lumber pile. She was reading her plans and simultaneously scratching Cooper under his chin.

"Hey, Coop, what are you bothering Hannah for?" Nathan addressed his dog in a tone that made the dog cock his head as if to say, "WTF, you sent me over here!"

"He's not bothering me. We were just discussing the best approach for getting this mounted in the tree." Hannah held her hand to shade her eyes from the sun as she looked up at Nathan.

"Do you need some help?"

"I will, but not quite yet. I don't want to impose on you. Some friends offered. I'll probably get them over here tomorrow evening."

"I'm around tomorrow if you need an extra hand."

"I might take you up on that. Once I get the support in-stalled, I can probably do the rest myself, but it's pretty impossi-ble to erect these braces on my own. What are you doing over there anyway?" She pointed to his pile of stripped logs.

"I'm making a wedding arbor. Check out my hands; it's been a chore stripping the bark." Nathan held out his ragged palms.

"Eww. Do they hurt?"

"Not at all, just dirty. But I'm glad that part's over. I'm be-hind schedule."

"When's the wedding?"

"A few weeks from now, second Saturday in July." As he said this, he felt the vibration of his phone in his pocket. He pulled out the phone and looked at the message. It was an alert from his mountain rescue squad. He had recently joined the team, which provided technical rescue in the local area. This was the first time receiving an alert since he joined.

"I'm such a girl. I love weddings," said Hannah.

Nathan peered down to read the message. A hiker was injured on Mount Mansfield. He felt a bolt of excitement course through his veins. He looked up at Hannah. He didn't want to cut the conversation short, but he needed to go. "You should come. It's not far away, over in Waitsfield, about fifteen miles from here."

"Yeah, I don't think so," said Hannah. "I think you'll be pretty busy at the wedding." She widened her eyes and tilted her head with a faint smile.

Nathan was furiously typing a message into his phone. "A little," he said, not looking up. "My entire family will be there, old friends, but if you like weddings and you don't have anything better to do—it might be fun for you. You said you weren't from around here." He finished typing and looked at Hannah.

"Thanks anyway, but I don't think so," said Hannah, abruptly looking down at her clipboard.

"Oh, okay. No, it was a bad idea. I—well, I gotta go." Nathan shook his phone in the air and said, "Emergency thing." He took Cooper by the collar and turned to his house. "I'm around tomorrow afternoon if you need another hand. Be happy to help."

"Bye," said Hannah.

"ARE YOU CRAZY?" Grace asked her brother later that evening.

"What's the big deal? It's dinner and dancing and drinking," said Nathan into the phone.

"You don't invite strangers to weddings. She must think you're nuts."

"Well, in the middle of talking to her I got a call out to a rescue. It was my first alert, and I got distracted. But she said she loved weddings. You gave me a plus one, so I just went for it. She seems . . . uh . . . interesting. It turns out she's single, or at least those aren't her kids. I wanted to invite her to do something. Plus, if Lindsey gets all batshit crazy, I'd have a buffer."

"I'm sure . . . what's her name, Hannah? . . . would love to know that she's going to serve as protection from your still-into-you ex. I'm glad she said 'no,' which makes me like her. All women love weddings, Nathan, but it doesn't mean you invite them to your sister's wedding when you just met them. Have you never seen a rom-com?"

"It doesn't matter; she said no. No harm was done, except now she probably thinks I'm weird."

"Ya think?" asked Grace.

"OKAY, I'M SEARCHING for him on Facebook. Does he look like a twelve-year-old boy? Is his dog black and white?" Sara asked.

"No, brown."

"Okay, that's not him. No *e* at the end of Wild, right?"

"No *e*. His name was on a box on his front step when I was delivering the wine. I can't believe he thought Nora and Owen were my kids. I was kind of mean to him after he mentioned I should go to his wedding. I was shocked. Who does that?"

"So bizarre. But you know, also super confident." Sara paused.

"Okay, the next one is someone dressed as a spaceman. Let's hope not. There's another with some kinda Wiggles cartoon . . . These are all kids . . . and there is one with no information, just one of the default heads. Okay, wait, I think I got it. This is it, I think. Okay, it says from Richmond, Vermont. One hundred and forty-six friends. The profile picture is from a distance, but he's in, like, a cave thing and has dark hair. Alone. AHH! Networks—Carnegie Mellon and MIT. There are only six photos—all big groups of people . . . maybe family. And one of him that's the profile picture. It doesn't say anything about being in a relationship. Nathan only shares some information publicly. If you know Nathan, send him a friend request. Aggh. Let me see his friends . . . Maybe he has siblings who are more active. Hmm. Ohh. Jackpot. It looks like it might be a sister. Grace. Wow, pretty. Engaged. Went to UVM and Cornell Vet School. Lives in Richmond. A few pictures . . . mostly of her and some guy and animals. Okay, so it looks like he's got a normal family, at least."

"Never mind. It's fine; there's just something about him. He was so obvious, sending his dog over to see me so that he could come over. It was cute. Then in the middle of telling me about his wedding, he gets a text and starts texting back, and then he runs off. God, maybe he's a drug dealer." Hannah laughed. "But on the other hand, he seems very, I don't know, solid."

"A cute, solid drug dealer with a nice family. I've seen worse," replied Sara.

Sixteen

Lea emerged from the minivan, clutching Claire in one arm and a sack of groceries in the other, with Ava and Tyler tagging along.

"Chris is right behind me," she said. "He's got his tool belt and testosterone on."

"Great. Let me help you there." Hannah took the bag of food and peered inside. "You didn't have to bring all this. I've got dinner going."

"It's just some brownies and ice cream, no biggie. Wow, it looks like you've made some progress here." Lea looked at the cross braces assembled and strewn across the driveway.

"I hope Chris and I can get these up by ourselves. I appreciate you guys helping me with this part."

"Hey, I plan on my kids playing in this thing for years. It's the least we can do." Lea brought the kids into the house, where she would keep the troops busy while Chris and Hannah installed the support structure.

Chris exited the red truck wearing worn-out jeans, a T-shirt, and a baseball cap and buckling up what appeared to be a brand-new leather tool belt.

"What you need done, ma'am?" he asked Hannah with a nod of his cap.

"Right this way, sir." Hannah escorted Chris to the staging area and showed him the plans and diagrams explaining what was next.

"The concrete footings for the legs are all set. There's a slight incline, so we'll want to put this leg in first." She pointed to one of the wooden braces. "I think we should haul them back there and lay them where they'll eventually go. Then, one by one, we can stand them up and put them together. I've already leveled the footings with the anchor brackets."

Hannah and Chris began hauling the assembled posts to the back yard. They were heavier than Hannah expected, but the two of them managed to move the support braces using the garden cart. It was clear that to stand them up and connect them, they would need another set of hands.

"I'll go get Lea," said Chris. He turned and yelled to Lea, who was on the deck with all five kids.

"Hey, babe, can you come help now?"

Lea looked warily at the children, told them to stay put, and made it all the way to the bottom of the deck steps before Claire started to whine for her. She went back up to get the toddler and headed back out to the yard holding Claire's hand.

"What's up?" asked Lea.

"We need you to hold this support in place while I hold up the other side," said Chris. "You just have to hold it for a few minutes while Hannah bolts it together. Okay?"

"Claire, honey, sit over here and don't move. Mommy has to help build the treehouse for a few minutes. Can you do that?"

Claire sat on the ground a safe distance away. As soon as Lea had the support in place, Claire got up and started walking toward the side yard.

"Doggie," she cried. Then she bolted, heading straight for Nathan's house to see Cooper.

"I'll get her," said Hannah. She ran after Claire, leaving Lea and Chris to hold up their respective beams.

Claire was fast and nearly into Nathan's yard by the time Hannah caught up with her.

"Claire! Stop," cried Hannah as the little girl moved toward Cooper. The dog was happy to see her. Cooper and Claire stood eye to eye, evaluating each other. Nathan stood in the yard too, with a Frisbee in hand.

"Hi," he called out to Hannah as she approached.

"Hi," said Hannah.

"Who's this?" Nathan looked at Claire and tapped his Frisbee on the side of his leg.

"This is Claire, the escape artist. She's my friend's daughter. We're putting up the treehouse support, and she's obviously not cooperating." She gave Claire a stern look while simultaneously smiling. Claire giggled.

"Need some help?"

Hannah was desperate to get the supports installed, and although hesitant to ask this favor, she went for it. "I hate to impose. Are you sure you're not busy? It shouldn't take too long."

"Clearly not busy," Nathan said, holding up the Frisbee and smiling. "Let me just put Cooper in the house, and I'll be right over."

"That'd be great. Thanks so much."

Hannah and Claire walked back to the house and found Chris and Lea sitting beside the tree, having given up holding the support brace, which now lay on the ground. Claire jumped on Lea's lap.

"I've enlisted some additional manpower. My neighbor offered to help," said Hannah.

Lea gave Hannah a sideways, knowing glance. "The Asshole?" she mouthed. Hannah nodded.

"Okay, then. This is going to be more fun than I expected," said Lea.

"Claire, tell your mother to be cool," said Hannah. Claire gently slapped her mother's face.

"Good girl," said Chris. He patted Claire's head.

A few minutes later, Nathan appeared in the yard.

"Nathan Wild," said Hannah, "this is Chris Harris . . . his wife Lea . . . and you've already met Claire."

Nathan grinned and shook hands with Chris and Lea.

"Thanks for coming over. These supports are pretty heavy," said Chris.

"Hellllooooo, Prince Charming!" Nora pleasantly wailed from the deck, waving her arms theatrically.

"Hi, guys," shouted Nathan back to the group on the deck.

Lea and Claire headed back to the house, leaving the trio alone with the supports.

"Okay, let's try it again," Hannah said. "Nathan, if you'd hold that support while Chris gets the other one, I'll lash it in place temporarily. The idea is to get the two front and back supports up and braced in place, then install the side cross braces. Then we can put these two deck joists between these two header joists." Hannah pointed out the various components to the men.

"Woman knows her stuff," said Chris, nodding at Nathan.

"Impressive," agreed Nathan. "Let's do this."

Hannah climbed the step ladder with a couple of clamps in hand. "I think these will hold it." She scampered down the ladder, moved it to the next corner, and repeated the task.

In no time, the structure was up, clamped together, and looking ready to go. "Do you think it's too close to the tree?" asked Hannah. "It's designed to be tree adjacent, not attached to the tree."

"Looks like there's plenty of room for further growth," Chris said.

"Not too close. But I think you're going to have to do some trimming to get those branches out of the way," said Nathan. He pointed to a cluster of light branches on the left side of the tree.

"True," said Chris and Hannah in unison, both standing with their hands on their hips.

"First we'll see if it's level, then bolt it together," said Hannah. Although Nathan was no longer technically needed to assist in the securing of the braces, the three of them worked together, leveling the joists and bolting them to each other.

An hour and a half later, Hannah stepped back, admired their work, and declared, "It's perfect. This is great. That was the hard part. It's all cake from here. Thank you, guys, so much."

"Looks good," agreed Chris. "I'm starving. Nathan, can you stay for dinner? We're doing barbeque."

"Yes," said Hannah, spinning to face Nathan. "You have to stay. We have to feed you. We couldn't have done it without you."

"Not necessary, but that sounds great. Would it be okay if I brought Cooper over and tied him up back here?"

"Of course," said Hannah. "The kids will love it."

"Okay. I'll go wash up and be over in a few."

Hannah and Chris headed back to the deck and informed Lea there would be another for dinner.

"Oh goodie," said Lea with a mischievous smile.

Nathan returned a short while later wearing longish shorts and a plaid shirt with the sleeves rolled up; he was carrying some beer. Lea had arranged the food buffet-style and was preparing the kids' plates when Hannah appeared from the back door. She wore a white sundress and carried a tray of glasses and a pitcher of Sangria.

Nathan stopped at the top of the deck stairs and stared at Hannah. "Hi."

"Hi," Hannah said, freezing and staring back.

Lea watched Nathan watching Hannah. "You both look like you stepped out of a J. Crew ad."

"Always wanted to be a male model," Nathan said.

"Me too," said Hannah. "Who wouldn't want a life of eating disorders and constantly being judged on your looks?" Hannah set the Sangria on the food table.

"I brought beer," said Nathan. "We'll have to pursue our starvation diets next week." He handed Chris the pack of beer.

"I'll take one of those," said Chris, pulling off a can. "I have no intentions or hope of ever being anything other than a plus-size model."

To Hannah's delight, the dinner conversation went remarkably well. The kids were sitting at their kid-size picnic table and managed to eat their dinners with few interruptions. The adult foursome chatted about the weather, the food, the highway construction project, Nathan's job at a tech company, Bernie Sanders's appearance at the Energy Expo, and a new paddle-board concession at the reservoir.

"Hannah tells us you're getting married in a few weeks. That's exciting," said Lea.

Nathan swung his head toward Lea. "Huh? I'm not getting married."

"You said you were getting married. You asked me to come!" Hannah said incredulously. Her cheeks were scarlet, and she shot a glance at Lea.

"I'm not getting married. My sister Grace is getting married." Nathan's face was pinched with confusion. He looked pointedly at Hannah sitting directly across from him. "You thought *I* was getting married and that I invited you to *my* wedding?"

"Well, you didn't say. I just figured. I saw you with your girlfriend at the coffee shop."

"That was my sister Kendall. It's my other sister Grace who's getting married."

"Oh." Hannah looked down at her plate. There was a moment of stunned silence as Hannah absorbed Nathan's revelation. "Well, I'm glad we cleared that up!" Hannah rose, headed to the food table, and began shoveling additional food onto her plate that she had no intention of eating.

Not getting married. He's not getting married. How did I miss that? She felt utterly foolish and simultaneously excited. *Single.* She wanted to jump over the table and throw herself on him. Instead, the four of them sat in silence until a voice rang out from the kids' table.

"Yay! Now Nathan can marry Aunt Hannah," shouted Nora. "I can be a flower girl."

All four of them swung their heads in Nora's direction and burst into laughter.

Today 9:23 PM

me: He's not getting married. Hes not engaged. It's his sister's wedding.

Sara: OMG What! What now??

me: Now what is I'm getting the hell outta town - going to my parents for the weekend I wish you were going to be there. gotta think about this

Sara: ok I'll call you after the weekend text me any updates xo.

JULY

Seventeen

Taking the kids to her hometown of Newton, Massachusetts, a three-plus-hour drive from Molly's house, for the Fourth of July weekend had been the plan for weeks—and Hannah was glad because an overwhelming desire to see her parents had struck her shortly after she learned that Nathan was not the one getting married. *Nathan Single. Need to Talk to Mom Now.* Bags were packed, car was fueled; she picked the kids up from camp Friday afternoon and headed south for the long Fourth of July weekend.

Home sweet home. Whenever Hannah pulled into the driveway of her childhood home, she whispered those words to herself automatically. She had not lived in this house for more than ten years, but to her it was still "base." The house had been in her father's family for over one hundred years, and Hannah loved that her paternal grandfather had once roamed the halls as a child.

The kids were sound asleep in the back seat. Finally. She wanted to leave them in the car and go inside to say hello to her parents before waking them. Before she even got her door open, Bob and Elizabeth appeared.

"Hey," she said softly, bringing her finger to her lips in a shushing gesture and pointing to the back seat.

"You made good time," her father said as he hugged her.

"Yeah, they were great. Nonstop chatter, but good. They fell asleep about fifteen minutes ago, so let's let them be for a few more minutes."

"You hungry?" asked her mom, rubbing Hannah's back in her usual manner.

"Yeah, pretty hungry. I fed them McDonald's drive-thru but couldn't bear to eat it myself. Molly would kill me if she knew."

"Yes, she would," Elizabeth agreed.

"GRANDMA!" Nora yelled from the car. "GRANDPA!"

The short nap recharged Nora and Owen, who were running all over the house with Bob on a long journey that would ultimately land them in their beds. Hannah and her mom sat on the couch in the family room, drinking red wine and recounting the days of their lives since they had last spoken on the phone.

"That guy I told you about who moved in next door helped me with the treehouse yesterday and stayed for dinner with Lea and the gang," Hannah said.

"The asshole who invited you to his wedding?"

Hannah nodded, pursing her lips. "Turns out he's not engaged. It's his sister who's getting married and who I've seen him with."

"Huh! So now what?"

Hannah sighed and dropped her head. "I dunno. I'm very, very intrigued, but I'm just not sure I want to start something. I've got a lot on my plate."

"Why are you overthinking this? Haven't you said that you hadn't had a chance to meet anyone your age? What's wrong with a summer fling anyway?"

"I dunno. We'll see what happens. I intended to spend my summer thinking about what I want to do next, and getting involved with someone seems like it might complicate my evaluative process."

"Geez, Hannah." Her mother laughed and threw a fake punch at her. "That doesn't sound like you. Wait, yes it does. You're a compulsive planner. But why don't you just relax, have fun? Just keep it light."

"You should see him. He doesn't look like a light-summer-fling kinda guy. He's smart and nice and helpful and somewhat serious. And I swear, Mom, there is some kind of crazy chemistry. I get all sweaty and nervous every time he appears. My heart goes all jumpy wumpy."

"That's unusual for you. Well, I guess you're going to have to see how it plays out. Maybe take it slow. Go to the wedding. What the hell, it'll probably be fun."

Hannah lay in her old bed in her old bedroom that night, staring at the ceiling. She thought about Nathan and why she was hesitating, for the first time, to start a short-term relationship. She was becoming preoccupied with him, she knew. It had started even when she was under the impression he was engaged. She had not been preoccupied with a guy for a long time. There was some sort of animal attraction, pheromones, taking over her body and drawing her in.

She had spent the entire drive chatting and playing games with the kids, so there had been no time for car dreams about Nathan. Exhausted, she closed her eyes and harnessed her inner Scarlett O'Hara. *I can't think about that right now. If I do, I'll go crazy. I'll think about that tomorrow.*

EARLY THE NEXT morning, Elizabeth and Hannah went for a run at the local park where Hannah once ran cross country for her high school team.

"I'm having flashbacks," Hannah said. They had just completed their three-mile course. She was panting and bending over with her head down, hands on her knees. "Thinking about the same things I used to think about when I was seventeen and ran these hills."

"Yeah? What things?" asked her mother, equally out of breath.

Hannah rose, now placing her hands on her hips. "You know how it's always hard for me to zone out and get the monkeys out of my brain. When I was running in high school, I was always plotting my future. In those days, it was more like what I was going to wear to prom, or what kind of hit my reputation would take if I joined Academic Decathlon, stuff like that. But once in a while, I'd think about what I was going to be when I grew up."

"Remember when you used to want to be an actuary? I didn't even know what that was. I had to look it up."

"Ha, I forgot about that. I didn't know what they did either. Ally Bouchard's mother was an actuary, and she was the coolest adult I knew, present company excluded," replied Hannah.

"Karen's still pretty cool. Hey, let's get lattes, and you can tell me what you were plotting on this run," suggested Elizabeth.

Over coffee and muffins, Elizabeth and Hannah reminisced about Hannah's high school days. Hannah loved spending time with her parents now that she had "grown up." There had been many battles from middle school through her junior year of high school, but she saw now that the clashes were mostly her fault, sprung from her ever-growing desire for independence. Retrospectively, she was glad that her parents were stricter than some of her friends' parents and imposed limitations. Spending the past few weeks with Nora and Owen had been a crash course in how powerful children can be in manipulating adults. Even Owen relentlessly tried to convince her that he could have dessert if he ate just four green beans at dinner.

Hannah had always been impressed by her mother's career fulfillment. She was executive director of a nonprofit devoted to lifting the reading skills of inner-city youth. She had a challenging job and still managed to raise a family while, for the most part, remaining a cheerful and calm person.

"What do you think about your future?" Elizabeth asked. "You've been pretty quiet on that subject on our phone calls."

"I told you about my vision board, and you know about the treehouse, which I had to add to the vision board because I hadn't included it. But it's made me think that anything in my future must involve at least some creativity. I've gotten a little sidetracked with the treehouse, but I had been spending a lot of time going through job postings. It's hard to figure this out, Mom. I just want to be doing something that moves society forward. I think that's my basic objective. It can't be anything where I'm not contributing. Did you read that book *Ishmael*?"

"I haven't," said Elizabeth. "But I think I've heard about it. Is it about a gorilla?"

"There's a gorilla in it, but that's not what it's really about. The gorilla is a spiritual advisor who helps a man understand the idea of 'takers' and 'leavers' and global problems. Anyway, you should read it; it's awesome. The bottom line is I want to be a 'leaver' and not a 'taker.' That's what I'm searching for, and that's tough to do and still make a living. When I was running, I was thinking about that book, and I'm going to reread it. So far, I've seen a couple of jobs that sparked my interest. One in Boise, one in Portland. The one in Boise looks pretty cool. I've always wanted to live out West. I know a couple of people from school out there who love it. At least that's what they're always projecting on social media."

"Ah, beware of Insta envy," said Elizabeth.

"Yes, I'm aware. But I'm resolved to live differently than I did in Boston. No job that does not make the world a better place. I'll hate being so far away from you guys and Molly and the kids, so that's a conundrum. But I think if I only did it for a few years and got it out of my system, that could be good too. My privilege is showing. Most people on earth don't have the luxury of employment choice. I want to be mindful of that as well."

"I get what you're talking about. You know that's why I've worked for so long. I keep thinking about retiring, but then I think, *But I'm not done yet! They can't all read on grade level!*"

"That's the kind of enthusiasm I want! Your job satisfaction has elevated my career expectations!"

"Yeah, I like to keep the bar high for you girls. C'mon, let's get out of here and see how Dad's doing with the kids."

"I'm so glad we came here this weekend, Mom. I love our chats and your perspectives," Hannah said as they left the café, throwing her arm around her mother's shoulder.

"I'm glad you came, and I love our talks too. You'll figure things out. I did. I've never regretted getting out there and trying to build my best life. Never perfect, not always easy, and there are no guarantees, but I don't think you can go wrong if you stay true to yourself."

Eighteen

"I'm so obsessed with Angry Birds . . . I'm, like, addicted. Do you play? What level have you gotten to? I'm stuck in Danger Above," said the woman tapping furiously on her phone. "I love flinging the birds."

"I'm sorry," Nathan said, "but I have no idea what you're talking about." He placed a big bowl of popcorn on the table and took a seat next to the woman.

"Angry Birds. It's a game on my phone. See?" She thrust her smartphone in his line of vision.

"Oh yeah, I've heard of that. Never played it though."

Nathan was on a date. Dylan, his best friend from high school, and Dylan's wife, Kim, had convinced him to go to an early dinner on the Fourth of July. Since Nathan's new house had an excellent view of the town's fireworks, the plan was to go there afterward for the show. The real agenda was for Nathan to meet Amber, a physical therapist and work friend of Kim's. Amber and Nathan sat at the table in the noisy bar area, waiting to be seated with Kim and Dylan in the main dining area.

"It's got, like, a million levels and just keeps getting harder. I play it all the time, between patients and waiting in line, but Boomerang Bird is being such a pain." Amber had to raise her voice to accommodate the loud din of the bar.

"That's too bad."

"I'm sorry. I'll put it away. The first part of recovery is admitting you have a problem."

Amber was attractive and sweet. Petite, with long dark hair, flawless skin, large brown eyes, and distractingly large breasts that seemed to pop out of her tight V-neck shirt.

Nathan had to keep thinking, *Eyes up.*

Dylan and Kim returned to the table, a beer in each hand, having made the first run to the bar, unwilling to wait for a server.

"It's their double IPA, one of my favorites. Hope you like," said Dylan to Nathan and Amber.

"How's the unpacking going, Nathan?" asked Kim. "I can't wait to see your house."

"I'm sorry it's taken so long to have you guys out," said Nathan. "I just finished a huge project at work and haven't even unpacked yet."

"You're so lucky to have a house!" said Amber. "That's so cool. I've been renting since college and want a house so bad."

"Mortgage rates are good right now," Nathan said. "Good time to buy if you can."

"I have no savings, so I could never make the down payment," said Amber. "But I'm going to start working on it."

"You're gonna have to give up your shopping addiction, girl," said Kim. She turned her head to face Nathan. "She's hands down the best-dressed employee at Fletcher Allen Hospital."

"I do love me my outfits," agreed Amber, raising her glass to clink with Kim's.

The evening had been fun, and Nathan was glad he had agreed to go. Amber was an enthusiastic person, although he found her obsession with her phone juvenile. They played darts, and she was surprisingly good. She was not shy about showing Nathan a few of her techniques, leaning into him and holding his arm and wrist, pressing her breasts against his back.

While Amber took her turn, Kim walked up to Nathan and leaned her head on his shoulder. "I'm glad you're back. We've missed you." She raised her head and nodded toward her friend. "So, Amber. Nice, huh?"

"She's great, Kim." *Not as great as Hannah*, he could not help but think. "Thanks for putting this together."

"She's a lot of fun too. Do you want me to make it so that you can drive her home tonight? I can make that happen."

Nathan looked at Amber, who was now standing near Dylan, watching him throw darts. He had not been with anyone for months, and he admitted to himself that he was attracted to this playful, outgoing woman with ginormous breasts.

"Let's go to my house and watch the fireworks and see how it goes," Nathan said.

Nineteen

Hannah was relieved Nora and Owen slept the last hour of the drive back to Vermont. She wanted them to get enough sleep, so they would be alert for the fireworks, but not so much that she would have trouble getting them back to sleep for the night.

It had been a wonderful weekend, and she was grateful for the conversations with her parents. She resolved to keep an open mind about Nathan and think "casual," as her mom suggested. It was clear that her family and friends wanted her to stay in New England but were supportive of her need to shift her career away from finance. All in all, the brief trip had been encouraging, if not enlightening.

Hannah unpacked the car in the near dark. Lights were on at Nathan's house, and the dull sound of voices and laughter filled the night. Fireworks would go off in town, and the houses were perfectly positioned to afford a distant view of the show.

Partying. She unloaded the last of the bags and beach paraphernalia. *And I'm stuck here.*

"Let's go get your jammies on before the fireworks start so you'll be all ready for bed when they're over." Hannah led Nora and Owen into the house.

She had never seen them get their pajamas on so fast. Hannah set up chairs and blankets on the deck and warmed milk with just a hint of chocolate. The fireworks started, and soon the sky was illuminated and the children thrilled. Hannah had not seen fireworks for as long as she could remember, and this was the first time in years she was into it as she watched them through Nora and Owen's eyes.

Nora suggested that they name the fireworks as they exploded.

"That green one is Exploding Kermit."

"Wait, wait, Dancing Mermaids."

"Palm tree."

"Disappearing flower."

"Christmas tree."

"Spiderman."

"Giant Silky."

"Pretty Pretty Parachute."

"Snowflake."

After about twenty minutes, the fireworks finale began, and the kids were finally showing signs of fatigue. Nora's last contribution, "Fountain of Orange Juice," was shouted, followed by a big yawn.

"Okay, guys. Bedtime now. Let's go." Hannah pushed the children through the screen door into the family room.

The earsplitting scream that came from Nora's small body made the fireworks finale seem tame.

Hannah spun to look at the girl. She was in the family room, jumping up and down, shrieking and pointing at the couch. As was typical, Owen started screaming too but without the commitment that Nora showed.

"Calm down, what's the matter? What's the matter?" Hannah hugged Nora to her and knelt beside her.

"THAaaaaRES Aaaaa GIAaaaaNT BUuuuuG!!" wailed Nora in a terrified voice. Hannah looked in the direction of Nora's pointing but saw nothing.

"It's okay, honey. I'll check it out." She gave Nora a final hug and peeled herself off her niece.

Hannah walked slowly toward the couch, looking around. "I don't see anything," she said. Nora screamed again.

To Hannah's horror, the "thing" flew out from behind the couch to the ceiling. It began a spastic dance above her head, flying silently but frantically around the room.

Hannah screamed. "What the hell?" Her heart was racing.

The projectile was a bat. With that realization and in a slightly less than calm voice, Hannah directed Nora and Owen to sit on the chairs in the kitchen. "It's only a bat," she said. The children bolted out of the family room and, still screaming, ran into the kitchen.

Hannah turned around to see the bat clinging to the wall of the family room close to the ceiling. What could she do to get it out of the house? *I'm on my own. I'm the adult. I have to fix this.*

"Everything okay in there?" came a loud voice from the side door. "We heard screaming." Nathan appeared in the family room, followed by a man and two women. Nora and Owen, afraid to venture further, peered into the room from the kitchen.

Hannah was so relieved to see Nathan. "We have a bat in the house, and we're a little freaked out," she said, pointing at the bat on the wall.

"EWWW," cried a woman standing next to Nathan. "That's disgusting." She folded her arms against her chest and backed against the wall.

"It probably got in through the side door. It was wide open when we walked up," said Nathan.

"Geez," said Hannah. She sighed and momentarily wondered who the additional people in the house were. "I guess I've got to get it out of here."

"Can't you just call somebody—like the Wildlife Department?" asked the same woman.

"This is Dylan, Kim, and Amber," said Nathan, ignoring the question and pointing to his friends. "I think we can get it. Can you get a bucket and a piece of thin cardboard and a step ladder or chair?"

Hannah paused. "Okay, MacGyver. Yeah, I got that." She ran out of the room, headed for the kitchen closet. The bat took off again, bursting from its perch and flailing around the living room.

There were now four people screaming—Nora, Owen, Kim, and Amber. Amber held a throw pillow over her head, diving and weaving with the bat's every move. Kim ran into the kitchen and hid behind the door with the kids. Dylan provided a running dialogue of the bat's movements interlaced with expletives: "He's over here. Watch out. Shit. Oh my god. Here he comes. Fuck."

The bat suddenly landed flat on the ceiling, hanging there as if by magic. Hannah returned with the bucket and shoved it at Nathan. "I'll go find some cardboard."

Hannah went back into the kitchen, and on top of the hutch was one of Nora's camp craft projects—a collage of African animals cut from magazines glued to a poster board.

"My animal poster!" whined Nora.

"It's an emergency, honey. We'll make another one, I promise."

Nora hung her head, putting on her most sad face, and said, "Okay."

"Are you sure it's all right, Nora?" asked Nathan. "It's perfect for catching the bat, but I'll have to rip it in half."

"Okay, Nathan." She looked at him with big sad eyes. "If you must."

Hannah pulled one of the kitchen chairs into the living room and tiptoed to where the bat was hanging. Stepping on the chair, she slowly brought the bucket up to the bat, pressing the top of the bucket against the ceiling, enclosing the animal. Nathan handed her the poster board, and Hannah slowly ran it along the ceiling, detaching the bat and forcing it into the bucket while keeping the bucket pressed against the ceiling. Nathan reached up and held the bucket as she carefully lowered it. Hannah held the poster board tight against the top of the bucket. As she stepped off the chair, Nathan put his hand over the bucket. "I've got it," he said. He smiled and gave her a nod, then slowly walked to the back of the house. Everyone followed him silently.

"Don't forget to close the door!" Nathan yelled as he exited and continued deeper into the yard. The rest of the group waited near the house.

Nathan set the bucket on the ground, removed the poster board, and walked back to the others huddled on the deck steps. All stood in silence, waiting for what would transpire next. Nothing happened for a minute, and then suddenly and silently, the bat flew out of the bucket and, spastically flapping its wings, was gone into the night.

Everyone started talking at once.

"That was so creepy."

"Good job, Hannah. You too, Nathan."

"Where's the bat?"

"I've never been so scared in my life."

"Bats carry rabies, you know, and some nose disease."

"I thought it was going to drink my blood."

"You're brave, Aunt Hannah."

"I appreciate you coming over and helping," Hannah said. She looked directly into Nathan's eyes. "You're a great guy to have in this kind of situation. You were so calm. Thank you!" She lingered for a moment, still holding his eyes.

"Glad to help," he said. He ran his hand through his hair and looked down, then looked back at her. "You did most of the work."

"I was on the edge of freaking out if you guys hadn't shown up," Hannah said. "The kids were so out of control. I think it's because it was so unexpected. They typically love wildlife and creepy things."

"I need a drink," blurted Amber as if she had contributed in any significant way. "What's your name? Do you wanna come have a drink with us?"

Hannah paused. Who was this woman who felt entitled to invite her to Nathan's?

"Thanks, I'd love to, but I have to get the kids to bed, or they'll never get up tomorrow." Hannah glanced at the clock and was thankful that less than a half hour had transpired since the fireworks had ended.

"Okay, well, bye," Amber said. She immediately turned and headed back toward Nathan's house.

"It was nice to sort of meet you. I'm Kim, and this is Dylan," said Kim, turning to Hannah and extending her hand.

"I'm Hannah. I'm sorry to intrude on your party."

"No problem. It was fun seeing you guys going all Steve Irwin on us," said Dylan.

"Thanks again, Nathan, you have a deposit in my favor bank. I owe you big time," said Hannah.

"Anytime," said Nathan. "Night."

"Bye," said Hannah as she watched the trio head out into the darkness.

"Time for bed," she said, ushering Nora and Owen back into the house.

Hannah chose to read *Stellaluna* to the children that night, embracing the battiness of the evening. The bat-friendly story did the trick, and Nora and Owen fell fast asleep, curled up in her bed. Hannah did not have the energy to move them. She extracted herself from the bed and the room, leaving the light on in the hallway in case they woke.

Hannah was skeeved out from being so bat adjacent. She took a shower and settled onto the couch to text Sara, but Sara was out and asked if they could talk the next day. She checked her social media feeds. The usual Fourth of July weekend posts —beaches, barbeques, fireworks, outdoor concerts. Everyone was having fun. It was good weather in New England, hot, but no rain. She did not feel jealous exactly, but she did feel a degree of loneliness. She wondered what was going on over at Nathan's house. The introductions to his friends had all happened so fast. *Was it Amber and Kim? What was the guy's name? Dylan? And he was with Kim, so that means Amber must have been with Nathan.*

Hannah got to her feet and headed to the open kitchen window to see if there were any cars in Nathan's driveway. An outdoor light shone onto a single truck. Hannah had not noticed if there were cars over at his house when she had returned with the kids, so she didn't know whether there had previously been more than one vehicle parked there. She turned off the light in the kitchen so as not to be seen from the outside. She jumped on the counter, put her feet in the sink, and faced Nathan's driveway, sitting comfortably while she staked out the car. It was almost eleven o'clock. How late would they stay out on a weeknight? She sat there staring out the window for ten minutes. *This is stupid.* She got off the counter, and just as she did, the beep of a car door lock pierced the silence. She jumped back on the counter. Three figures walked toward the truck. Amber's distinct voice rose above the others: "Bye, Nathan, see you soon, I hope." She was not staying over. Hannah was pleased. She could go to bed now.

Her last thought before she fell into a deep sleep was how synchronized she and Nathan were in capturing the bat. What a team they made. They had spoken few words and yet moved in total harmony once he had said the words "bucket and cardboard." She breathed deeply and smiled. *I like him.*

Twenty

Hannah was staring at the partially erected treehouse, contemplating her plan for the day, when Cooper suddenly appeared next to her and silently leaned into her leg.

"Cooper, hey, buddy. What are you doing here?" she said, scratching him under his chin as he lifted his head up in delight.

Nathan appeared in the driveway and began calling, "Cooper, Cooper."

"He's here," shouted Hannah.

"What are you doing over here again?" reprimanded Nathan as he walked up to his dog. "Are you putting your moves on Hannah? He loves leaning on people so they pet him."

"That's what he's doing," said Hannah. "He knows I love him."

"How's the project going?" asked Nathan, pointing up at the treehouse frame.

"Pretty good. I'm going to fill in the deck today—lots of sawing, so it'll be kind of noisy over here."

"Do you need any help?" asked Nathan.

"Not right now, but can I take a rain check? I could have you do step number forty-seven, which looks impossibly complicated," Hannah said, waving her clipboard at him and smiling.

Nathan reached for a stick that Cooper had dropped at his feet and did not immediately reply.

"You know," she added, "I can't tell you how much I appreciate your helping us out the other night. I'd like to think I could have handled the situation, but I don't know what I'd have done if you hadn't shown up. I want to do something for you. Can I make you dinner or something? I could take you out to dinner. Chris and Lea said they would babysit anytime. Maybe we could go out to dinner Saturday night? Does that work for you?" Hannah was talking so fast, and it was all out before she knew it.

"This weekend is my sister's wedding," said Nathan. "So I can't."

"Oh," said Hannah. "Of course."

"What about midweek? We don't have to go out," he suggested.

"Nora and Owen aren't the most sophisticated dining companions," said Hannah. "And getting them to bed takes up most of the evening. How about you come by after I get them to sleep some evening this week and have a drink, and we can figure out dinner for some other time."

"Tomorrow night?" asked Nathan.

"Yeah, that'll work! Come around eight thirty, but be quiet so the kids don't hear you. Just come in the side door, and hopefully, they won't wake up. They should be down and out by then."

"Got it. C'mon, Cooper, let's let Hannah build her treehouse. See you." Nathan gave a little wave and left the yard with Cooper in tow.

A few minutes later, she noticed Nathan pull out of his garage and drive away. She sat on the pile of wood and laid her head back against the garage door. She was stoked at the prospect of Nathan coming over. Amber must not have been too serious if he was setting up a date with her. *I think it's a date.* She would have to get some decent wine, figure out something to wear, and get the kids to bed without having them suspect anything. Would it be too much to hope that things would go well, and they could have their first uninterrupted conversation? She loved having something to look forward to.

Hannah settled into the work of the morning and began bolting the railing posts into the header joists. This chore first required reinforcing the deck corners with a metal bracket. The project had many little tasks that were incredibly time consuming, but Hannah did not want to take the time to build something unless it was built right. By the time she completed all four corners, it was already noon. She had hoped to get a lot more accomplished in the last two days. As she wolfed down a turkey sandwich standing over the sink, she worried that she was falling behind schedule.

Hannah made better progress that afternoon, and before Nora and Owen rolled in with Lea, she had finished cutting all the deck boards. She also made the cutout for one of the several special surprises planned in her design, a "hidey hole." Within the floorboards, there was a secret hiding place between the deck joists that would be covered with a trap door where Nora and Owen could hide treasures. She knew Nora would love it and its inherent drama potential.

WHEN NORA AND Owen arrived home from day two of "Olympic Week" at camp, they were exhausted. And they were cranky. Nathan was due that evening, and Hannah was determined to remain calm and get through the evening with children without becoming exhausted and cranky herself.

As Hannah prepared dinner, Owen sat on the floor, leaning against the kitchen wall, and Nora sat at the kitchen table, coloring. Hannah walked over to Owen and sat down beside him.

"How are you doing there, Owen?" Hannah asked. "You look a little sad."

"I tripped and France lost the race," said Owen, sinking his head.

Hannah looked at Nora with her look that said, "Translate, please." Nora explained that Owen's country, France, was in a relay race to the flagpole, and Owen tripped during the race. He felt responsible for France's losing and "only" getting a silver medal.

"Can I see your medal?" Hannah asked. Owen reached into his pocket and pulled out the crumpled paper medal on a ribbon and handed it to his aunt.

"That's great, Owen. You should be proud," Hannah said. "How about we hang it on the refrigerator, and let's not forget to show it to Mom and Dad next time they call."

The gesture lightened Owen's mood, and Hannah was relieved that dinner was accomplished without incident, although bath and bedtime were the usual challenges. Why did kids resist the luxury of sleep? Hannah managed to get them tucked in by eight o'clock, giving her a half hour to prep for Nathan's "popover." Earlier, she had run to the store and bought two kinds of good wine and a raspberry cobbler and chosen an outfit. She selected a sundress that would look good with a light cardigan. It had been a warm day, and she hoped the evening temperature would be just right to sit on the deck.

AT EXACTLY 8:29, she was ready with wine glasses, the bottles, an opener, plates, forks, napkins, a knife, and raspberry cobbler on a tray. Feeling anxious, she wanted to gulp down a whole glass of the wine to calm her nerves, but she knew the better plan was to take it slow and not get drunk on their first "date."

A few moments later, a light tap on the side door announced Nathan's four-minutes-after-the agreed-to-time arrival. *Perfect.*

"Hey," said Hannah, gesturing to Nathan to follow her to the kitchen. She picked up the tray and led him to the back deck, noticing he was carrying a small shopping bag.

They made their way to two Adirondack chairs on the far end of the deck, away from the windows of the sleeping children upstairs. The sun didn't set until quite late these days, and it was still light outdoors. Hannah had arranged several candles on a small table but had not lit them yet.

They both agreed on red wine, and Hannah deftly opened the bottle and poured two glasses.

"Cheers," she said, raising her glass to meet his. "Here's to men who aren't afraid of screaming children or bats."

"To women who don't *bat* an eyelash when faced with a challenge!" said Nathan, clinking her glass and drinking a hefty gulp.

"Here, I brought you something," said Nathan, handing Hannah the bag.

Hannah peered inside and saw a book.

"It's actually for Nora and Owen. It's a book about African wildlife. I felt bad about ruining Nora's project, so I figured they might like this. It even has a bat in it."

"That's so nice. They'll love it, thank you." *What a thoughtful gesture.* "But why don't you hang on to it and give it to them in person?"

"Sure, good idea. So . . . speaking of Africa, you mentioned you learned how to build houses in Kenya. What was that about?"

Hannah commenced with the story of her childhood, how obsessed she had been with wildlife, how all her books were either about animals or natural disasters. When the *Lion King* movie came out, she already knew all about Timon, precisely what a meercat was, its range, diet, and habitat. She told him how her parents would push their two daughters outside every day, no matter the weather, and they were forced to use their imaginations. "Pioneers" was the most popular of their adventures, and she and her sister donned bonnets and long dresses and created elaborate scenarios where they would befriend Native American families and fight alongside them against the white settlers.

"My family is very politically correct," she said. "But I was always confused by these storylines."

Her love of wildlife had made traveling to Africa a high priority, and thus, after graduation from college, she raised the money to go on a gap year before her plan to start graduate school. Living in Kenya was difficult, but she had been wildly happy there and loved the challenge of the day-to-day life and her work with Habitat. While there, she confessed, she considered herself supremely put together and capable.

She had been talking for a long time, but Nathan seemed interested. He kept asking questions. He liked the details. He laughed in all the right places.

"You had no electricity? How did you deal with food? How did you cook?" he asked.

"There were markets once a month, and you had to think hard about how you'd make things last. We had these little coal stoves. You had to source the coal though, which meant you had to figure out what day the coal guy came through town and guess how much you'd need until he came through again. I subsisted mostly on rice and vegetables.

"It was the hardest thing I've ever done and the best thing I've ever done," she said. "I stretched it out to two years, and then I landed back in the States, broke and homeless. Well, I'm the independent, proud type, so I didn't want to move back home with my parents. I ended up moving in with my friend Sara in Boston. The next thing I knew, I was working at a finance firm making good money and eating crappy takeout food on my way home from work every night. I was living a life I never imagined for myself."

She told him how she sometimes felt like the main character of another version of the movie *Sliding Doors*. "I went through one wrong door when I got back from Kenya, and it set me on a trajectory that was beginning to turn me into an apathetic corporate cog."

"So, you quit?" asked Nathan.

"Nope. I got fired. Laid off, technically," said Hannah. "I'm getting a severance payout, and I'm eligible for unemployment when that runs out. It stung when it happened, even though I basically asked them to fire me. I wanted out, but now here I am, thinking about what to do with my economics degree from UMass. Problem is, I've found I really have a loathing for all things that have to do with money."

"If you hate money, why did you major in economics?" Nathan asked.

"Good question. I trace it back to organic chemistry. I couldn't pass it. I was trying hard to be an environmental science major, but I couldn't do the hard science. I never even got to physics, but I'm sure that would have been a disaster too. It's funny—I'm okay at math, but not science. I had taken a couple of economics courses related to environmental policy and found it interesting, so I just changed my major. It was sophomore year, and I was partying a lot. I mean, I wasn't too focused on my career objectives at that point."

They had finished the bottle of wine and eaten the raspberry cobbler. Over an hour and a half had passed, and nearly the entire conversation had been about the kids and Hannah. She had not meant to talk so much about herself, but Nathan kept commenting and asking her follow-up questions, so it made it seem like he was contributing to the conversation. Now she felt like she had just finished a therapy session. He made it easy to talk. The only thing she had learned about Nathan was that he was a good interviewer.

"Okay, your turn now. I need to know about the life and times of Nathan Wild. Spill," she said.

"Wait, we didn't get to the good part yet. You didn't mention any boyfriends or what you wore to the prom or your celebrity crushes," said Nathan. He was pouring the last bit of the bottle of wine into their glasses and smiling.

"I'm not saying another word until I get some real information out of you," Hannah shot back.

"How about we meet here again tomorrow night, and I'll let you query me on my absolutely fabulous life as a computer programmer?"

Hannah did not have to think about it much before replying. It was getting late, and she was tired. She was not much of a night owl these days, but having a second "conversation date" with Nathan was not something she would pass up.

"You're on, and I think you should know I'm going to be ruthless in my questioning. I'll make *you* talk for two hours nonstop. I'll delve deep."

It was now dark, with only the light radiating from inside the house illuminating the deck. They had been so engrossed in their talk that Hannah never lit the candles. As they rose from the chairs, Hannah stumbled, and Nathan gently grabbed her arm.

"Careful," he said.

"Lotta wine," she said.

"You okay?" Nathan asked, still gently holding her shoulder. Hannah looked up at him, realizing it was the first time they had touched. A tipsy fall save wasn't particularly romantic, but she felt electricity run through her, nonetheless.

"I'm good," she said. "Just went to my head for a sec. Haven't been drinking too much this summer."

They gathered the tray of remnants of their evening and walked into the house, stopping in the kitchen to set them down. Hannah anticipated that the departure part of the evening would be both exciting and awkward. Would they hug? Would he try to kiss her?

"Same time tomorrow night?" asked Nathan as he walked to the side door. "I have to go to Burlington all day."

"Yup, this worked out pretty well. Do you think maybe I should text you when the coast is clear in case I run into some resistance from the kiddies?"

"Good idea," said Nathan. "Let me give you my number."

Hannah went for her phone and pressed the buttons to arrive at "new contact" and handed the phone to Nathan, who entered his number.

"See you tomorrow night," he said. He turned for the door but paused with the doorknob in his hand. "I'll bring something to drink. Would you like wine again?"

"Maybe something non-alcoholic. Surprise me."

"Sounds good," he said. "So long." Nathan opened the door and left.

Hannah felt relieved that it had happened so fast, with no odd handshake or attempt at a kiss. It felt right that he just left, but she could not help wondering what it meant. Didn't he like her enough to *try* for some contact?

Twenty-One

The following evening, Hannah sensed that getting Nora and Owen to bed would be more challenging than the previous night. They both had passed out in Lea's car on the short drive home from camp and crashed on the couch for an additional half hour before she poked them awake. They eventually rallied and, with their batteries refreshed, were fairly wound up throughout the dinner of "Mom's Pasta Special," their grandmother Elizabeth's specialty and a family favorite.

Molly and Ted had scheduled a video call for after dinner following their return from skiing at a nearby mountain. They were attempting to show the kids some photographs, but the pictures were on Ted's computer, which they held up to the video conference camera of Molly's computer. Everything was very blurry, and everyone was frustrated by the effort, which used up a lot of time.

Then Nora detailed and performed the ribbon dancing/gymnastics Olympic event that she had done at camp that day. Owen kept trying to dance with Nora, and each time he interrupted, Nora insisted on starting over. Hannah smiled through it all, but she felt pangs of impatience. *Wow, this is only cute for about two minutes, not ten.*

After the call, she got them in the tub, and as soon as she did, she texted Nathan and let him know that they were on schedule. By the time they were tucked in, it was already the appointed time with Nathan. She ran downstairs to be ready to greet him without so much as a look in the mirror. She answered the door, a little disheveled, and Nathan entered with a pitcher of something brownish and a paper grocery bag.

"They're Arnold Palmers, half iced tea, half lemonade," he said, handing her the pitcher. "But my mom calls them 'Kerri Wilds' because she claims she invented them first. I also brought brownies."

"I love Kerri Wilds," said Hannah. "I'll get some glasses."

In a repeat of the previous evening, they settled on the Adirondack chairs and watched the sun setting over the mountains. "Okay, I'm ready for my inquisition," said Nathan after they poured their drinks.

"Let's see, where do I begin my line of questioning," started Hannah.

"Hey! What's going on out there?" came a child's voice at the screen door. "Who's that?"

"What are you doing out of bed?" exclaimed Hannah, getting up and walking to the door. "Get yourself back in bed right now."

"But I can't sleep. I'm all wound up," said Nora. "Hi, Nathan!" she said with a little wave.

"Hi, Nora," said Nathan, giving the child a wave back.

Hannah was frustrated. She knew from past similar incidents that this could be an hour-long battle of wills to get Nora back to bed and sleep.

"I'm thirsty. What are you drinking? Can I have some?" Nora asked.

"No," said Hannah. "Honey, you have to go to bed. You have a big day tomorrow."

Hannah put her hand on Nora's back and led her back into

the house and toward the staircase. Owen, too, was up and walking down the stairs, dragging his favorite sleeping silky behind him.

"Okay, you guys, back upstairs. Nathan, I'll be right back," she said over her shoulder to Nathan, who was standing by the screen door.

"Why is Nathan here? What are you guys doing?" asked Nora as they climbed the steps.

"He just stopped by for a visit . . . an adult visit . . . no kids allowed. It's late, and you have to go to bed."

Hannah put the kids in their beds, threatening them with no TV for the next day if they did not stay in bed. She rushed the process and ran down the stairs to Nathan, who was back on the deck.

"Sorry about that. I had a feeling they might be trouble tonight. They slept on the couch after camp, and it screwed up their schedule," she said, taking her seat.

"It's okay, no problem," he said.

"It can be so hard with kids. There's no reasoning with them sometimes, and it can make me crazy," confessed Hannah.

"I don't have a lot of experience with kids, not since I was one myself," said Nathan.

"You have two sisters, any nieces or nephews?" asked Hannah.

"Nope. I have a brother too. Grace is the first one to get married."

"There's four of you. Wow, that must have been fun growing up. Where are you in the line-up?"

"I'm the oldest, then Grace, then Adam, who's twenty-four, and Kendall is the youngest," said Nathan.

Above them, a window creaked. Hannah shot her head to the window and abruptly jumped out of her chair. Nora and

Owen were now standing on her bed, trying to sneak a peek at them.

"Excuse me," she said in exasperation. "They're up again."

Hannah disappeared upstairs and scolded the children firmly to stay in bed. Threatening them one more time not to move a muscle, she left their rooms and headed back down the stairs, pausing for a minute to calm herself. She was so disappointed and irritated. She had been in Vermont for over a month, and this was the first time she had anyone her age to hang out with, let alone a guy—a guy she was anxious to get to know. She walked out on the deck but did not sit down.

"I'm sorry, but I don't think tonight is going to work out. They're really wound up, and I think I'm going to have to read them a story to get them to sleep," she said.

"You want me to read to them?" asked Nathan as he stood up.

"I think you being here is making it worse," said Hannah kindly but emphatically. "I think we're going to have to call it. I'm really sorry. I was looking forward to my inquisition."

Nathan wore a dejected look on his face, and she felt panic rush through her veins. *I'll never see him again.*

"I feel bad." She tried to think of something else to say, but she could not think of anything.

"It can't be helped. I'll just have to stay the mysterious guy next door," he said, widening his eyes and turning his head slightly.

"No way. You're going to talk, mister. I want the lowdown." Perhaps he was just as disappointed as she was in the turn of events.

"If you really want to learn about me, you'll come with me to Grace's wedding on Saturday. I know it was weird of me to ask. My sisters were horrified and said for sure you'd think I was psycho for even suggesting it. But I'd like a date for the wedding, and I'd really like that to be you," Nathan said, looking her straight in the eyes.

"I wouldn't know anyone. But a wedding would be fun. No kids for the first time in four weeks." She paused. "Okay, I'll go. But I'll have to make sure Lea can watch the kids."

"Awesome!" said Nathan. "It'll be a great time. Everyone in my family is extremely outgoing and friendly. You won't be uncomfortable, I promise. The wedding starts at four thirty . . . but let me figure out what else I have to do that day, and I'll let you know about the transport."

"I can drive myself if that makes things easier."

"There's a bus involved to take people, so that's an option, but let me get back to you on the details."

"What's the dress?" asked Hannah.

Nathan looked at her, appearing perplexed. "Wedding dress?" he said. "I mean, I guess just wear what you wear to any wedding. It's not super formal. She definitely keeps saying that the ladies should not wear high heels."

"Okay," said Hannah, wondering what she could pull together from the "summer clothes collection" she had brought with her. Most of her clothing and accessories were at her parents', including most of the dresses she had worn to weddings over the past few years.

"I'll be in touch tomorrow," said Nathan as he turned to leave. "Sorry tonight didn't work out, but I'm glad you'll come on Saturday."

"You admitting that inviting me was weird helped. You realize that everyone will think we're a couple?" asked Hannah. "Normal people don't just bring someone they just met to a family wedding."

"Let 'em," said Nathan, flicking his head back. "I already told them about Owen calling me an asshole, so they've heard of you. Also, I need some street cred with this gang. They'll be impressed that I got you to come. I'll see you. Good luck," he said as he pointed upstairs and closed the door behind him.

Today 10:37 PM

Sara: Nathan update pls

me: He came over again. Nora and Owen got out of bed and were super wound up and kept interrupting us so I agreed to go his sister's wedding!!!!!!

Sara: OMG

me: I can't believe it either. But I asked him to go home so that I could get them to bed and he just talked me into it. It'll be fine. It'll probably be fun

Sara: You're going to sleep with him. I can tell

me: There won't be any sleeping together

Sara: What the hell—why not?

me: Aunt Flo is arriving on Friday and she doesn't like to be up close with any boys at that time

Sara: O no Bloody Mary messing up your good time

me: Yes I'll be riding the Cotton Pony

Sara: Shark week is the worst

me: Gonna be checking into the Red Roof Inn

Sara: It could be a Red Wedding

me: I'll be surfing the Crimson Wave

Sara: Ok let's video chat outfit choices etc - text me when you can talk

me: Perfect ❤

Hannah tossed her phone aside and dropped on the bed, placing one hand on her belly and the other over her head on the pillow. Her brain flooded with thoughts about the wedding—who would be there, who would she meet, would it be awkward, what would happen with Nathan? She remembered her mom's advice and heard her words: *"Relax, have fun, keep it light."*

Throwing her legs onto the floor, Hannah sat up, then jumped to a standing position. *I can be light.* She headed to the closet and, for the next two hours, tore through every article of clothing, footwear, and lingerie in the house.

Twenty-Two

"Aunt Hannah," Nora said. "You look so pretty! But I wish it was a fancy gown."

"It's not a fancy gown kinda wedding. It's going to be outside and in a barn for dinner and dancing," Hannah explained as she inserted a pair of Molly's gold earrings into her ears. "What do you think of these?" she asked, pulling back her hair.

"Perfect touch." Nora had been scampering around Hannah all afternoon like a bird helping Cinderella get ready for the ball. Several times she asked if she could also go to the wedding and fulfill her lifelong dream of being a flower girl. "I already have a dress," she said. "I've been waiting and waiting to be asked."

Nathan had suggested that Hannah take the hired bus from the local hotel to the wedding venue, where he would meet her. Hannah got the impression that he now realized that family weddings could be complicated. Lea would drive her to the hotel and keep the kids overnight.

"Lea will be here in a few minutes; do you have everything you need for your sleepover?" asked Hannah.

"Yes, but I'm going to go get Samantha so Ava and I can play at her house." Nora skipped out of the room to find her American Girl doll.

Hannah, wearing a mask of apprehension, looked at herself in the mirror. She had been surprised to find a beautiful dress in Molly's closet, and she hoped it would be appropriate for this wedding. It was a great shade of blue, flowy, and fit her well. She managed to get a last-minute haircut and blow out appointment, which made her feel festive even though she had to bring the kids to the salon. She primped her hair a final time with her fingers, slid on her metallic flats, grabbed her clutch, and left the room, pleased with the result.

THE MINIVAN PULLED into the Best Western Hotel, where a school bus idled in front of the main entrance. "That looks like your ride," Lea said. "Call me if you need an extraction. We'll come get you."

Hannah leaned over and kissed Lea on her cheek, then laughed. "I'm pretty sure that won't be necessary. Thanks so much. I'll text you and give you updates, and please let me know if you have any problems with them. Bye, guys. Be good," she said to the gang in the back of the van. "Have fun at the pool."

Hannah approached the bus. She stopped. *What the hell am I doing here?* Guests were boarding, and she headed for the line and joined them. This was not the first time she had taken a bus to a wedding, but it was the first time she had done it alone. She sat in the first available seat located by the window and, with a nervous smile, glanced around to see with whom she would be spending the next several hours. They were like most of her contemporaries—happy faces filled with excitement, phones at the ready to capture every moment.

"Hi, everyone. Can I have your attention?" said a young woman at the front of the bus. "I'm Melissa. I'm Grace's cousin, and I'd like to welcome you on board. It'll take us about twenty minutes to get to the ceremony site, and I just want to let you know that this evening the bus will make two runs back here to the hotel. So just enjoy yourselves, and we'll make sure you get home safe!"

"Hell ya," shouted a guy from the back of the bus.

As the bus pulled out, Hannah's seat companion leaned across the aisle to speak to a woman sitting catercorner to them.

"Hey, Linds . . . you nervous about seeing Nathan? It's been a while, right?" he asked. At the mention of Nathan, Hannah perked up and leaned in to listen.

The woman gave him a sharp look. "Nathan and I broke up a long time ago. We're still good friends. It's no big deal."

Hannah turned and stared dumbly out the window, concluding that this girl must be an ex of Nathan's. *"Linds," probably Lindsey. Well, this could be awkward.* Hannah had seen this girl boarding the bus, dressed in a short pale aqua strapless dress and, despite warnings to wear flats, four-inch heels. From Hannah's vantage point, she could see only the side of her face, but her long dark hair was gorgeous, and her skin was flawless.

"Seat companion" turned back around and gave Hannah a look and said, "Hey, I'm Neil. How ya doing?"

"Hannah," she said. "Nice to meet you."

"How do you know Grace and Nick?"

Hannah felt her stomach drop away, fearing that "Linds" might hear her response. "Family friend. What about you?" she asked, hoping to divert the focus from what the hell she was doing at this wedding of a stranger.

"College friends. A bunch of us here went to UVM together," he said.

Thankfully, his phone buzzed, and with an abrupt "excuse me," he answered and began talking. When he finished, he turned to report to the others around him that Harry had missed the bus and would be late, as usual. Laughter erupted, and the group began to share memories of Harry's previous inability to get anywhere at the appointed time.

The bus slowed and turned onto a gravel road. "Wow," said Neil. "This is awesome." The guests peered out the bus windows at the sizable Dutch-style barn situated on a hill. The cloudless day provided a stunning view of the mountains in the distance.

Hannah stepped off the bus and immediately spotted Nathan walking toward her in his groomsman's outfit—a navy-blue suit with a white shirt and gray tie. There was a flower sprig in his lapel. "Hi," he said, giving her a brief kiss on the cheek. "You look amazing."

"Hi," said Hannah, a shiver running through her as she received his kiss. "And look at you—wow! Are you in the wedding party? This place is so incredible . . . look at this view." Hannah paused to take in the magnificent expanse before her. There were rolling fields as far as she could see.

"Yeah, I am," he said, gesturing to the lapel flower. "Wait until you see the ceremony site. C'mon, let's check it out." Nathan grabbed Hannah's hand and they abruptly headed away from the bus and toward the barn, where guests gathered. She felt his hand in hers, and a giddy wave of excitement ran through her. He didn't let go of her hand until he dropped it to give a bear hug to an older gentleman using a walker.

"Pop," Nathan exclaimed. "I've been looking for you."

"Nathan! Got a ride in a golf cart from the parking lot," said the man. "I could use one of those at my house."

"That'd be convenient," said Nathan. "Pop, I want you to meet Hannah Spencer, a friend of mine. Hannah, this is my grandfather, James Wild."

"Hello, Hannah. Good to meet you," said James. "You look lovely."

"Thank you, Mr. Wild," said Hannah. "It's very nice to meet you too."

"Hey, Nathan," came a voice from behind. "Connor's going to take Pop up the hill to the tent. Is this Hannah?" Hannah turned to see a woman about her age dressed in a sleeveless, long rose-colored dress.

"Kristy, Hannah . . . Hannah, Kristy, my cousin," Nathan said by way of introduction. "Kristy is the most irreverent of all my cousins, so I'd highly recommend you sit with her while I do my thing during the ceremony. She'll provide excellent commentary."

"Looking forward to it," said Hannah. She smiled at Kristy.

"Yeah, I can tell you all kinds of stuff about Nathan," said Kristy, smiling back.

"Don't believe any of it," said Nathan. "Hey, I gotta go. See you after the ceremony. Thanks, Kristy."

"Break a leg, Nathan. C'mon, Pop. Let's go see Gracie get married."

The threesome headed toward the golf cart. Connor, Kristy's husband, was seated in the driver's seat and jumped out to meet Hannah and assist James into the seat beside him. Connor drove James the short distance to the ceremony site atop the knoll.

Kristy and Hannah walked along the freshly mowed grass path toward the big tent adjacent to the meadow. As the two women walked, Kristy explained that the wedding venue was a former working farm owned by an old family friend. The old barn and small house were the old farmstead, and the fields once grazed both cows and sheep. Now hayed by a local farmer, it was indeed a quintessential New England barn wedding site. The view of rolling farmland with the Green Mountains in the distance was unspoiled.

"How lucky they are to have such perfect weather today," said Hannah.

"I know. It's amazing. Look!" said Kristy, pointing to the edge of the woods a short distance away, where a small herd of deer stood frozen, staring toward them. "Fangirls."

"So cute," said Hannah, stopping to admire the scene. A quartet of musicians set up nearby began to play a lively tune, and the startled deer abruptly turned and darted into the woods.

They reached the tent, where tables were set up, some with beverages and some featuring framed photographs. Hannah and Kristy helped themselves to glasses of lemonade and walked around the tent. James and Connor were standing at one of the tables, and James caught Hannah's eye and beckoned her over.

"This is a picture of my bride and me on our wedding day," he said, handing Hannah a framed photo. "She was the love of my life for over sixty years, a wonderful woman. She was a nurse . . . one of the first working mothers. She made everything special."

"She's beautiful," said Hannah. "What was her name?"

"Hannah was her name, but her family called her Anna," said James, peering over his glasses and smiling at Hannah. "You remind me of her."

"Ahh!" Hannah exclaimed. "I've always liked my name. Did you know it means 'grace'?"

"I didn't know that," said James. "But maybe my son did, since that's what he named his firstborn daughter."

"You look happy and handsome on your wedding day," said Hannah. "You must miss her very much, especially on days like today."

"Yes, yes, I do," said James, looking at the picture. "She loved the gathering of the clan."

Hannah looked at the photographs with James as he explained who was who and where and when the shots were taken. Hannah was impressed with his recall and deep love for his family. Many of the photographs were of the groom's family, and he was even familiar with many of their names.

"Hey, Pop, time to get seated," said Kristy. "Show's about to start."

They walked James to a seat in the front row and took their places a few rows back. Hannah scanned the crowd and felt the anticipation growing around her. She looked around for "Linds" but couldn't see her. Although she still felt a little out of place, everyone she met so far had made her feel entirely comfortable. *So far, so good.*

Music played by the quartet suddenly stopped and, after a few moments, began again with "Jesu Joy of Man's Desiring." Hannah watched as the procession started with the seating of the bride's and groom's mothers. Hannah assumed the woman in the peach silk dress must be Nathan's mom, as there was some resemblance, and Nathan escorted her. Nathan and his mother were both wearing broad smiles and occasionally whispered to each other as they strolled down the aisle.

The remaining groomsmen and groom slowly appeared in front of the arbor that Nathan had built. White gauzy fabric was draped over the arbor and fluttered in the gentle breeze. The arbor, the striking wedding party, and the mountain backdrop made for an incredible, picturesque ceremony site, like something out of a magazine.

Nathan, standing with the other groomsmen, looked particularly handsome. He gave her a little nod and smiled, and she grinned back at him. Hannah seriously loved weddings. She loved the ceremonies and the ripple of anticipation that moved through the guests as they waited for the bride to walk down the aisle. Even though she was sometimes skeptical about the enduring nature of the relationships, weddings made her feel hopeful. She especially enjoyed the dressing up, the dancing, and the attention to detail that the couple put into planning. But most of all, she loved seeing the families, knowing that the couple had all the people they treasured in one place. She turned to watch Kendall and the other bridesmaids walk down the aisle and felt the giddiness grow inside her. Kendall could have been Grace's twin, and for a moment, Hannah was confused as to which one she had seen at the coffee shop and which she had seen at the hardware store.

The music turned to "Canon in D," and Hannah watched as Grace and (presumably) Nathan's father began to proceed down the aisle. She was breathtaking. Her gown of lace was both formal and appropriate to the outdoor setting, gracefully flowing as she walked to her groom who stood under the arbor. As Hannah watched the bride and her father, she glimpsed "Linds" seated in the midsection, not looking at the bride but staring at the wedding party standing alongside the arbor. She was watching Nathan.

The bride approached the arbor, kissed her dad and mom, and clasped Nick's hands. To Hannah's utter surprise, Nathan stepped forward and addressed the guests.

"Good afternoon, everyone. My name is Nathan Wild, brother of the beautiful bride, Grace, and I'm so happy to be the officiant today. A warm welcome to all of you who have come here today to witness and celebrate the marriage of this couple, Grace and Nick. I want you first to take a moment to admire this setting. What a beautiful day to start a marriage. You are here today because we are each a part of the story of Grace and Nick.

And whether you have known one of them since birth or be-friended them more recently, they're delighted that you're here to share this celebration." He had given a slight nod to Hannah as he said the word "recently."

"This relationship didn't start, nor has it flourished, in a vacuum. Each couple lives in the context of their culture and community. This personal network of family members and close friends make up what we might call their pack. You, here today, are Nick and Grace's pack."

Hannah sat mesmerized as Nathan continued the service with such poise and ease. She was captivated by the ceremony. There were meaningful readings by friends and family and a ring-warm-ing ceremony where the wedding bands were passed amongst the attendees who gave the couple a little wish or prayer over them. There was a humorous and touching exchange of vows, during which Nick and Grace each expressed unique hopes and promises. Nathan completed the ceremony with a fun twist.

"Nick, Grace . . . ," he said as he handed each a small crystal cordial glass. He poured a small amount of Scotch into each glass. "Will you, Nick, take this woman to be your lawfully wed-ded wife?"

"I will," said Nick, beaming and raising his glass.

"And will you, Grace, take this man to be your lawfully wed-ded husband?

"Absolutely," said Grace, glowing and raising hers.

"Now that you have given yourselves to each other with solemn vows and the giving and receiving of rings, in front of your pack, all assembled here . . . it is with great joy that I pro-nounce you husband and wife. You may begin your marriage the same way your relationship began: with a shot of whiskey in the middle of the day! Cheers!"

Nick and Grace downed the shots and Nathan said, "And now . . . though you may have kissed each other countless times, this is the one you'll remember for the rest of your lives. Please seal your vows with a kiss to last a lifetime."

As Nick and Grace kissed, the crowd jumped out of their seats and erupted with applause. The recessional music began, and Hannah knew she had just experienced something quite special. During the entire ceremony, you could have heard a pin drop. It was meaningful, filled with humor and love. The joy was palpable.

Not sure exactly what to do, Hannah stood next to her seat while others filed passed her on the way to the cocktail hour under the tent. Nathan was still standing at the arbor greeting guests, who were gushing with compliments and praise for his performance, and he motioned to her to come toward him.

"That was the most thought-filled, heartfelt exchange of love and commitment I've ever seen. It was a remarkable thing to witness," Hannah overheard one middle-aged woman say to Nathan. *Exactly.* Nathan's words, Grace's and Nick's words to each other, all authentic, so intimate—and not in a creepy way but in a "we're all rooting for you" way.

When he broke away from the well-wishers, Nathan took Hannah's hand, turned them toward the tent, and said, "I need a drink!"

"That was mind-blowing. I was so surprised. You didn't tell me you were officiating," Hannah said.

"Yeah, I didn't want to say anything to you. I guess I didn't want you to have any expectations. I've been kind of anxious about it. It's a lot of responsibility," he said with a goofy smile.

"You should take that show on the road. It was amazing. I've never seen wedding guests so completely engaged and attentive. It was beautiful."

"Thank you. I'm glad it went well and even happier it's over. Now we're going to party. I'm so glad you're here with me," he said, holding her hand up and shaking it in the air. "I want to eat and get drunk and dance. You in?"

"Absolutely," said Hannah. They headed to the bar and food stations under the big white tent. He hadn't let go of her hand. Hannah ordered a gin and tonic and made a mental note to pace herself. She wanted to let loose but maintain control. A little tipsy, not drunk, would be her goal. Nathan got a beer, and they turned away from the bar and immediately found themselves facing "Linds."

"Hello, Nate." Lindsey stared at him with a sly smile.

"Hi, Lindsey, this is Hannah," he said, abruptly pointing to Hannah. "Hannah, this is Lindsey."

"Nice to meet you," said Hannah, face to face with Nathan's ex.

"You too." Lindsey quickly turned to Nathan. "I hope you aren't uncomfortable that I'm here—Grace insisted I come. We've been friends forever; I couldn't have missed it."

"No, it's fine. Glad you made it."

Lindsey turned to Hannah. "Is this your first Wild event, or have you and Nathan been going out for a while?"

Whoa, lady, slow down. Hesitating before she spoke, Hannah gave a quick glance to Nathan and said, "Yup, it's the first time I've been able to get to a party where *everyone* was here." She was pleased with herself for giving this answer, which was truthful but left room for interpretation.

Before she could be interrogated any further, Nathan took her arm and said, "And I want to introduce her to everyone she hasn't met yet, so have a great time, Lindsey. Good to see you."

As they walked away, Nathan slid his palm into Hannah's

and gave her hand a little squeeze. When they were a safe distance away, he spun her around and pulled her close to him.

"Sorry for that, and thank you," he said.

"She's a fierce one." Hannah looked up at Nathan.

"You have no idea," he said. "I used to date her in college. I'll tell you about that later, but I'm glad we got that out of the way. I want to introduce you to my family. C'mon, let's start with my parents."

He leaned down and kissed her softly on the lips. It was a brief kiss, but it was enough for Hannah to want to tackle him to the ground and ravage him. She did not. Instead, she brushed her hair behind her ears and looked to the ground, smiling, as he grabbed her hand and they walked to the tent.

Nathan escorted Hannah around the tent during the cocktail party, and she met the entirety of his family, including the bride and groom. They were a lively, open "pack," and there was a lot of humor. A few looked surprised when they met her and teased Nathan about being too busy for women. Nathan didn't seem to mind. She didn't feel nearly as out of place as she'd expected, and before long a bell rang, and everyone was encouraged to head into the barn for dinner.

Nathan and Hannah took their seats at the cousins' table, which included Nathan's siblings, Kendall, and Adam, along with Adam's girlfriend, the Wild cousins Kristy and Melissa, and their spouses. The groom's brother gave a heartfelt toast mentioning all the reasons why Grace was too good for Nick. That was followed by Kendall's hysterical toast for her sister, featuring anecdotes about their younger selves and pointing out how nice Grace was compared to the rest of the family.

"Most people notice immediately, one of Grace's defining qualities is her kindness. She's just *good*. Like, if she were to go for a walk in a forest, all the woodland creatures would come out and sing with her. Her sweetness was always considered an anomaly in our extended family, and as my mom always said, 'That's not how she was raised.'

"Don't get me wrong, she tries to fit in, but even if she calls you a bad name, you can tell her heart's not in it, and it comes out sounding like a compliment. But no matter where this strange quality of kindness comes from—it could be from my dad, but he doesn't talk enough to really know—we appreciate that she balances out the rest of the family."

At the table, Nathan's cousins and siblings were welcoming to Hannah. She sat next to Kristy, who went out of her way to talk to her and appeared to be doing some interrogation. Every time Kristy asked her a personal question, the cousins would lean in to listen to her response. "We're pretty curious about you. Sorry. Nathan doesn't bring women around too much," Kristy said with a smile to Nathan.

"True," Nathan said, shrugging his shoulders and smiling at Hannah.

Hannah was getting the vibe of the family. There were a lot of inside jokes and much reminiscing, but they were a fun gang, and the laughter was contagious. Also drinking. There was a lot of drinking.

At her seat, Hannah had a direct sightline to Lindsey, sitting with some of the group from the bus. When Hannah looked over, Lindsey was staring directly at her. She didn't look back again for fear they would lock eyes.

The couple had their first dance, and then Grace and her father danced to "Gracie" by Ben Folds. Hannah, Nathan, and nearly everyone in the barn wiped away tears watching the sweet father-daughter dance. Before long, the barn's floor filled with guests dancing to the band from Boston playing classic rock, Motown, and the "good" wedding songs. Happy to be letting go, Hannah danced with abandon for the first set. During the second set, the band played a swing dance. Nathan twirled her, pulled her close, and said, "How do you like my sweet dance moves?"

"Not bad, Wild." She laughed.

He pushed her back, twirling her away and then pulling her in and finishing with a deep dip. Hannah popped upright, threw her arms around his neck, and kissed him on the mouth. Out of breath and jubilant, Hannah pointed to the bar, indicating she wanted a drink. Nathan led her to the bar, and then, drinks in hand, put his arm around Hannah's shoulder, and together they watched a dance circle form. Guests danced in and out of the circle as others clapped and danced around them. Before long, Lindsey tripped into the circle and began shaking her hips from side to side. But then she took it one step further, shimmying and shaking and performing moves that would make a stripper blush. She gyrated over to one guy after another and pressed her pelvis to theirs, swinging her hair and mashing against them. People were laughing and egging her on, but there were also awkward gazes and uncomfortable looks. She threw her arms around one guy and started making out with him. Nathan abruptly handed his beer to Hannah and raced to the dance floor, where he took Lindsey's hand, spun her around gently, and embraced her in a slow dance. He led her off the dance floor, tango-style, and the two of them disappeared out of the barn.

It all happened incredibly fast. Hannah stood there, stunned, with two drinks in her hand. *What am I supposed to do now?* She walked away from the bar and headed back to her table, which was empty. Embarrassed, she pulled her phone out of her purse and texted Lea, hoping to look purposeful to any on-lookers. After a brief exchange of "all goods," Hannah slid her phone back into her purse and leaned under the table to stash it. A warm hand touched her shoulder.

"Miss Hannah, are you having a good time with the Wild clan?" It was James, Nathan's grandfather.

"Hey there, Mr. Wild." She spoke loudly so he could hear her over the music. "Yes, I'm having a great time. I haven't had this much fun for months."

"Where's my grandson? I can't imagine why he'd ever leave your side," he shouted.

"I have no idea where he's gotten to," said Hannah. She was fuming, but she didn't want James to hear it in her voice.

"Would you mind helping me outside to get some quiet for a few minutes?" he asked. "I can only take so much of this volume!"

"Sure." Hannah was happy to have a mission to distract her from her growing annoyance. Nathan had basically abandoned her to get up to god knows what with his former girlfriend. Hannah escorted James through the barn and out into the night air. The sky was incredible—clear and starlit. The moon was nearly full, and the air crisp. About a dozen people were gathered around a bonfire, sitting on hay bales. Hannah and James walked toward the fire, and Hannah picked up a couple of folding chairs, arranging them a short distance from the others.

"This is nice," James said. "Such a beautiful night."

"It is," said Hannah. "I have fallen in love with Vermont summers. Do you live nearby?"

"Yes, I'm at a wonderful place near Burlington, in Shelburne, actually. An assisted living facility. Been there for about seven years. My wife and I moved there when she started ailing, and after she passed, I stayed."

"It must be nice to live near the lake," Hannah said.

"I hated it when we first got there. It was full of old people. Then one day, I caught a glimpse of myself in the mirror in the hall, and it hit me like a ton of bricks. I was an old person! I was just like the rest of them. So, I started giving the place a chance and have come to love it. Got a lot of good friends, but they could go at any minute, so I try not to get too close," he laughed. It was a wonderful laugh.

"I wish my Nana would go to a place like that," said Hannah. "She lives all by herself in her lifelong home in Pennsylvania, and she won't budge. But her friends have either passed or moved near their children or into a place like yours, so I fear she's lonely. She has a live-in aide—my parents insisted on that—but she despises her. It's so frustrating. She thinks this is less of a burden on my folks, but from what I see, it's a huge burden of worry. She only has one person to interact with all day. We all try and visit when we can, but it's not a good situation."

"That's too bad," said James. "But I understand her thinking. I didn't want to leave my home either. But one thing I'll tell you, Hannah, it's not the place, it's not the stuff you've accumulated, it's the hearts you've accumulated. The people you have brought into this world and the people who they've brought into the world. They're who I want to surround myself with now. Today has brought me such joy to be here with my entire family having such a wonderful time."

"I'm so glad you have this day, James. They're quite the gang. I like every Wild one of them. Except right now, I'm wondering about Nathan." She looked around the field.

"I'm sorry, I'm keeping you from him," he said. "Why don't you go back inside and resume your dancing."

"Nathan disappeared. I'm not sure where he went. He literally swept his old girlfriend off her feet and left the barn with her. What do you think I should make of that?"

"Ha, Lindsey? That young lady cannot hold her liquor. Was she drunk? There were many family parties where she was. Sweet enough, but not a lot of substance. I'm not sure where Nathan is, but don't fret about it. That boy is character through and through."

"Good to hear," said Hannah. But a terrible gnawing doubt was growing in the pit of her stomach. She thought her friend Derek had had character too, and then he had cheated on Kaitlyn. She shook it off. Her grandmother in Pennsylvania used to love to say, "Don't borrow trouble." And so, she would not, not yet, not when it was so pleasant sitting outside with James. The two of them fell quiet for a couple of minutes, gazing at the fire. Hannah could see a shadowy figure walking away from the house on the property. It was the house the wedding party used to get ready for the ceremony. As the person came closer to the barn and the bonfire, Hannah was certain it was Nathan. What had he been up to in the house? Where was Lindsey? What should she do now?

"I think that's Nathan," said Hannah, pointing to the barn door, which Nathan was now entering.

"Looks like," said James. "Why don't you run along. Melissa is right over there, and she'll take me back in when I'm ready."

Hannah rose and leaned to give James a peck on the cheek. "Thanks for the lovely talk, James. I'll tell Melissa you're over here." She let Melissa know her grandfather was outside and that she was returning to the barn. Melissa immediately rose to help him over to join her group. It was touching how all the cousins almost fought over who could be more helpful to James. Kristy said it was a constant competition to be James's favorite.

Nathan had not noticed her out by the bonfire, so Hannah proceeded to the barn to join him. The dancing was still in full force, and she spotted Nathan near the bar, scanning the crowd. He spotted her, and they walked toward one another.

"There you are," he said.

"There *I* am?" she said with a raised eyebrow and a cock of her head. She did not mean for it to come out so snarky, but he had been gone for at least twenty minutes, and in I-don't-really-know-anyone-here time, it was half-past polite and a quarter to rude. She kept her gaze on him to gauge how he would respond. He held the gaze, took hold of her hand, and asked her if she would like to take another walk outside so that he could explain. She agreed but pulled her hand away from his.

They walked toward the tent in the field, away from the bonfire and barn.

"I'm so sorry I left you like that," he said.

"Lindsey is your ex?" asked Hannah. She could feel her cheeks burning, but inside she was cold, almost shivering.

"She was my college girlfriend. She's an old and good friend of Grace's, so I knew she was going to be here, which was why I was so interested in having a date tonight. I know it may sound like I was using you, which I sort of was." He gave her a sheepish smile. "But it's more than that. I like you, Hannah."

"Oh my god. This guy I used to see, Seth, would say that to me all the time. 'I really like you, Hannah.' Is there some website or app out there full of lines you pull out when you're in trouble? You like me? Which is why you grabbed her off the dance floor and left?"

"No, no, no. Let me explain." Nathan ran his fingers through his thick crop of wavy brown hair. "Lindsey had a tough time with our breakup. I mean, she didn't used to be like this. If you'd known her before—long story—but she has a history of getting shit-faced, and lately she gets pretty inappropriate. I think you could probably see it was going in that direction the way she was dancing. I didn't want a scene at Grace's wedding." Again, he ran his fingers through his hair. "I just wanted to abort a potentially embarrassing situation. I took her outside and brought her to the cottage and put her to bed. She passed out almost immediately when she hit the mattress. Some of the wedding party is staying there tonight, so they can deal with her. They're all good friends."

Hannah listened quietly and did not respond immediately. The story was straightforward enough, but it was still kind of messed up. He was gone a pretty long time, and there was about fifteen minutes not accounted for . . . It didn't take that long to walk to the cottage. What had transpired? She hated being made a fool. Nathan seemed like such a great guy, but to abandon her in the middle of their date was not okay. She wondered what everyone in the barn must be thinking about her, about him, about Lindsey.

"Hannah?" Nathan asked, reaching for her hand and clasping it with his other. He looked at her without breaking his gaze.

"You wanted me to come to this wedding with you, and I was hesitant because, obviously, I don't know you very well," Hannah said. "I was having a good time, but this whole thing makes me uncomfortable. I mean, I get the part about you not wanting a scene, and I guess that did work."

Nathan nodded. "I'm so glad you came, and I'm sorry that happened. Lindsey is nothing to me, just a part of my past that unfortunately shows up at family stuff sometimes. But even Grace is getting tired of her, so I don't think it's going to be a problem much longer. Can we pick up where we left off? Let's go get some more drinks and dance. And, we haven't even done the photo booth yet."

She looked at Nathan. Was it a mask of sincerity he wore, or was he truly sincere? A movie reel of all the dick guys she had ever known flashed through her brain. She was fairly sure he wasn't one of them.

"I do love a good photo booth," said Hannah. "Okay. What the hell. But don't abandon me like that again." She lightly punched his arm.

"Promise," said Nathan. He pulled her close to him, wrapping his arms around her. "Thank you for not bailing. I'm really happy you're here with me tonight. Unless you tell me otherwise, I'm going to kiss you right . . ." Nathan leaned in a little closer, smiling, and then his lips were on hers, softly, and then she was returning the kiss. He held her head in his hands and they kissed tenderly and then more enthusiastically.

"I could do this all night, but I think we better go back," said Nathan quietly when they pulled apart after a few minutes.

Hannah's "lady parts" were on fire as they walked hand in hand back to the barn, and not because she had her period. Despite the events of the last half hour, the make-out session had hurled her hormones into overdrive.

"Drink first?" asked Nathan as they approached the barn door.

"Yup," said Hannah. They walked to the bar and each ordered a beer, took a few swallows, and headed for the dance floor, leaving the bottles on a ledge of the barn wall. They danced for an hour, working up a sweat, occasionally grabbing their beers to quench their thirst.

Clapping and exhausted as "Living on a Prayer" wound down, Nathan and Hannah stayed in the middle of the dance floor. The band leader announced, "We're going to slow things down now as we close out the evening."

Nathan pulled Hannah close to him for the last dance. Hannah breathed in his scent, a comforting, woody smell. Her hand went to his shoulder, and she leaned her head against her hand. They held each other, at first barely moving and then slowly stepping from side to side, his hand on her back as they swayed to Etta James's "At Last" and let the music wash over them. She closed her eyes and savored the feeling of being held by a man. Nathan bent down and kissed her gently on the mouth. It felt strange and, at the same time, familiar. And it was in that moment, she thought later, as their lips touched and her hands caressed the muscles in his back, that her guard slipped, and her body began to yield to the joy of human touch. Hannah could not stop smiling.

THE BUS PULLED up to the barn for the last run of the evening back to Waterbury. Nathan asked the driver if he could drop them off at a crossroads to his house on the way to the hotel, and the driver obliged. Taking the bus would mean he would have to go back to the barn in the morning to get his car, but that was better than driving himself. Of course, it might mean running into Lindsey in the morning. Thankfully, she had not reappeared yet, not since she passed out in the cottage.

Nathan and Hannah jumped out of the bus along the road leading to their houses to shouts of "Bye, Nathan," "Go get ya some!" "Great ceremony" and began the half-mile walk home.

"This walk will sober us up," Nathan said, leading Hannah along the road in the moonlight. "You okay?"

"I'm fine, but I'm glad I brought this sweater. That was a blast, Nathan. Thanks for badgering me into going."

"Ha, you're welcome. So now that my family has been revealed in all their crazy glory, will you hang out with me again?"

"How can I avoid you? Your dog is obsessed with me."

They walked along in silence for a while. The road was quiet and all Hannah could hear were their footsteps.

"Watcha thinking about?" Hannah quietly asked Nathan.

"Just recalling the evening," Nathan said. He reached in the dark to find Hannah's hand to hold as they walked. "I feel good about how it all turned out."

"It was great," agreed Hannah. "I like your family."

When they got to the driveway of Molly and Ted's house, Hannah stopped and turned to Nathan. He smiled and stepped back, pulled her hand toward him, and tilted his head toward his home. Wordlessly, they turned toward his house.

As they got to his doorstep, Hannah paused. "I gotta tell you before we go in. I can't sleep with you. Not tonight, maybe some other time, but not tonight. I just want to say that before we go in. We can hang out, but don't push it, okay?"

"Hey, that's fine," he said, without hesitation. "I wouldn't push it, ever. No problem. Let's just hang."

Hannah was relieved. It was the first time she'd ever flat-out said something like that to a guy so early in a "relationship." Even with the Lindsey drama, it had been a great date, and, in her experience, that would typically end with sex.

Hannah entered Nathan's house as if she were entering a museum. It was cluttered and untidy. She immediately began scanning the living room to assess the habitat. Some items gave a hint of what Nathan was into. She saw pictures, objects d'art, a small original oil painting of Mount Mansfield, an upside-down map of the world that made it not so Eurocentric, a turntable, and LP collection. His laptop had a sticker of a fluffy white cloud and the phrase THERE IS NO CLOUD, IT'S JUST SOMEONE ELSE'S COMPUTER. On the coffee table was a pile of books, *The Warmth of Other Suns* on the top. There was a large framed photograph on the wall of a man rock-climbing up an enormous cliff face. She looked at it closely.

"Is that you?" she asked, pointing to the photograph.

"Yup. It's in the Gunks over in New York State." He studied the photo with her.

"You climb the sides of mountains for fun?" she asked.

"Not as much as I once did, but I was way into it in high school and college. I spent my summers working as a climbing instructor. I took a bunch of instructor courses in mountain guiding, wilderness first responder, stuff like that. I never wanted to do it as a career, but I like to play outside. I just joined the Mansfield Mountain Rescue Squad."

"Wow. What does that involve?"

"It can be intense. We do rescue missions, like backcountry stuff and wilderness searches. People go out hiking or backcountry skiing and get turned around, lost, or hurt, and we rescue them. Occasionally it goes very bad, and we have to do a recovery. I'm new to it so haven't done much yet. Oh yeah, we also do water rescues in swift water."

"That's very cool. It also sounds a little dangerous."

"We do a lot of training—it's a very professional group."

"And what's this?" she asked, picking up a framed photo on a side table of young Nathan and a woman. The woman appeared to be Christiane Amanpour, the British CNN journalist. "Is that Christiane Amanpour?"

"Yup."

"Yeah, so how did you come to meet her and get this?" Hannah waved the framed photo in the air.

"That's a long story. Do you want something to drink? Water, coffee, tea, beer, wine?"

"Water, please. Tell me about Christiane!" demanded Hannah.

Nathan went to the kitchen and poured two glasses of water, carried them back to the living room, and placed them on the coffee table in front of the L-shaped sofa. He patted the sofa seat next to him, inviting Hannah to sit.

"My dad was a journalist. He still actually does some freelance work. When I was a kid, CNN was on all the time in my dad's study, and I'd go in there and watch. And while my prepubescent self didn't give a hoot about Wolf Blitzer, I was infatuated with Christiane Amanpour. My friends all thought I was a freak, because they were obsessed with Britney Spears but not me. Christiane was everything to me."

"That's freaking hilarious. Go on."

Nathan put his arm around Hannah and snuggled in, moving his legs onto the couch and pulling them both down to a prone position. Hannah was still holding the picture.

"Basically, my dad knew a guy who knew a guy who worked at CNN, and for my birthday—I think I was turning twelve—my parents took me to Atlanta and got us a tour, and there she was. My dad planned for us to be there when she would be available, and she was incredibly nice to me. I was so starstruck, I don't even know if I said anything."

"Look at your face." Hannah stared at the picture. "You're ecstatic. So, Nathan Wild, are you still crushing on Christiane?"

"I pay attention when she's on, but it's not the same after you've spent time with real girls."

Twenty-Three

What the hell? Hannah's deep sleep was ended abruptly by a piercing and persistent dinging. *Phone alarm.* Her body, draped over Nathan's on the couch, stirred to life, as did his. They groggily sat up and looked for the phone, which was right next to them on the coffee table.

"Damn," he said. "I was out cold." He looked at Hannah, slumped on the couch. He leaned back and brushed some hair out of her face, saying, "It looks like you were, too."

"I guess we better get going. I need some coffee," Hannah mumbled.

"Lots," agreed Nathan, rising. They had stayed up late after talking about Christiane, eating leftover pizza, and sort of watching a repeat of *Saturday Night Live*. They kissed for a while, then fell asleep with the TV on. At some point, one of them must have switched it off, but Hannah could not remember.

Hannah looked up at Nathan walking away from the couch. *Oh my god, he doesn't have pants on.* She was fully clothed, sans shoes. *When did he take his pants off? Why did he take his pants off? Oh, boxers. Good.* Her head was spinning; she was anxious but sure nothing much happened. She remembered eating and kissing (she smiled, that was fun), but they must have just fallen asleep.

"It's eight. I've got to get to my parents' house in Richmond by nine. I promised," said Nathan. He nonchalantly put on his pants. "I'm so sorry to wake you so early."

"It's fine," said Hannah, not meaning it. She was tired.

"Do you want to come along?" He sat beside her on the couch and drew her close to him.

"Hmm, late night and breakfast?" She tilted her chin to her shoulder, smiling coyly. "What would your family think?"

"They'd think, *Yay, Nathan*." He gave her a little squeeze.

"I think you have to go this one alone," she said. "I need to rescue Lea from the kids."

Hannah sensed there was a seismic shift in their relationship. There was a sudden ease in the way she spoke to him and the way he casually touched her. As they said their goodbyes after a quick cup of coffee, Nathan gave her a long morning-breath kiss and asked if he could stop by later to see how she was doing. "You might need a hand with the kids, what with the hangover and all," he said.

"Maybe. Text me when you get home, and I'll let you know," she said.

Hannah returned home, showered, dressed, ate a banana, and managed to pick up the kids by ten o'clock. Lea was her usual organized self, and they were all playing in the back yard when she arrived.

Lea approached Hannah, tilted her head, and said, "Sooo?"

"It was great. I had so much fun. Nathan's family is great, and it wasn't as awkward as I thought it'd be," said Hannah, staring off into the back yard as she answered.

"Where'd ya sleep last night?" She was still staring at Hannah. "You look a little . . . tousled." Lea smiled at Hannah and gave her a side-eye.

"It was all respectful. We spent the night on the couch at

Nathan's. Nothing happened," she said with a friendly arm punch to Lea.

Hannah shepherded Nora and Owen into the car and set out for home, wondering when Nathan would be back from the brunch and if he would indeed come to see her. She was tired from the late night but couldn't wait to see him again. She was so intrigued by him, and she liked everything she knew about him. But that was the thing—she did not know much. Like, what did he actually do? She knew it was techy, but nothing more specific. Maybe he worked for the government and was some sort of hacker. She would have to get more details.

"Aunt Hannah, can we go to the big pool today?" asked Nora when they were eating their lunch on the deck. "It's so hot."

"That's a great idea," said Hannah, but doubted if Nathan would want to join them at the community pool. As she picked up her phone to text him, it buzzed with an incoming message.

Today 12:34 PM

Nathan: hey, did you get the kids? how are they

me: good, we're going to the pool

Nathan: i think I'm going to stay here this afternoon

lots of relatives still here . . . call you tonite?

me: sounds good have fun

Well, that's that. She could not shake the feeling of wanting to see him again, but it would have to wait.

The Waterbury Community Pool, located in town, was busy on a hot Sunday afternoon. But with tons of kids and lifeguards, Hannah was happy to know the kids would be safe, active, and hopefully exhausted by the end of the day.

Nora and Owen ran into the pool and soon found friends to play with in the shallow end. Hannah sat on the one available lounge chair near them. She spent the afternoon texting wedding pictures she had taken to Nathan, Sara, and Molly. Nathan sent her back some of his family. She could identify nearly everyone in the photos, which surprised her.

They returned home from the pool exhausted, and once the children were fed, bathed, storied, peed, watered, sang to, and watered again, Hannah finally plopped in front of the TV to stream an old season of *The Amazing Race*. It was her secret dream to someday become a contestant on the show, if only she could find the right partner. *Would Nathan be interested in that kind of thing?* A few years ago, she had told her mother that the right guy for her would have to agree to go on *The Amazing Race*, in theory, if not in reality. Elizabeth had smiled but confessed that she was also puzzled because they were discussing the characteristics of a good mate. Elizabeth had contributed suggestions such as "treats his family well" and "willing to share in household responsibilities." Hannah explained that all those qualities were also the qualities of someone who was game to go on *The Amazing Race*. He would have to be a willing partner, ready to evaluate her strengths and weaknesses, willing to be evaluated himself. And he could not be shy about letting a woman excel. He would need to be athletic, adventurous, handy, competitive, not opposed to adversity, flexible, happy to travel, sturdy, daring, and able to be pleasant in front of others even when he did not feel pleasant at all. One needed these qualities to win the Amazing Race *and* to win her love. And it was not all about winning the million dollars! It was the experience of trying that appealed to Hannah. Her mate needed to feel the same. Her mother could not help but agree when she laid it all out that way.

Five minutes into the show, Hannah's phone buzzed.

Nathan: Hey, can I call you?
me: Sure

"Hey!" Hannah answered on the first ring.

"Hey, I just wanted to check in and see if you wanted some company."

"I'm just hanging out, watching *The Amazing Race*. Want to come over?" asked Hannah.

"*The Amazing Race*! Be right over. I've always wanted to be on *The Amazing Race*."

Hannah smiled, hung up the phone, and raced to the bathroom to primp. She exited the bathroom just as Nathan was tiptoeing into the house.

As they watched the show, they assessed the remaining contestants—trashing the obnoxious ones and evaluating the potential of the nicer ones. They were mostly in-sync, but Hannah favored the all-girl teams (except for the overly bubbly cheerleaders), and Nathan rooted for the father-daughter team. The season was one that neither of them had seen, and they vowed to watch it together until the end. He stayed awhile after it was over, and they kissed on the couch. She was grateful the kids did not emerge from their beds and discover them. Nathan told Hannah he would be traveling to Boston for a couple of days and Cooper would be staying at his parents' house. Hannah reminded him that her parents were visiting on Friday for a long weekend.

"Does that mean you're unavailable for the weekend?" he asked.

"No, actually the opposite. They want me to go off and have

fun. You are, however, my best and only new friend around here. I have no real plan, but I do want to take advantage of them being around," she said.

"As your best and only new friend, I'll make a plan for us for Saturday or Sunday," Nathan said.

"Awesome," said Hannah. "Way to take a hint."

Twenty-Four

"Aunt Hannah?" Nora asked, walking into Hannah's room early Monday morning. "If you could have any superpower, what would it be?"

"Wow, it's a little early for such a big question. Why do you ask?" Hannah was just out of bed, pulling on her shorts. She sat on the edge of the bed and faced her niece.

"It's Superhero Week at camp, and I want to have a super good superpower," said Nora. "Everyone always says flying or being strong or invisible, but I want something super super."

"Let's see, you can make it so you could walk through walls, or you could talk to animals and understand them," suggested Hannah.

"I don't need to walk through walls. I can use the door. The talking to animals is a good idea, but I want something *powerful*." She twirled in place, ending with a Wonder Woman pose, chest out, hands on hips. Hannah laughed.

"Powerful. I know—how about the ability to always mimic, you know, copy people who are the best at things. Like, if you wanted to be the best at running, you'd be able to copy the fastest runner on earth, and then you could mimic other things as you needed them."

Nora paused and tapped her finger on her upper cheek. "That's good because then I could copy all of the other kids' superpowers!"

Hannah patted Nora's head. "I don't think that's keeping with the spirit of the activity, but yeah, you could."

Owen made a mad dash to Hannah, leaping on her and nearly knocking her down.

"I miss Mommy and Daddy," he said, putting his head on Hannah's shoulder.

"I know, pumpkin," Hannah said soothingly, stroking his back. "It's hard for you with them gone so long. But guess what? Their work project is already half over. They will be home in just a few more weeks. We've got some extra time this morning. Would you like to call them and say 'hi' on the computer?"

"Yay, yeah, let's do it!" said Owen. He pushed away from Hannah and leaped off the bed. He walked to the desk and flipped open her laptop, knowing exactly which keys to press to access the video chat setup. Hannah had to assist with the actual connection, but in no time, Nora and Owen were telling their parents about their expectations for "Superhero Week" at camp. Molly and Ted were all smiles, staring at the children on the screen, who were mostly acting goofy. When the kids flew out of the room, Ted began to tell Hannah about his research project involving beavers in Tierra del Fuego, Argentina. Although they were based at the University of Chile in Santiago, they would be flying south in the upcoming week to assess the damage beavers were doing to the ecosystem. Hannah found it fascinating but could not concentrate as Nora and Owen flew back in and kept interrupting. Nonetheless, it was a mood-lifting call. Everyone said their goodbyes and I love yous, and Hannah disconnected.

Generally, the kids were coping with their parents' absence well. Still, there were occasional situations when one of them would be desperate for them, and it was distressing. Hannah did her best to comfort them, acknowledge their feelings, and find a new activity to distract them and change course. Sometimes, this did not work, and there would be prolonged weeping, which usually caused the other child to cry as well. Stereo sobs. Thankfully, this was not one of those times.

"Okay, you two, we've got to get going now," said Hannah as she snapped the computer shut. "Lea will be here soon."

When the minivan full of kids rolled out of sight, Hannah strolled to the back yard with her coffee to assess the progress of the treehouse. The kids were impatient and wanted it done. With the summer half over, she needed to pick up the pace of construction. The decking was complete, and the railing posts installed. She toyed with the idea of insulation—it was New England, after all—but she would forgo that idea to keep it more rustic. It was easy to get carried away. She was determined, however, to provide electricity for lights and had figured out a way of installing a small solar panel on the south-facing roof. The panel would increase the project costs and further deplete her nest egg. Still, she was familiar with the steps to make it happen, and it was a rather straightforward addition. Plus, she wanted the challenge.

Hannah worked all day on the treehouse, framing the walls. This was her favorite part of the project so far. It took great accuracy in measuring and cutting but was satisfying as the small building began to take shape. The day went well, and by the time Lea pulled in with the kids, all four walls were completed. However, she had assembled the walls on the ground and needed assistance to heft them to the treehouse deck. She hoped her father could help her over the weekend. Seeing the walls framed out but not attached to the deck was frustrating for Nora and Owen. They begged to climb it, but Hannah flatly refused, promising them they would be able to check it out soon.

Taking advantage of decent weather, Nathan's absence, and her desire to show off her project to her parents, Hannah made tremendous progress by Thursday afternoon. She completed the "safety stairs," cut all the roof rafters (including the tricky notches), and installed the pulley mechanism, which could hoist a bucket to the treehouse.

Nathan texted he was delayed in Boston and proposed his plan for the weekend. He suggested they go kayaking at his favorite water spot in the area, the Green River Reservoir. Hannah was thrilled at the prospect of doing an outdoor activity at more than a preschool pace and quickly replied she would love to go.

She spent the rainy Friday morning cleaning the house, food shopping, and planning a simple welcome dinner for her parents. They arrived midafternoon and were stunned by the treehouse project. The assembled lumber parts were scattered across the lawn, and Hannah was proud to explain the project and how it all fit together.

"This is terrific, Hannah. Much more elaborate than I envisioned," said her father. "Why don't we take care of getting it up now while we have a break in the rain?" It did not take long for the three of them to hoist the pre-assembled walls onto the decking, which was convenient since it started raining right as they were completing the task.

As they sat talking in the family room, awaiting the arrival of the children home from camp, Hannah told her parents about her plans for the kayaking date with Nathan. She came clean with the entire plan and boldly disclosed, "I'll be back on Sunday by lunch. Is that okay?"

"Sure," Elizabeth said. "Will we be meeting your neighbor friend this weekend?"

"I don't know—could be awkward for him," she said. "Why

don't we play it by ear. But whatever you do, don't let Nora and Owen know where I am. They're mad for him and will want to come too, and I'd like to spend some alone time with him. He's great as far as I can tell, but all our time together is interrupted by the needs of the kids. I don't feel like I have gotten a full picture yet."

"Any red flags?" asked Elizabeth.

"Nothing. Nada. Wait. His house is kind of a mess the few times I've seen it. I think he might be a slob. But mostly, he seems too good to be true. I guess I have to dig deeper and see where the flaws are!" Hannah said. "It's an odd time to be dating someone. I don't want to lead him on because my options aren't around here."

"You know, I recently read that because of the limited number of young people in Vermont, the unemployment rate here is lower than the rest of the country," said Elizabeth. "Have you looked here?"

"You'd like that, wouldn't you?" said Hannah. "Both your babies right here, one-stop shopping to see us. I don't know. This is a great place to visit, but I've never considered it as a place to live. It doesn't seem to have much going on. What would I do?"

"You'll never know unless you look," said Elizabeth.

"I'll think about it, but the weather!" she said, looking out the window at the rain. "And the winters are even worse than Boston. You really have to enjoy the extremes."

Twenty-Five

Early the next morning, Hannah drove her car to Nathan's, and he waved her into his garage to hide her car from Nora's curious eyes. Nathan's SUV was parked in the driveway, filled with paddles, life preservers, coolers, bags, and chairs. Two kayaks were strapped to the roof top.

"Wow," said Hannah. "You must have been up since dawn getting this all together!"

"It didn't take too long. I have it pretty much down at this point."

They set off for the reservoir while there was still dew on the grass because Nathan wanted to get there in time to participate in the annual Loon Survey. Hannah was not one hundred percent sure what that was, but she was game and used to getting out early. She wore water sandals, a quick dry T-shirt, and running shorts under hiking pants.

The day was all sunshine and white puffy clouds as they traveled along a scenic byway through the town of Stowe. The rhythm of this summer was unlike any she had experienced in, well, forever. Vermonters were more chill than the hurried citizens of Boston. They were friendly and conversed with her, especially when she was with the kids. She listened to public radio while she worked on the treehouse and was surprised by the topics covered. Instead of constant crime reports, there were reports about initiatives underway to lift the state's residents, like getting local food to needy people, or stories about unexpected heroes. When there were crime reports, they were robberies, assaults, and deaths mostly connected to the continuing opioid crisis. Not perfect, but it was a more peaceful environment than other places she had lived.

"Do you listen to NPR?" Hannah asked Nathan as they drove through the rolling green hills toward the reservoir.

Nathan turned his head toward her with his eyes peering over his sunglasses, cocking his head with a "seriously?" look.

"Sorry, of course you do." Hannah laughed. "Did you happen to hear the segment the other day when they were talking about the new solar array in Essex?"

"Yeah, I caught that. Solar's huge in Vermont. There's another system going up over in Milton. I've been thinking about getting some panels for my house eventually."

"I remember the first time I saw a solar panel," said Hannah. "This guy in our neighborhood had two of them, and he was so proud. I was just a kid, but I remember every time our family walked by his house and he was outside, we'd say hello, and he'd invariably brag to my dad about how much he was saving on his electric bill and saving the world from greenhouse gas.

"I'm fascinated by them," Hannah continued. "When I was in Kenya, they were getting popular and made a huge difference in the villages. I'm thinking about putting a panel on the treehouse. I don't know how to go about it exactly. I've done some research but need to do more. There's one section on the roof that gets sunlight, so I think I could use a small panel, or I may install one remotely. I want them to be able to use it at night, so it'd be great if they could have lights."

In the town of Morrisville, they stopped at a red light. Nathan turned to Hannah. "What I can't understand is why there's been such a big delay in getting this technology going. It seems ridiculously simple and would cut us off from such dependence on fossil fuels."

"Right? It gets me so angry. Why aren't we already driving solar-powered cars by now? We barely have electric cars. But we know—it's all about corporate greed associated with cars, electricity, oil, power generation. Our country has to figure this out."

"You're preaching to the choir, man. This is at least a hybrid," Nathan said, tapping the dashboard. "I have a good friend who works over in Montpelier, and he's working on getting a new solar company going, so maybe I could put you in touch with him. Maybe he could direct you to where to go around here for the panels and stuff you need."

"That'd be great. If it wouldn't be too much trouble."

"Not at all. He's a good friend and would be cool with it."

"Hey, look," she cried out, pointing to a hillside off to the left. "Is that a moose?"

"I'll pull over and we can have a better look." Nathan turned the car onto the side of the road, and Hannah rolled down the window and held out her phone to take a picture.

"I wish I'd brought a real camera. He's so cool," she said.

The antlerless moose stood on the edge of a pond in a swampy area about three hundred feet from the car. It looked up but did not run off. In fact, it stared at them for a long moment, and they stared back.

"I've never seen a moose!" said Hannah.

"They're kind of elusive. A lot of people who've lived here for years have never seen one. Lucky day," Nathan said.

As they drove away, Hannah stared out the window and thought how different this summer was from last year. *What was I doing last summer at this time?* Martha's Vineyard with Sara,

Aaron, and seven others. They had rented a large house on the beach, which had cost a fortune, even sharing. Their days were spent sailing, lunching, shopping, and lying on the beach. The nights were all about eating lobsters, making bonfires, and drinking. When the week was over, she was exhausted, and it had not felt like a vacation at all. It had been a blast, though.

When they arrived at the reservoir, Nathan was all business. He pulled the car to the boat ramp and jumped out, and before Hannah had finished applying her lip balm, he was pulling one of the kayaks off the roof. She lent him a hand, and after they got both kayaks down and filled with the gear, Nathan went to re-park the car in the lot. Hannah turned on her phone. No cell service. It didn't matter. Her parents were with the kids, she was with easygoing Nathan, and it was a beautiful morning. She had been so "on" for the past few weeks it was hard to believe this whole day, and maybe night, was all hers.

It took a while for Nathan to come back, as it was surprisingly crowded at the small park. He explained that parking was on a first-come-first-served basis, and everyone arrived as soon as the gatehouse opened.

"This is perfection," said Hannah, looking out over the reservoir. "So unspoiled. It's like we are a million miles away, yet we only drove thirty minutes."

Hannah was, thankfully, an experienced kayaker. It was, in fact, one of her favorite ways to engage with water. She told Nathan about the first time she had kayaked as a teenager while on vacation with her family in the Adirondacks. She would never forget the feeling of paddling out to the middle of the lake and stopping to experience the quiet and solitude. "It made me feel like a duck, floating peacefully on top of the water," she said.

As they paddled along the shoreline, campsites came into view, and campers were hanging out along the water.

"What a great place to camp," she said. "I want to do that!"

"It's incredible. Now that I'm back, I'm planning to make it an annual event. You have to make reservations way in advance, and you have to bring all your gear by boat, as it's the only way to access the campsites. I have a site reserved over Labor Day," he said.

Hannah's first instinct was to offer her availability. But perhaps he already had people he intended to bring, so she said nothing. It hung in the air, though, her wanting to go and him having the means.

"If you're interested, I'll keep you posted on the plans," Nathan said.

Hannah smiled at him and nodded her head up and down rapidly.

"Loons!" said Hannah, pointing off to the right about one hundred yards. "Let's get closer."

They quietly paddled toward the animals, knowing they should keep a wide berth, excited to see several chicks swimming in a row behind the mama.

"They are so beautiful. Such exquisite markings," said Hannah. The mother loon, black with white flecks and a ring around her neck, glided seemingly effortlessly through the still water.

"How I long to see the silvery moon, on the crystal-clear lake with the call of the loon," Nathan said in a singsong voice.

"Are you reciting poetry to me?" said Hannah.

"It happens to be the only poem I know, may not even be a poem, just a quote, so don't be too impressed," said Nathan.

They paddled around the reservoir, counting the loons, and Nathan recorded their numbers in a small notebook. After about an hour of quiet paddling, he led them to a small beach area. They got out of their kayaks and dragged them ashore. Nathan pulled two dry bags out of the kayak hatches and proceeded to arrange a sizable picnic on a thin silk camp sheet.

"I wasn't sure what you liked for lunch, so I brought a variety," he said.

"A variety" was an understatement. There was a loaf of fresh-baked bread, four different kinds of cheese, two bottles of wine, grapes, olives, hummus, sausages, almonds, and a small box of chocolates. Hannah dug into the food with abandon. "I'm starving," she said, biting into a hunk of cheese and tearing off a piece of bread.

"Here's a souvenir from the day," Nathan said, handing her a sticker with a picture of a loon. "It's your participation award."

"So pretty," Hannah said. "Thanks."

Nathan screwed off the top of a bottle of wine and poured them each a paper cup. "Cheers. Here's to loons and pristine water," he said, bringing his cup to hers.

Hannah said, "Cheers" back and leaned in to kiss him. The move surprised her, but the urge to kiss him was real. They kissed slowly at first, and then Nathan pulled her toward him, and they became locked together before breaking apart, breathless and beaming. Their paper cups of wine spilled out on the sand.

"I was wondering, Hannah Spencer—would you like to have dinner and an adult sleepover tonight?" asked Nathan, brushing Hannah's face with his fingers.

"Why, yes, Nathan Wild, that'd be lovely," said Hannah, smiling. "I even packed my pajamas and toothbrush."

They gathered up the remnants of their lunch and launched the kayaks to head back to the car. Nathan pointed out an osprey diving for a fish, but they did not encounter any more loons. As they loaded up the kayaks, Nathan suggested they stop for extra dinner provisions at a nearby market.

Hannah maintained a high level of anticipation about how the evening would unfold. If the kissing at lunch was any indication, she was in for a good time. At the market, Nathan stopped before a rack of DVDs near the checkout.

"What do you think about a movie?" he asked, flipping through the selection. "Drama, adventure, comedy?"

"Something fun," said Hannah. She began scanning the titles. "No torture."

"A little torture, but fun," said Nathan. He held up a copy of *The Princess Bride*.

Hannah's eyes widened. "Yes, please."

"As you wish," said Nathan, nodding at her and tossing it into the basket.

Once home, and after they unpacked the car and groceries, Nathan invited Hannah to take a shower in the upstairs bath and said he would take one in the downstairs.

The shower was refreshing, and Hannah was glad he did not suggest they take one together, as she wanted to get herself together for the evening. Co-showering was not her ideal way to be seen naked for the first time. When she finished, she wrapped herself in the towel and walked down the hallway. Nathan was coming up the stairs, his towel wrapped around his waist.

He took two steps toward her, and before either of them could say a word, Hannah dropped her towel to the floor and said, "Is now good?"

"Now's good," said Nathan.

"OH MY GOD, you didn't?" Hannah was laughing convulsively as they entered hour six of their sleepover. They never watched the movie and had only climbed out of bed to pee or get food and drinks. They were cuddled up, Hannah's head on Nathan's chest.

"Yup, serious miscalculation," he said. They were exchanging stories of their past, the latest being Nathan's retelling of his study-abroad romance. He had been hooking up with one of his fellow students while in Spain, and the relationship was fun, but he lacked strong feelings for April, who attended college in the Midwest. It was nearing the end of the semester, and April was beginning to drop hints about continuing their relationship when they returned to the States. Nathan, who had seen the whole thing as a casual fling, did not want to hurt her feelings, but he needed to let her know he was not interested in continuing long distance. They were returning by train from the south of France to Paris to fly home the next day, sitting in a packed compartment with their classmates.

"It seemed like a good time to say something. We were in those kinds of seats that faced each other. I was making jokes about being on the Hogwarts Express. And so, as soon as the train departed the station, I turned to her and recited the words I had planned all week. 'April, this has been such a fun semester. I'll always look back on it fondly, but I think the end of this semester should also be the end of our relationship.'

"What I didn't factor into the situation was that I was trapped with her in a crowded train car. I imagined I would say these words, and she would see the obvious sense of them and agree. But I didn't think past that moment. I never considered she would be sitting there with me, fixed into the seat, facing other people, for three hours. It was three horrible hours. She cried at first, then she got angry, then she cried some more, then she called her friend and said mean things about me right in front of me, and everyone around could see and hear this whole thing play out. For a while she got silent, then she would suddenly blurt out these super cruel statements like, 'I can't believe I put you on that video call to my little sister—she's going to be so heartbroken.'"

Hannah laughed and snorted all the way through his story.

"I'm sorry for April, but that's really funny. It could have been a conversation of, like, five minutes if you had waited until the end of the trip," offered Hannah, a few years too late.

"Yes, that's pretty much what everyone in my life says when I tell this tale," said Nathan.

"I had to keep giving her napkins to blow her nose, and she was so upset. At one point, I almost considered saying 'never mind,' but thankfully, I stayed strong."

"Why weren't you into her?" asked Hannah.

Nathan stroked Hannah's hair. "She was pretty and ridiculously smart, but I don't know, something was lacking, like an intangible quality, maybe chemistry. We were there and going through the motions of hanging out together and doing it and all, but we never really connected. I expected to have a non-emotional breakup since the entire time we were together it was entirely unemotional. Boy, did I get that wrong."

Hannah said, "I had a thing for an Australian while I was abroad."

"Really?" said Nathan. "Go on."

"To this day, he's still one of the nicest, most genuine people I've ever met. His name is Ricky. He lived in the town where I worked in Kenya and was in the program the year before I got there, so he was still always around helping. We started playing pool at the local pub, and I don't know—he was so appealing in the cerebral sort of way but attractive and exotic as well. It was the last night before my flight home, and I thought, *It's okay— I'm leaving*, and what was fascinating was that he didn't want to go for it. That's the kind of guy he was, although he might have been gay, don't know. Anyway, we stayed awake and talked all night, and he gave me a peck on the cheek the next morning and sent me on my way. We kind of stayed in touch on Facebook for a while, but not so much anymore. He has a child, no wife, and he seems fairly involved with his son, which is good. I guess I have a type," said Hannah, rolling on top of Nathan and staring into his face. "Nice."

"Nice? What about funny? Don't you value my incredible sense of humor? Isn't that what all women want?" Nathan tickled her in the ribs.

"God, no." Hannah giggled at the tickles more than they actually tickled. "We women just say that so we don't seem shallow. We want handsome, nice, and rich with a six-pack. Hey, I got one for you. Who's your celebrity freebie?"

"Ah, the celebrity freebie," said Nathan. "Obviously, Christiane. You?"

"Damn, I was going to say one of the Hemsworth brothers, but now I feel all superficial. I like Ezra Klein."

"That political journalist? Oh, now you're just trying to impress me." He paused and grew more serious. "What do you want, Hannah? What do you think you're going to do after this babysitting gig?"

Hannah rolled off Nathan, landing on her stomach with her head resting on her folded arms. She turned to look at him. "Good question. I've been job searching on the internet and trying to think about my next move. I have some ideas. Seattle, Boise, Colorado. I'm even looking at something in London." At the moment, she didn't feel like leaving this bed with Nathan in Waterbury, Vermont. Ever.

"What kind of jobs?" he asked.

"You know, it's all abstract at the moment." She was deflecting. "Right now, I want to be employed on this." She threw her head under the covers and squirmed down the bed.

Twenty-Six

This was going to be a challenge. After her thirty-second "drive of shame" and reuniting with her family, Hannah already missed Nathan and wanted to see him again. She hated leaving his house, and her libido was off the charts. She went about the business of telling her family about the kayak trip, the moose, and the loons. She left out the part where they had incredible sex and stayed up all night talking. She thought about calling Sara and telling her everything, but for the first time in her life, she did not want to disclose the details to her best friend.

Her energetic parents took Nora and Owen to the pool for the afternoon, leaving Hannah time for a much-needed nap. In the bathroom, changing her clothes, Hannah found the loon sticker Nathan had given her in the pocket of her shorts. Facing the mirror, she saw the vision board hanging on the opposite wall, and her eyes landed squarely on the photo of the people lined up staring at the ocean. She noticed for the first time that it was kind of a lonely picture, even though the caption said, "Happiness is not a goal—it's a byproduct." She stuck the loon sticker over the photo. *Better.*

BEFORE LEAVING FOR home, Bob and Elizabeth bathed the kids so that all Hannah had to do was feed them the dinner her mom had made and put them to bed. Exhausted from the pool, they were out like a light in no time.

No sooner had she lain on the couch and begun reading than her phone dinged.

Today 8:34 PM

Nathan: you up? I've always wanted to text that. I saw your folks leave. want some company?

me: Yes, give me 15 mins to make sure the kids are down

No games with him. Hannah wanted to spruce up the house as well as herself. She took the world's fastest shower and put on a T-shirt and shorts. No bra. She headed to the basement to execute the plan she had concocted.

When Nathan came to the door, he gave her a quick kiss on the mouth.

Hannah asked, "Want something to drink?"

"A beer would be great. I should've brought some over."

"I bought something new for my dad, so we are set." She opened the refrigerator and handed Nathan a can of local beer. "I really want to check out the Hill Farmstead brewery over in Greensboro. We should go sometime. Lots of good craft beer around here. I've been to the Alchemist, and Heady Topper is my favorite. But I'd like to check them all out." She was talking rapidly and without breathing. *Why am I acting so spazzy?*

"Love Heady. It sounds like we need a brew tour." Hannah and Nathan cracked open their beers and took a sip. "It's good," said Nathan.

"Pretty hoppy."

"Enough small talk." He pulled her close and kissed her intensely.

Hannah broke away and said, "Come with me."

Nathan followed her to the basement door, and she led him

down the dim staircase. At the bottom, she flipped the light on to reveal her interior-design achievement.

"Welcome to my sex dungeon, Nathan Wild. No kids allowed."

A cozy pile of quilts, sleeping bags, and pillows were arranged in the corner of the room, forming a surprisingly comfortable-looking bed.

"That'll work," said Nathan, taking her hand and leading her to the lair.

THEY HAD SEX twice that night, and Hannah admitted to herself that it was quite possibly the most fun she had ever had. After the second time, Hannah leaned over to Nathan, elbow bent and head resting on her palm. She looked at him with a slight smile. "We appear to be in a rapidly evolving situation here."

"Yes," said Nathan. He rolled over, mimicked her position, and faced her. "Very rapid. Could you please make a list of all your faults and flaws before we take it any further?"

"Sure," said Hannah, taking him seriously and adjusting the pillows to sit up against the wall. "Let's see. For starters, I'm super judgmental. I hate that people say, 'Don't be judgmental' all the time. If people weren't judgmental, how would we compliment one another for something positive or a job well done? Who started this whole 'can't be judgmental' thing anyway? Can you imagine if you told me I was nice, and I replied, 'Stop being so judgmental'? Anyway, I like judging things—actions, choices, ideas, outfits. Don't even get me started on public policy. I try not to say my judgments out loud, but I assure you they're happening."

"Good to know. Continue. What else?" said Nathan. He, too, was sitting up against the pillows and held her hand.

"I say 'sorry' too much. I hate that. It's something girls are trained to do, to apologize for taking up space. I notice guys don't do it. And from a physical standpoint, I think my chin is a little pointy and my eyelashes are virtually invisible. I do, however, have a super metabolism and almost no hair on my legs." Hannah shot both legs up into the air.

"Good metabolism—hence the ability to drink lots of beer." Nathan stroked her leg, looking for nubs. She knew there were none.

"Yup. But don't worry about me becoming an alcoholic. The best advice I ever got was from my mom, who said you should just drink reasonably, and it can be a lifelong pleasure. Makes a lot of sense, right? My mom keeps a strict mental record of how many alcohol units she has every week."

"That's good advice, but I want another beer now," Nathan said.

"I'll get them and check on the kids." Hannah stood up from the bed, fully naked, and reached for her shorts and shirt. "Get thinking about *your* flaw list while I'm gone."

She returned from her mission with two beers and a large bag of pretzels to find Nathan lying faceup, staring at the ceiling. The sheet covered him from the waist down, but she paused to admire his physique from the waist up. He was fit and lean. She was fit and lean. She liked that they matched in that way, since being active was a big part of her life.

"They're still out cold," she said, flopping on the makeshift bed and handing him the beer and pretzels. "Okay, Buster, your turn. Spill the bucket of flaws."

"I don't want to scare you off too fast, so I'll start slow. And I'm serious here. I have some stuff."

"Everybody does. I don't know any flawless people."

Nathan spoke slowly. "I can get reticent. I'm not sure how to explain it exactly, but you experienced my family. They're all borderline hyperactive. Always talking, always moving. I find sometimes I don't exactly match their level of enthusiasm. Growing up, it was always noisy, and I found it to be overwhelming at times. I would retreat to my room and hide for a half hour or so, and then I'd be fine and get back into it with everyone. But none of them ever had to do that, just me. And, if I ever got caught, they didn't understand why I'd want to lie on my bed and read a comic book instead of fight over a game of kickball with the neighborhood kids. Even at Grace's wedding when I brought Lindsey to that cottage, I needed a break, so I sat on the porch for a few minutes."

"So, what you're saying is you're a sociopath." Hannah laughed. She was lying on the quilts with her arm across her forehead, listening carefully. "C'mon, Nathan, don't be so hard on yourself. I get it. You need to step away sometimes and recharge."

"Exactly," said Nathan. "They're all great and they'd do anything for me, but it's like our name is a badge of honor they feel they have to live up to—The Wild Kids—and I never had the same level of stamina for constant motion."

"I get that. To tell you the truth, I'm glad you told me about Grace's wedding. I was wondering what took you so long with Lindsey that night. Okay, what else you got for me?"

"See this tooth," Nathan said, pointing to his front tooth. "It's not real."

"Wow, that's amazing. It looks perfect," said Hannah, peering into his mouth. "How'd you lose it?"

"Cousin's house, ice hockey."

"Bummer."

"Actually, that's a lie. That's what I've been telling everyone for twenty years. What happened was that the game hadn't even started, and this asshole, Howie Bechler, walked over to me and shoved me, and I fell over on my face. Never found the tooth. When we went to school and my face was kinda messed up, Grace told everyone I did it playing ice hockey and that we won, but I lost a tooth. That story became our truth. That's how they are. No one ever said anything different, even when they were mad at me."

"Your family is great. Totally intense, and you can feel the love a mile away." Hannah moved in to snuggle closer to Nathan. "I'm lucky too. Even though Molly is older and so much more settled than me, and really different in a lot of ways, we are really close. She has been so influential in my life, and I don't know what I'd do without her."

"I'd like to build a family," Nathan said. "I've been thinking about it more positively lately. I used to think it'd be a drag to have kids and never get to do what you wanted. But for the past year, I've come to think maybe creating your own family can give you direction. It's interesting. Life has so many phases, and it's astonishing how quickly you get over one phase and on to another."

"True," said Hannah. "I've been thinking about it more this summer too, spending so much time with Owen and Nora. Half the time I think it's exhausting and stupidly annoying, but there are other times when I'm in awe of them and so curious as to what they'll grow into. I've never not-wanted kids, but I've never given it much thought until this summer."

"This conversation got deep quick. I guess we settled that then. We both don't hate the idea of children, running kinda sixty-forty in favor now. Would you say that's accurate?" asked Nathan.

"Spot on," said Hannah. They had been cuddling for over an hour, and she was pleased that Nathan had not bolted immediately after sex. Hannah liked to talk, and she very much wanted to listen. It was getting late though.

"Speaking of children, I think you have to leave now. I've got to get some sleep, as they'll be awake and raring to go in about five hours."

"I don't want to go." Nathan threw the covers over his head. "I want to live in your basement and always be available to fulfill your every desire. You know, I haven't even shown you my best stuff yet. I didn't want to peak too soon."

Hannah laughed. "You can come back tomorrow night if you bring me dessert."

"Cake, pie, ice cream, what do you want? I'll bring you anything." Nathan rolled her on top of him, squeezing her tight.

"I like everything, not kidding. Surprise me," Hannah said, kissing him quickly and pitching herself off their nest. "I have to run to Burlington tomorrow afternoon. I'll text you after dinner tomorrow night when the coast is clear."

Twenty-Seven

Nathan stumbled out of bed and headed to the kitchen to start the coffee. In a pre-coffee haze, he poured Cooper's food into his bowl, waited for him to finish, and hooked him to the lead in the back yard. His lack of sleep was catching up with him. He had spent the last three evenings at Hannah's, staying up later than usual.

Checking his email while drinking his coffee, Nathan opened a message from Grace. The "sneak peek" of her wedding photos was attached. He scrolled through them, looking for pictures of Hannah, and finally found a couple at the end. They were candid shots, one of the two of them at the cocktail hour—grinning at the camera, his arm around her—and another of them slow dancing. Her eyes were closed, and her head was resting on his shoulder.

Was he reading too much into what was going on between them? This was where having sisters you were close with was particularly helpful. Grace had called Nathan after the wedding to tell him of her great first impression of Hannah and how glad she was that he had brought her after all. She was anxious to rehash what had happened with Lindsey. He told her about taking her to the cottage and leaving her there. Grace reported that she heard Lindsey had fallen asleep in a bed reserved for one of the groomsmen. When the guy got to the cottage at the end of the night, he just pushed her over and got in bed with her. Apparently, they were dating now.

Nathan told Grace he was seeing Hannah regularly and expressed his concern about "where it was going."

"Why does it have to go anywhere, Nathan?" asked Grace. "Just go with it and don't overthink it. Let it roll."

"Okay. But I don't want to mess this up. I really like her."

"Here's an idea," suggested Grace. "Be honest with her. I mean, don't go professing your love and your desire to have her children, but don't play games. Carry on like she wants the same things you do—unless she tells you otherwise. I don't think people do that enough."

"Okay, that's good advice. I can be chill."

"You're chill in so many other ways. You can do this. Hey, gotta run. Keep me posted."

Nathan downloaded the two pictures of Hannah and saved them to his hard drive. He was falling for her, that much he knew for sure. There was no use denying it. He'd just have to manage it, because the last thing he wanted to do was scare her off.

He was confident she was into him, evidenced by her creating the basement hideout and welcoming him over all week. Wanting to spend as much time with her as possible, he had even invited her and the kids over for dinner. His mom had given him his old collection of Legos when he moved in, and he brought them out with the idea that they could all build something together. He and Hannah dived into the activity and became completely immersed in building the X Wing Fighter from the Star Wars series. The children, though, lost interest quickly and begged to go home.

"God, who invited them?" Hannah had said. Nathan laughed and promised Hannah they could finish another day.

She's the full package. She even loves Legos.

But Nathan knew he was courting on borrowed time. Hannah was leaving town in less than a month. He would have to make the most of their time while still giving her space to work on the treehouse. He had a lot of work himself. He had just started a new project. Ten days from now he would leave for Chicago for a full week. He could not expect that he had a future with Hannah. He told himself firmly to live in the present. *Disappointment comes from expectations.*

Twenty-Eight

"Aunt Hannah, Aunt Hannah." Nora shook Hannah's shoulder early Friday morning as she lay sound asleep. "Something's wrong with Owen."

Hannah bolted up in the bed. "What? What is it?" She threw off the covers and jumped to her feet.

"He says his belly hurts," said Nora.

It was Friday, the last day of "Mad Science Week" at camp. Owen was looking forward to the culmination of the festivities, which included the launching of the kids' rockets. He would not fake a stomachache to stay home. He had tried that a couple of times on rainy days when there was too much "arts and craps" and not enough outside time.

Hannah entered Owen's bedroom and knelt beside his bed. "Hey, buddy. You're not feeling well?" asked Hannah, stroking his head. "Tell me about it."

"My tummy hurts so bad." He was curled in the fetal position with tears in his eyes.

Hannah felt his forehead. Warm, but not too hot. He had taken off his pajamas sometime in the night, and now he lay curled on his side in his underpants, not looking at Hannah.

"Do you have to go potty?" asked Hannah.

"Nooo," wailed Owen. "It hurts."

Hannah looked at Nora, who was looming over her brother on the other side of the twin bed. "Do you know if Owen has been hurting for a long time? How long have you been awake?"

"I heard him crying and then I woke up," said Nora. "And then I came to get you. Momma always says to wake her up if we're sick, and so that's what I did. Is Owen very sick? Should we go to Dr. Varma?"

Hannah went downstairs and found her phone and the note on the refrigerator with the pediatrician's name and number. She first texted Lea to tell her Owen would not be going to camp. It was too early for the pediatrician's office hours, but she called anyway.

The answering service at Dr. Varma's office said they would have a doctor get back in touch with her as soon as possible. Within five minutes, Hannah's phone buzzed. She described Owen's symptoms to Dr. Varma. The physician asked about Owen's temperature and bathroom history for the past forty-eight hours.

"Owen, honey, did you go poopy yesterday at camp?" Hannah asked. "Can you remember?"

"I went poopy after swimming." He lay on his back, seemingly relaxed for the moment. "It was so cold in the bathroom." He hugged his belly and returned to the fetal position, moaning.

"He said he had a bowel movement yesterday at camp. He seems to be getting waves of pain—like cramps. He feels a little warm, but I haven't taken his temperature."

"How about you bring him into my office at nine, and I'll take a look at him," she said. They hung up and Hannah sat with Owen, stroking his back. She briefly thought about calling Molly and Ted but dismissed the idea as soon as it popped into her head. She was the adult in the room. She could manage this (hopefully) small medical situation.

Loving any kind of drama, Nora was all business, getting herself ready for camp as Hannah stayed with Owen until Lea arrived. Hannah had taken his temperature, and it was higher than normal. Lea arrived on the scene a few minutes early and assured Hannah and Nora that Owen would be fine. "My kids are always getting bellyaches. It usually means they ate something that didn't agree with them," Lea said. She did admit to Hannah it was somewhat unusual for him to have a fever along with the bellyache and was glad they were able to get in to see the doctor.

"Keep me posted when you find out what's going on. I'm headed to St. Johnsbury to visit my aunt, but I can get back to you if you need me."

Owen and Hannah arrived at Dr. Varma's office, and the nurse ushered them in right away. Hannah marveled at how at ease Owen was with the older doctor, who had been seeing him since birth. Hannah admired how kind, but all business, she was with the child, taking his temperature, asking him questions, and palpating his abdomen.

"I don't want to alarm you, Hannah, but Owen's symptoms, fever, and overall agitation make me want to run a few tests to rule out anything serious, like appendicitis. I think this would best be handled at the hospital," she said.

Hannah was speechless. The concept of something seriously wrong with Owen frightened her to the core. "Hospital. Wow, okay. Do I take him? Do we have to get an ambulance?"

"No ambulance necessary. Just go now and drive safely. I will call ahead to the pediatric gastroenterologist and let them know you are coming. They will likely be able to meet you in the emergency room. They will do a blood test to see if he has an elevated white blood cell count. They will probably do a urine test to rule out a urinary tract infection. They may perform a CT scan or ultrasound as well if they suspect appendicitis."

"Okay," said Hannah. She tried to process everything while jotting notes on the back of an envelope.

"Am I going to the hopsital?" asked Owen. His thumb was stuck in his mouth, something he had all but given up until now.

"Yes, honey," said Hannah. "It's going to be such an adventure."

As Dr. Varma left the room, Hannah texted Nathan that she was going to the University of Vermont Medical Center's ER with Owen, and she would not be able to make their lunch date. She scooped up Owen and headed to the car while wondering if she should call Lea and disrupt her day with her aunt. Instead, she called her father, who was a hospital administrator. He was the closest thing to a doctor in her family.

Bob assured Hannah she was doing the right thing by taking Owen to the hospital and gave her a couple of questions to ask the doctors. Hannah promised to update him as soon as they spoke with the gastroenterologist. With Owen periodically moaning and crying out, Hannah drove away and was at the hospital within a half hour.

Once inside the ER, the triage nurse was quick to attend to the paperwork. She let them know they would bring Owen into a room shortly. As Hannah turned to take a seat in the waiting room, Nathan burst through the double glass doors.

"Hannah," he called out. "How is he?"

"What . . . what are you doing here?"

"I was just heading out for a bike ride when I got your text. Hospitals and kids. I figured you must be worried, maybe even freaking out. I sent you a text, but you didn't respond, so I just came. I hope it's okay."

"Yes, yes! Thanks so much for coming." Hannah gave him a brief hug and turned to Owen. "Look who's here with us!"

Owen looked up and, barely audible, said, "Nathan."

A nurse appeared in the doorway of the waiting room and called out, "Dumont, Owen Dumont."

Nathan picked Owen up in his arms, and the threesome followed the nurse into a bay. Nathan gently placed Owen in the bed.

Things happened very fast once they were in the interior of the emergency room. Hannah suspected that when young children were involved, there was a more elevated sense of urgency. A nurse came in and took Owen's vitals and, while that was happening, Dr. Johnson, the pediatric gastroenterologist, entered their curtained compartment.

"Hello, Owen," Dr. Johnson said. Owen was lying in the fetal position again, looking vacant. "I hear you're not feeling so well today."

Dr. Johnson proceeded to examine Owen and told Hannah they would take some blood and get a urine test. The whole while they were in the bay, Nathan held Hannah's hand or laid his hand on her shoulder. She felt comforted by these gestures, and she was grateful he was by her side. Dr. Johnson said he would return after the results of the preliminary tests to decide the next steps. A new nurse entered, introduced herself as a phlebotomist, and began to prepare the instruments for taking blood. Owen watched her with trepidation, giving her a sideways stink eye. The nurse was experienced with drawing blood from children and talked him through the whole procedure. She patiently explained how the tourniquet worked to make the vein pop and how she used "magic cream" to numb the inside of his elbow before inserting the needle. He was a trooper, fascinated as the blood filled the tube.

"Okay, Owen, you were so good with letting me get the

blood. I need you to do me a big favor now," said the nurse. "I think you're going to be able to do this because you're four years old. We don't let three-year-olds do it, but because you're four, I think you can."

Owen sat up, intrigued by the favor being proposed.

"See this little cup?" she asked, handing him a plastic specimen cup. "I'm going to need you to pee into it. Do you think you can do it? Daddy can go with you and help."

"That's Nathan," he corrected her, taking the cup.

"Okay. Nathan, could you help Owen pee into this cup?" she asked.

"Sure. Is it cool if I do it?" he asked, looking at Hannah.

"Do you want Nathan to help?" she asked her nephew.

"Yes," said Owen.

Nathan lifted the boy out of bed and headed to the restroom nearby. Hannah was thankful that Owen was not whining for his parents and that he seemed comfortable having Nathan help him. She debated whether to contact Molly and Ted at this point, but without a real diagnosis, she decided to wait.

After what seemed like way more time than necessary to get Owen to pee in the cup, Hannah walked to the restroom. Laughter, Nathan's and Owen's, rang out from behind the closed door.

"I can do it again," said Owen. He giggled gleefully.

"Noooo, not again," Nathan said, but his tone was clearly meant to encourage Owen to do it, whatever "it" was, again.

Hannah put her ear against the door. Extreme farting was followed by extreme laughter.

She knocked on the door and asked, "Hey, everything good in there?"

"I'm farting, Aunt Hannah. I got so many farts in me."

Nathan opened the door a couple of inches and addressed

Hannah. "You *do not* want to come in here. It's bad. He's been farting like crazy. I think he's feeling better though. He thinks it's hilarious."

Hannah could smell the evidence from outside the bathroom. "Okay," she said, backing up. "Take your time."

Nathan and Owen emerged from the bathroom moments later. Owen ran to where Hannah sat in a chair next to his hospital bed, and jumped on her lap.

"Aunt Hannah, I farted sooo much. I had so many farts," he said, grinning from ear to ear. "Nathan didn't have any farts."

"Gee, Nathan, not any?" she asked, looking over at Nathan. "Owen, honey, are you feeling better?"

Owen immediately stood and started jumping up and down on the hospital bed. "My tummy doesn't hurt anymore. Can we go home? I wanna go to camp." He continued to jump as Hannah held his hands.

"Looks like someone is feeling better." The nurse appeared in the bay. "Owen's blood test came back normal, and we're waiting on the urinalysis."

"Owen experienced some . . . flatulence while I was obtaining the urine," Nathan said to the nurse. "It was an explosion of gas that could light up a city had there been a match. It was an epic farting event the likes of which I've never witnessed."

"My goodness, I guess perhaps he had severe gas pain." The nurse paused and then burst out laughing. "His fever is peculiar. I'll retake his temp and speak with the doctor."

Phbbbt. "That's my last one, I think," said Owen, releasing one more.

The trio cracked up, and Hannah was relieved. She leaned down and picked up her nephew. She pulled the boy in close. She was satisfied that the crisis was over. And what's more, she'd done well in coping with the unplanned situation. She had not called Molly and Ted, and now the report would be something that started scary and ended with a gigantic fart. She laughed just thinking about it.

Impatient to get home, Owen repeatedly jumped up and down on the hospital bed until the doctor returned. He told Hannah to watch his fever, which was almost normal, and then Owen was finally released. He desperately wanted to go back to camp for the afternoon. Hannah knew that was not allowed, so she suggested they all go out to lunch at Skinny Pancake, a family favorite.

Once home, the day shot, Hannah stuck Owen in front of the TV while she hustled to do some chores and get dinner started before Nora arrived. She wiped down the counters, lined up the ingredients for the night's simple pasta, and then tidied up the house. In the kids' room, she corralled some dirty laundry into the basket and stripped their beds. As she pulled the fitted sheet off Owen's bed, an unfamiliar object peeked out near the headboard. She reached under to retrieve it and discovered a pressurized can of whipped cream. An empty can. A can that had been full and in the refrigerator the night before.

Twenty-Nine

On Sunday, two days after the "$800 fart" (*Thank god for good insurance*, Hannah thought), Nathan appeared at Hannah's door. Nora and Owen greeted him.

"Who wants a fish dinner tonight?" Nathan asked.

Nora and Owen jumped up and down, shouting, "We do, we do."

"Then we better go catch some." Nathan stepped outside the door and grabbed two child-sized fishing poles resting against the house. He handed one to each of them. Nora beamed when she saw that hers was a Dora the Explorer–themed rod.

"I got Spiderman," screamed Owen, jumping up and down. "Spidey! Spidey!"

The foursome spent the afternoon at the reservoir, swimming, and fishing. Nathan was patient with the kids, showing them how the rods worked and teaching them how to bait the hooks. Hannah was impressed that neither child was squeamish about the process. They caught a brook trout and two yellow perch and threw back three smaller fish before they lost interest—a good haul for a first effort.

Back home, Nathan cleaned and gutted the fish. He grilled them while Hannah made the rest of the meal.

While they were eating, Nora proudly announced she had a joke to tell. She glanced at Nathan with a sly grin.

"Go ahead," said Hannah.

"What did *Cinderella* wear on her feet when she went swimming?" asked Nora.

"I don't know," said Hannah. "What did she wear?"

"Glass flippers," said Nora. They all roared with laughter.

"I have a joke," said Owen. "Me next."

"Tell us, tell us," said Nora.

"How do fishes go places if they don't have a car?" asked Owen. All were quiet and waited for his response. He looked at Nathan with a grin.

"An Octo-bus." Again, they all laughed. "Nathan taught us the jokes," Owen said. "Octo-bus. That's so funny."

Hannah was surprised how quickly the children finished their dinners, clearly proud that they had contributed their catch to the meal. Owen ran off to the back yard as Hannah cleared the table. Nora sprang up to help.

"Aunt Hannah, what is having sex?" she asked as she gathered her dishes and utensils and circled the table to get Owen's plate.

"Excuse me?" said Hannah, darting her eyes at Nathan. "Where did you hear those words?"

"At camp. Some of the counselors were talking about having sex in the woods. I don't know what that is. What is having sex in the woods?"

Hannah plopped into her chair and set the dishes back on the table. Nathan sat up in his chair and looked at Hannah with a bemused expression.

"Having sex is a thing you should talk to your parents about when they get back," said Hannah. "Why don't you just forget about it until then?"

"You can tell me. It sounds fun. They were laughing a lot when they were talking about it."

"Where did you hear them talking?" asked Hannah.

"While we were waiting for Lea to pick us up. Some of them were sitting on the bleachers, and Ava and I were sneaking around and spying on them. We love spying." Nora raised her eyebrows up and down, grinning. "What does it mean? Tell me."

Hannah paused, trying to think of a simple way to explain sex to a six-year-old that would bring the awkward conversation to a close quickly. "Sex is a way that grown-ups show love for each other. It's a special kind of snuggle."

"Do it," Nora said. "Do it with Nathan. Show me."

Nathan and Hannah simultaneously burst into laughter.

"I have a better idea," said Hannah. She stood, turned toward the yard, and yelled out to Owen, "Who wants ice cream? Let's go get ice cream!"

"Yay," both children screamed as they ran to the car.

THE NEXT MORNING Hannah sat on the deck overlooking the mountains of the Worcester Range, thinking that she would soon be leaving Vermont. It was a spectacular day: bluebird skies, low humidity, and a perfect sixty-eight degrees. Drinking coffee and stretching out her legs, Hannah evaluated her life-overhaul progress. She had managed to do a considerable amount of online searching, telephone networking, résumé tweaking, and cover letter drafting over the last couple of weeks, despite her dedication to the treehouse and time with Nathan. She had applied for two jobs: one in Boston and one in Denver. If contacted, she was hoping it would work out for her to do the in-person interviews in mid-August. She had two other prospects, one in Boise, Idaho, the other in San Francisco. The position in Boston was not so different from her last job but at a smaller company. She considered this her "I'm desperate" job, the one she would only consider if the others did not pan out.

The Denver opportunity intrigued her the most. She had gotten a call from Miki, her former country manager from Kenya, who was still with Habitat for Humanity. Miki told Hannah that one of their big donors was interested in creating a nonprofit in Denver dedicated to providing affordable housing for single-parent families. They were staffing up, and he had contacted Miki looking for recommendations. Miki immediately suggested Hannah, and now Hannah was scheduled for an online interview for a finance position with the well-endowed organization.

Denver was one of the country's cool cities—young, vibrant, walkable but with good transit, and close to amazing mountains. Hannah constantly mulled over the pros and cons of relocating to Denver, Boise, San Francisco, or back to Boston. She only knew one person in Denver—Travis, a good friend from high school—so getting acclimated could be a process. But at least she had a gateway friend. The housing job, if she got it, was exactly what she was looking for. Boise, Idaho, was the great unknown. Everything she had read about it made her think it would be a good fit, but she would be entirely on her own, as she would not have one friend or relative there. That could possibly be a good thing. She had countless friends in Boston, not to mention her parents, but she had "been there, done that" and she feared she would end up right back where she started.

Then there was Nathan. She had no fantasy about doing a long-term, long-distance relationship. That was crazy talk as far as she was concerned. She actively compartmentalized her connection with Nathan. Nathan was here and now and fabulous, but when summer ended, so would their relationship. It would go down in her personal history as a wonderful summer fling. She constantly looked for flaws in him but found few, none of which were deal-breakers. That would have made it easier to imagine it all coming to an end in a few short weeks. But his most annoying personality trait was that he would drop everything and abruptly leave whenever his phone beeped an emergency and he had to go rescue someone. *What a loser!* She stopped herself every time she found herself trying to work out a way to both live out of state and not break it off with Nathan. He had only recently relocated to be near his family, so she did not think he'd want to uproot himself again so soon to follow her to wherever the hell she ended up.

For the past year, she had begun to take charge of her own life, making proactive decisions based on a clear set of values she mulled over, and she was not going to stop now. The prospect of going back to Boston was depressing. It would be, at best, a lateral move, at worst a slide backward. But she had to get a job. Her student loan debt, while not astronomical, needed to be repaid. She toyed with the idea of staying in Vermont. Beautiful as it might be, she was quite sure the job prospects were less than excellent, although she had not investigated thoroughly. *Maybe I should at least give it another look.* She rose from her chair and headed to dress and get working on the treehouse.

When Hannah entered the bathroom, she glanced at her vision board. She had not studied it for a while and now stared intently at the photograph of a dazzling rooftop restaurant filled with glamourous people dining alfresco with the caption "Eat Well." *That's not what I meant.* She took a Post-it Note from her dresser, drew a picture of a fish perched on an apple and the words "Eat Well/Eat Local," and stuck it over the restaurant pic. *Better.*

AUGUST

Thirty

Hannah perched on the deck of the treehouse, tightening the railing screws. Nathan was mowing his lawn, the hum of the motor piercing the tranquility of the day. "Moovin' and Groovin' Week" was over, and when Nora and Owen came home from camp, they would have their first chance to explore the treehouse. The weeks of precision measuring and sawing and tedious hammering and bolting were over, and Hannah had only whacked her fingers about five times. The entire structure was sided, the roof was shingled, and the steps and railings were now fully installed. Hannah deemed it safe for Nora and Owen to enter.

Ready as it was for their first sneak peek, there was still so much to do: build the Dutch door and bunk beds; install the electrical work and solar panel; and paint the entire thing. There were two weeks until Molly and Ted returned, and Hannah was confident she would get it done.

Hopefully, with all the moving and grooving, they would come home from camp exhausted again, and Hannah and Nathan could continue to take advantage of the basement. He had been coming over with Cooper nearly every night, staying a couple of hours, and slinking home around ten o'clock. Twice Nathan joined them for dinner, and Hannah appreciated him being such a good sport with the kids. Nora interrogated him incessantly.

"What are your five favorite words to say?" ("guacamole, diabolical, mediocre, iambic pentameter, malarkey")

"Why do you have a house with no one else in it?" ("Cooper lives with me, and he likes the yard")

"What's your fourth favorite dessert?" ("apple pie")

"Have you ever kissed Aunt Hannah?" ("yes")

"Do you think snakes know no one likes them?" ("absolutely")

Owen enjoyed that, despite Molly's warning to do otherwise, Nathan would happily get on the floor with him and play cars. Owen seemed open to Nathan's play scenarios and less insistent on doing it his own way. It warmed Hannah's heart to hear the laughter coming from the living room while she prepared dinner. And everyone was crazy about Cooper.

Nathan was leaving for a work week in Chicago on Monday. She had enjoyed the adult company and was excited that Sara and Aaron would be coming for a visit on their way to Montreal while he was gone. Since college, she and Sara had never been separated this long except for when she was in Kenya. She missed her friend and their marathon talk sessions about everything under the sun. It was unfortunate that they would miss meeting Nathan, as Hannah would have liked her best friend to meet the guy she had been talking to her about all summer.

When he heard about Sara's planned visit on her way to Montreal, Nathan had suggested he and Hannah go away on a weekend trip to Canada after Molly and Ted returned. He said he always wanted to go to Niagara Falls or Ottawa. Hannah had never been to either place. While she was intrigued, traveling together was a big step from aggressively cuddling in her sister's basement. It was fun to think about going on a road trip with Nathan, but she was not ready to commit to the trip. "That sounds like fun, but let me see how my interview schedule looks," she had told him.

"Hey," Hannah shouted now from the deck, waving at Nathan. He cut the engine of his lawn mower. She beckoned him over, and he immediately trotted to the deck.

"Hi there." He gave her a peck on the cheek. "What's up?"

"Was wondering if you want to eat here with me and the kids tonight? I'm going to barbeque some chicken and make a big deal out of letting them go up in the treehouse."

"That'd be great. I'm trying to use all my perishables before I go away, so I'll bring them over. And, I've been meaning to ask you, I have to bring Cooper to Grace and Nick's tomorrow. If you don't have anything else planned, we could bring the kids, and they could see their farm. It's small, but it has a bunch of animals—chickens and goats and llamas and sheep."

"They'd love that. It's supposed to be rainy, though."

"It'll be fine. They have a big barn. We could go in the afternoon. I think it'll be clear by then."

Nathan left to finish mowing the lawn, and Hannah spent the afternoon working on the Dutch door. This was the part of the project that was the most fun—figuring out all the details that gave the treehouse character and the "wow" factor she desired. The idea had come to her as she fell asleep one night. Cut in half, the door would allow more light into the interior. She made a peephole in the top half, which was covered with another tiny door decorated with a carved turtle. It reminded her of the gatekeeper's peephole in *The Wizard of Oz*. She'd kept in mind the children's heights (and future growth) as she positioned the peephole. She installed the mermaid knocker from the reuse store on the wall adjacent to the door.

She was not quite finished by the time Lea pulled up the

driveway, but Hannah ran to the car to greet the kids. Whispering to Lea, she asked if she had time to spare to let her gang check out the treehouse, and Lea said, "Absolutely."

Hannah shouted out to the little people in the car, "Hey, everyone! Do you want to go in the treehouse?"

The five children could not get out of their car seats fast enough. Running to the back yard, they all scampered up the stairs and shrilled with delight. Even Claire managed to climb up the steps.

"It's not finished yet. I still have a lot to do," said Hannah. "But you can check out the hidey holes and the bucket and pulley." She put some snack bars in the bucket and showed the kids how to pull the rope to bring the bucket up to the deck of the treehouse.

Nora immediately launched into a play setup, saying, "This is our castle in the sky. Ava, you are my sister princess, and, Claire, you're our pet dragon." The others joined without hesitation.

"This is amazing, Hannah," said Lea. "Just so cool, so sturdy. Look, it doesn't budge an inch." She clutched a post with two hands and attempted to shake the structure. "It's so well made."

"Thanks. I'm getting to the 'carried away' phase where I turn it into every fantasy I've ever had about a playhouse. I want to finish it completely by the time Molly and Ted get back. I've been vague with them about how the progress is coming so they'll be surprised. I'm glad it's nearly finished. What do you think about color? The siding needs to be protected, so I'll have to stain or paint it. I can't decide if I want to make it pop out or blend into the natural environment. I was thinking of kind of a rustic bark color, but part of me wants to paint it something fun."

"Hmmm . . . How about a combo? Do the majority rustic but put some pops of color on it."

"That's a great idea." Hannah stood back and stared at the treehouse. "Yes, that's it; that's perfect. I can paint the turtle and the door and maybe parts of the trim with some color."

After the Harris gang departed, Hannah allowed Nora and Owen to stay in the treehouse while she got dinner started and set the table on the deck. She could see the kids from the kitchen window. Nathan came over, dumped his bag of vegetables on the counter, and ran to join the kids in the treehouse.

Brrrinnng, brrrinng. Hannah was startled by the abrupt ringing of her laptop indicating a video call coming through. She lifted the lid of the computer, and a slightly out-of-focus image of Molly's face appeared.

"Hey, you, how's it going?" said Hannah.

"Is this a good time?" asked Molly. Ted entered the screen, pulling up a chair behind his wife.

"Good, good, good. Kids got home a little while ago, and I'm making dinner. They're out in the back yard. Do you want me to get them, or do you want to talk to me?" she asked.

"We just wanted to say hi. I thought it might be a good time —end of the week and all. Maybe they can tell me what happened at camp. But you go ahead first and tell me what's going on."

"Let's see," Hannah said. "Things are great, a really, really good week. I guess you talked to them on Wednesday, so since Wednesday . . . Owen has been great about not sucking his thumb—that's the most incredible thing. I keep telling him the treehouse is the reward for him quitting sucking his thumb, and he seems to be getting it and is trying hard. Nora had a good week too. They both liked the 'Movin' and Groovin" theme and came home every day super exhausted, which was awesome because, well, I've been kind of busy at night."

"How *are* things with Nathan?" Molly asked. Hannah could hear the teasing in Molly's voice. Ted stood and disappeared from the screen.

"Pretty good, easier now, actually. But I don't know if it's getting kind of . . . I don't know. Oh, Molly, I can't wait for you to come back so I can talk to you about this in person. I like him, but you know I've got to get going with my life. I have to find a job. I'm trying hard not to let him influence any of my decision-making, but he's such a good guy. We're trying to keep it light, and he's been good about it. Anyway, we can talk more when you get here . . . we'll see. I've got some applications going out—what I told you about. I'm looking at one in Boise, Idaho, as well."

"That's progress. Boise, wow. I'm getting antsy to get home. Sometimes it seems like we've been gone forever and sometimes like we just got here. I'm so happy we've done this. It's amazing, but god, I miss my babies. I've been crying a little bit at night, mostly PMS this week. During the day when I'm crazy busy, I'm fine."

"They're fine too, they are. Weather has been off-and-on rainy but nice for the most part, and the summer is flying by," Hannah said. She wanted to put her sister at ease. "Okay, let me go yell for them to come in and talk to you."

"Why don't you bring the computer out there and let me see the treehouse?" asked Molly.

"I don't want you to see it on the computer. I want you to see it all perfect, all done when you get here."

"Come on—I want to see it," pleaded Molly.

"No—please? I want you to see it in person. I took a couple of pictures, and it doesn't look very impressive in the photos. Be patient, woman! Today was the first day the kids got to go into it, but I still have a lot of work to do."

Winning the argument, mainly because she controlled the computer, Hannah changed the subject to other events. "Before I get the kids, I have to tell you something that Nora said the other day. We were driving down to town, and she says, 'Aunt Hannah, do you have voices in your head?' And I asked if she meant thoughts? And she says, 'Yeah but there's, like, two guys in there, and one of 'em is telling me to be nice all the time, and then there's this other guy who says to do something naughty.' Then she said, 'Mostly I do the nice things, but sometimes I really want to do the naughty things.' So, I asked her what kind of naughty things, and she says, 'Well I really wanna say "damn it" when I get hurt, but I just say "ouchie."' I think when you get hurt, you should be able to say 'damn it' even when you're six.'"

"Oh my god. She is so funny. She's obsessed with cursing. Probably because Ted and I talk about it so much in front of them. We're allowed only one curse a day in front of the kids. It's a low bar, but we want to lead by example."

"She's pretty funny with what she comes up with. The other day she told me that I was in love with Nathan, and I told her that that was not true. So, she turned around and said, 'It doesn't have to be true. It's my opinion.' Where does she get that stuff from?"

"She's an observant one," said Molly. "I can't wait to actually meet this guy. Two more weeks!"

"Which means I've got fourteen days to wrap up my summer of self-discovery."

"You're such a boss! I'm not worried. You'll figure it out."

"Aw, thanks, Mol." Hannah yelled out to the back yard for the kids to come in and talk to their parents. They were reluctant at first but ultimately came when she promised to let them go back when they were done. Nora was first to run to the laptop, while Owen ran to the bathroom.

"Hi, Mommy. Hi, Daddy," Nora said. She grinned at the computer, waving both hands at them. "Guess what? It's so exciting. Aunt Hannah let us go in the treehouse. I love it. It's up SOOO high. Hannah did a marvelous job. She's such a good builder. I can't wait for you to play with us in it." Nora looked away from her parents toward Nathan, who was standing off camera in the hallway. "Hey, Nathan, come meet my mommy and daddy." She turned back to her parents. "Nathan is here. He's having dinner with us again."

"He is? Isn't that nice? I guess you see a lot of Nathan," Molly said.

"Yes, we do. He's here a lot and sometimes he stays in our basement," said Nora.

"Really. The basement?"

"Yes, he has a room there now."

"Okay, why don't you go back out and play in the treehouse," said Hannah. She pulled Nora away from the screen and pushed her toward the back door.

"So," Molly said when Hannah came back to the computer. "Nathan lives in our basement?"

"Of course not. I don't know what she's talking about." She turned toward Nathan. "Hey, Nathan, want to come here and meet my sister and Ted?" She stood up out of view of the camera and waved for him to come. Nathan gestured with his hands frantically and mouthed, "No, no." Hannah responded with a wide-eyed look that said, *Get over here and meet my sister.* He must have read the seriousness in her eyes because he obliged and walked to the computer and sat down.

"Hi, Molly. Hey, Ted. Nice to meet you online." Nathan waved at the screen.

"We've heard so much about you! So, you live in our basement?" Molly's grinning face filled the screen.

Hannah leaned into the computer, hiding Nathan's face with her own. "Hey, Molly, I'll explain it all to you later," she said. "It's fine, I assure you. He doesn't live in the basement." Hannah pulled away, putting Nathan's face back in front of the camera.

"Welcome to the neighborhood," interjected Ted from behind Molly's head. "It'll be good to meet you in person."

"Looking forward to it," said Nathan.

After a few more awkward pleasantries, a quick chat with Owen, and a promise to call again over the weekend, they all disconnected from the video call.

"What the hell?" said Hannah. They were both looking out the window at the children in the treehouse. "What did Nora see? When?"

"It might have been that night they weren't quite asleep, and I came upstairs to use the bathroom."

"But I'd have heard her on the monitor."

"She's kind of sneaky. She might have been stealthy. I'm certain she never saw us, because we always locked the basement door from downstairs."

"I'll try and get it out of her. She's pretty bold about reporting on her activities."

After dinner Nathan made a point of saying goodbye and leaving the house so Nora could bear witness. Hannah gave the children a bath and, while cuddling with her in bed, began a gentle grilling of her niece. With a little sweetness and assurances that she would not get in any trouble for answering, Nora sang like a canary.

"If you're as quiet as a church mouse, you can wander all over the house at night when everyone thinks you're sleeping. It's when I play spy games. But I only do it when the lights are on, so I'm not scared of the dark. Once, I tried to turn the TV on, but Mommy and Daddy caught me, so I don't do that anymore," she confessed.

"I saw Nathan come out of the basement one night. He was in his underwear for some reason, and then he went to the bathroom. I was sitting right there on the couch reading a book with my flashlight, but he never saw me. So, I just figured he sleeps in the basement now. Which is weird cause he has a house, and I don't know why he just doesn't sleep there and use his own bathroom."

Hannah gave Nora a final kiss on the forehead and said goodnight without further discussion. Once behind the closed door, she paused for a moment, shaking her head and quietly laughing. *We'll have to up our security game*, she thought.

Thirty-One

Awake earlier than usual, Nathan lay in bed, staring at the ceiling. *It's over tomorrow.* He curled up into the fetal position. *It's over.* He had spent hours, days, thinking about how it could work out with Hannah going forward. He had met up with Dylan and Kim for beers earlier that week, and they both convinced him not to put pressure on her regarding their relationship. Nathan respected Hannah's determination to pursue a new life for herself, but he wished that new life could happen in Vermont. He had made a point over the last few weeks of showing her that a "slow, deep life" could be more rewarding than a "fast, shallow life" and be fun. He wasn't sure she had noticed, though, since her employment prospects were all still in places with a lot more action than he could offer.

"Aren't you afraid if you take a finance job in Denver, you'll end up feeling like you did in Boston?" He had asked this question on one of the rare occasions they had spoken about her job hunt.

"Not this time," she said confidently. "I'll do it differently. I won't get sucked in like I did before. I'll refuse to stay late and work weekends, and I'll make sure it's more about my work quality than how many hours I clock. No more eating lunch 'al desko.' If I move to Denver, I'm going to make the most out of the mountain life and hike and ski on the weekends. I'm going to be more particular about who I befriend. I'm not going to make the same mistakes."

Nathan could not argue with how Hannah felt about work-life balance. He had ventured out beyond the Green Mountains when he attended college in Pittsburgh and grad school in Boston and moved to Chicago for his first job. Emotionally, he had found life in those cities colder than the top of Mount Mansfield in January. But Denver was different. Denver was some solid competition for the life Hannah envisioned for herself. He was going to lose her.

He even had the audacious idea to follow her if she would have him. His job was telecommute-friendly, and, theoretically, he could uproot himself and move practically anywhere. But, damn it, he just bought a house that he wanted to fix up. He wanted to be near his family and was ready to stay put. He was reconnecting with old friends and loving the mountain rescue team. His grandfather had heart problems. He was pretty sure Grace was pregnant or soon would be and he'd have a niece or nephew. Was Hannah worth giving all that up for? Would she even want him to?

He would have to heed Dylan and Kim's advice and not pressure her. All he could do was let her know exactly how he felt. That wasn't pressure; that was just honesty. He would do it. He would tell her.

Thirty-Two

The Ramones' tune "I Wanna Be Sedated" was running through Hannah's brain and quietly out her mouth after the morning routine. She wanted to get to the airport and get on a plane before she went insane. Nora and Owen had been distracted all morning, refusing to cooperate. Finally, Lea pulled away with all five kids headed to camp, and Hannah breathed a sigh of relief. She would join the kids at camp in the afternoon for the awards ceremony and end-of-summer party.

In many ways, it felt as if she had just arrived in Vermont. The summer had flown by, especially the last two weeks. She had practically finished the treehouse the week Nathan was gone. Sara and Aaron's visit had been full of all the tourist favorites with the kids in tow. They hiked the trails at Trapp Family Lodge, took a tour of the Ben & Jerry's ice cream factory, and had a farm-to-table dinner at an organic farm. The past week was spent putting the finishing touches on the treehouse, planning her upcoming travel, and sleeping with, but avoiding significant conversations with, Nathan.

Her parents were driving up, and everyone would go to the airport tomorrow to greet Molly and Ted. She was, as the Ramones suggested, ready to get out of there. Truth be told, Hannah was tired of taking care of Nora and Owen. Molly was right. Kids were exhausting, and she was looking forward to a different kind of challenge. Her interview schedule was finalized, and all she had to do now was say hello and goodbye to Molly and Ted, and she would be off. Oh, and say goodbye to Nathan.

They would have two more nights together, and she would leave for Boston first thing Sunday morning. They had been skirting the issue of her departure for weeks. The closest they had come to sharing their feelings about her leaving was him saying things like "I'm going to miss this" after a particularly good time in the basement. She was deliberately avoiding thinking about him and planned to focus her day on wrapping things up.

She had one more item to finish on her punch list for the treehouse before its "reveal" to Molly and Ted. The drop-down ladder for the top bunk of the bunk beds had been difficult. She designed the bunk beds so that the lower bunk could be used as a table when it was not being used as a bed. She had made a ladder that was stored under the top bunk and could be pulled down as needed. It was on a pivot mechanism that wasn't working. She needed to figure out how to get it to operate correctly, and then she would be done.

When she finished the ladder, she sat down to write a thank-you card for Lea and Chris. Hannah's gratitude for their help all summer was enormous. By way of thanks, she had bought a gift card to the most sought-after restaurant in the area. Conspiring with Chris, she made a reservation for them, and Hannah and Nathan would babysit while Lea and Chris enjoyed a special night out. She was appreciative of Nathan's willingness to participate in a less than peaceful evening. Generally, the Harris kids were well behaved, but there were three of them, and Hannah remembered how Nathan admitted he could get overwhelmed by his own family. She wondered how he would cope with what could be a challenging evening. But he had assured her he was game. "I don't mind. You're only going to be here two more days, and then my life will get decidedly unexciting. I can handle some crazy."

HANNAH PICKED LEA out of the crowd as she walked toward the rowdy scene at the day camp. The place was packed with parents, kids, and camp staff. The basketball court was filled with chairs, and a podium and stage were erected under one of the nets. "Hey," Hannah called out, waving at Lea. Lea walked toward her.

"Do you have a sec? I want to talk to you—where are the kids?" Hannah looked around at the mayhem.

"I don't know, I don't care. I only have about a half hour more of freedom until this camp officially ends and they'll be home all day until school starts in three weeks."

Hannah laughed. "Come here." She took Lea by the arm and led her to the unoccupied picnic bench near the parking lot. "I have something for you."

Hannah pulled out the gift bag from her backpack and handed it to Lea.

"What's this?" Lea peered into the small bag.

"Hang on. Before you open it, I just want to say a few things." Hannah paused. "Thank you doesn't begin to express how grateful I am for all your help this summer. There is no possible way I could have done it without you. Nora and Owen are alive because of you. Well, maybe I could have done it, but I'd have been much crankier. And I would never have built a treehouse or spent time with Nathan. And you helped me figure out my life. You taking the kids back and forth to camp was so great, and the sleepovers and rescue calls and everything. I love the way you remain cheerful and calm through all the chaos that is your life. I am in awe of you, Lea."

"It's the drugs and alcohol. Makes it all chill," said Lea calmly, splaying her arms in front of her.

"You're such a liar. You and Chris have built a sweet family, and I know you have given up a lot of your ambition to stay home these past few years. I love the way you guys interact with each other with humor even when the kids are, like, real jerks. That's a rare thing."

"Thank you. You are so sweet. Parenting can be a thankless job, and it can be so tough on a marriage. You can read all about it in my memoir—it's kind of like *Eat Pray Love* but I'm calling it *Cook Clean Cry.*"

Hannah laughed. "And you're hilarious. Anyway, this is a small token of my appreciation, but I hope you'll be excited." She nodded at the package.

Lea opened the gift and pulled out the note and gift card to the restaurant.

"You're going tonight. Nathan and I will babysit, and you have a six thirty reservation. Chris is in on it. We made it on the early side in case you want to go listen to some music or something after dinner."

"Oh my god. I have been dying to go to Hen of the Wood. Thank you so much. I can't believe you got a reservation. I can't believe I'm finally going!" She squealed and threw her arms around Hannah. "I'm going to miss you so much. I wish you'd just move in with Nathan and live next door to Molly and be my friend forever." She waved her hands in front of her face. "Okay . . . too much. But I am going to miss you tons."

Hannah and Lea returned to the basketball court, their arms around each other's shoulders. They took seats with the other parents as the awards ceremony began. The children all sat on the ground in front of the stage. Hannah thought it was great that the counselors gave "awards" to everyone and said nice things about each child. The awards were cute—a paper plate with the achievement and the child's name: *The Amazing Attitude Award, The Cheerful Camper Award, The Super Kind Award.* Nora received *The Incredible Imagination Award* and Owen got *The Very Determined Award,* perhaps in honor of his finally and permanently quitting thumb sucking. Molly and Ted would be thrilled that he had finally managed to kick the habit.

Thirty-Three

"There they are!" Nora was jumping up and down in the tiny arrivals room at the Burlington Airport. "MOMMY, DADDY!" she screamed, frantically waving her hands. Owen was jumping up and down screaming too, as well as running around in a tight circle.

Molly and Ted, with enormous smiles, ran through the doors to reunite with their children, dropping their bags without regard to their fellow travelers right behind them. Molly burst into tears as soon as she wrapped them in her arms. Ted, too, was tearing up. The happy reunion of the family talking over one another lasted through baggage claim and the loading of the two cars. Ted opened a carry-on and presented the children with the first of many souvenirs they had brought back for them—two stuffed llamas.

"Buying them presents assuaged my guilt for being away, plus I got to support the local Chilean economy in a big way," said Molly. She handed her parents and Hannah packages of chocolates.

Hannah could not wait to show her sister and brother-in-law the treehouse. It had turned out to have more of an impact in the back yard than she originally anticipated. You definitely noticed it. She hoped they would not feel it detracted from their view of the mountains. The consensus from her parents, Chris, Lea, and Nathan was that it did not. The day before, when she showed it off to her parents, they were effervescent in their praise and impressed with the level of finish work and detail. Her father snapped pictures and sent them to his brothers, and her mother took a video with her phone. Hannah was proud of what she had created, and that was a feeling she had not experienced for a very long time.

"This is remarkable. If I hadn't seen you work on it, I don't know if I'd have believed you did it yourself," Bob had said. He beamed with pride, throwing his arm around his daughter's shoulders and squeezing her. "You're something else, Hannah Spencer."

As the car came to a halt at home, Nora and Owen jumped out of their car seats and insisted their parents go immediately to see the treehouse.

"Hurry, Daddy, hurry," yelled Owen. Ted wasn't following him but surveying the front yard and looking at his home. Ted turned to oblige his son and headed for the back yard.

"WHOA!" whooped Ted. He gazed in wonder at the treehouse, stopping in his tracks and grabbing his head with his hands. "Oh my god. This is fricking amazing, Hannah! Freaking unbelievable. Wow." Ted trotted to the treehouse, and the kids and Molly ran after him.

"This is so cool. I am blown away!" exclaimed Molly. She looked up at the structure while Ted circled it, pushing and pulling on the support posts, just like Lea had done. Hannah stood, watching them admire her work with a joyful grin on her face.

"Look, Mommy, there are so many surprisey things. Look, here's my special peephole." Nora stuck her head out of the little hole in the door. "Come in here and see my secret hiding place where I can keep my treasures." She pulled Molly through the door. Molly looked around the room to see the hidey hole and the bunk beds, the top one adorned with two red foam mats and two brightly covered pillows. Nora flicked on the light.

"Is that a solar panel?" Ted asked, standing on the deck, appearing astonished and pointing at the roof.

"Yeah. I wanted it to be a net-zero situation. It has one outlet and one light. Sorry, no internet or running water."

"Daddy, Daddy, here's my favorite thing." Owen reached over the railing and began pulling the bucket up on the pulley. "We can pull up lunch and treats and toys."

"They really like it. They have been playing in it quite a lot. I think it's a good bonding thing. Owen is totally getting into Nora's imaginative play. She still runs the show and bosses him around, but I hear him expressing some original ideas, and she's receptive."

Molly scampered down the steps of the treehouse and threw her arms around her sister in a fierce embrace. "You are freakin' amazing," she whispered into her ear.

Hannah took a triumphant pause. "Thanks, Molly."

"HELLLOO, NATHAN," Nora yelled. Nathan was in the back yard, throwing a Frisbee for Cooper. Nora peered into Nathan's yard, giving him her signature crazy wave. Despite Hannah's best intentions to avoid it, there was a vantage point into Nathan's yard from the treehouse deck. Nathan didn't seem to mind. "C'mon over and meet my mommy and daddy."

"I guess you're all going to meet Nathan now," said Hannah. She climbed to the deck of the treehouse and stood next to Nora.

"Can you come over?" Hannah yelled.

"Sure," Nathan yelled back.

Hannah smiled, watching as Nathan ran his hand through

his hair and checked his fly as he walked over. Cooper tagged close behind. She was as excited about her family meeting Nathan as she was about them seeing the treehouse. *Stop that*, she said to herself.

"Hi, Ted. Hi, Molly. Welcome home," Nathan said as he approached the group. "Mr. and Mrs. Spencer." He extended his hand to Hannah's father first, then her mother.

"Bob and Elizabeth, please," said Bob. They shook hands and looked at each other squarely in the face.

"So nice to finally meet you in person." Molly moved in and embraced Nathan in a warm hug. She reached down to pet Cooper. "Hey there. You must be the famous Cooper."

"I'm looking forward to hearing about your trip," Nathan said. "I've always wanted to go to South America, especially Patagonia."

"We're giving the PowerPoint, just the highlight reel, tonight after the kids go to bed and before Hannah leaves town. You're welcome to join us," Ted said. He gave a quick "I hope that's okay" glance to Hannah.

Hannah looked at Nathan. "Can you? They've taken some amazing photographs."

"I'd love to, thanks." Nathan turned to Ted and pointed at the treehouse. "So, what do you think?"

"We're blown away. To be honest, I wasn't sure what to expect, but this is incredible. It'll be the envy of the school. She could start a business building these," said Ted.

"We love it," agreed Molly. "I can't believe we got this as well as free childcare and a dream trip."

"She worked hard. The first time I met her was when she told me about her plan to build it," Nathan said. "I have to confess, I was skeptical."

"One thing about Hannah; when she makes a plan, she follows through," said Molly.

"I've noticed," said Nathan.

Thirty-Four

After the excitement of the day, Nora and Owen fell asleep earlier than usual, curled in their parents' arms. Molly hung a sheet against the wall in the living room to serve as a screen for the presentation. Nathan and Hannah arranged the furniture, so everyone had a comfortable seat facing the "screen." Ted explained they would show them the "friends and family" lecture, and it would take about an hour and a half. "We can make it shorter if you want." Everyone agreed they wanted to see the talk in its entirety.

Ted began, explaining that, despite being one of the world's last remaining pristine wilderness areas, the sub-Antarctic ecoregion was full of human-introduced, exotic, and often invasive species. Nathan had only ever given passing attention to invasives, but he was immediately captivated by Ted's presentation. His research centered on the havoc beavers were unleashing in the area.

Nathan had no idea that Canadian beavers were introduced into South America in the 1940s to create a fur trade. Ted said that it never took off, but the beavers reproduced rapidly because there were no natural predators. Now, the region was being destroyed by two hundred thousand beavers.

"The bottom line is that the beavers have to be substantially eradicated, and it's a tough situation because they're so darn cute." His final photograph was an image of an adorable baby beaver.

"That was awesome," Bob said as everyone clapped. "My all-time favorite Ted Talk."

"Haha. Now all I have to do is pare this version down to thirty minutes," said Ted.

Molly spent the summer working on a paper called "Patagonia Is Melting" and presented next. She began with a lot of charts and graphs. "The people of the area are concerned, and rightly so. The ice fields in southern South America are rapidly losing volume and, in most cases, thinning at even the highest elevations. This is contributing to sea-level rise at substantially higher rates than observed from the 1970s through the 1990s." Her glacier photographs were spectacular. The jagged peaks glowed with every shade of blue: aquamarine, cerulean, robin-egg blue, teal, pale gray blue, periwinkle, and an otherworldly nearly fluorescent blue.

"There's ongoing research about how this melting will affect populations downstream who depend on the ice fields as a reservoir providing their water supply for drinking and agriculture. I spent some time at the Center for Climate Studies, where college students do research on climate change impacts, glacial dynamics, and conservation," Molly said.

"That was both fascinating and a little bit depressing," said Nathan when her speech was done. "It makes me want to pack my bags and go right now. It's incredibly beautiful. What an experience for both of you."

"We couldn't have done it without Hannah. And, well, if you have any feedback you want to give us on the PowerPoints, we'd be grateful. Some of this is in the technical presentations, and we want them to be perfect, so don't be shy," said Ted.

"It was fantastic," said Hannah. "I think they're both interesting, and the photography is amazing. Kudos to the photographers." She shot out both arms and pointed her fingers toward Molly and Ted, gun-style.

The group continued awhile longer, discussing the presentations and learning more about their time in Chile and Argentina. When it became clear that Ted and Molly could no longer stay awake, they said their goodnights, and Hannah and Nathan departed for Nathan's house.

As soon as they entered the house, Hannah reached into her tote bag and drew out a nicely wrapped package. "I have something for you."

"What's this? A going-away present?"

"Don't look at it like that." Hannah scowled, then smiled. "I didn't get it together until now. It's just a little something."

Tearing off the paper, Nathan held the gift in his hands, staring at it silently. He felt tears of emotion forming.

"Wow." He stared at the hinged frame with two five-by-seven photos. The first picture was of him and Cooper sitting side by side in his back yard on the grass. The second was a full-body shot of just Cooper. He was cocking his head, completely adorable. The image depicted his entire personality.

"Did you take this one from the treehouse?" Nathan asked, pointing to the one of him and the dog.

"Yup. And I used a real camera with a zoom. I saw you and Cooper playing catch when I was photographing the treehouse for posterity. I felt like a stalker, but you guys were so cute."

"Thank you. You are a great photographer. You captured him so well. It's a wonderful gift. Look at that face; he's such a ham."

"You're welcome." She nuzzled closer to Nathan. "Sorry to report that I only started hanging out with you because of your dog."

"Duh," replied Nathan.

Thirty-Five

Hannah slipped quietly into the house the next morning and found her mother sitting at the kitchen counter, a coffee cup in her hand.

"Mornin'," a sleepy-looking Elizabeth mumbled.

"Hey, Mom, you're up early," Hannah whispered.

"It's my age. I don't sleep well anymore. Fucking menopause."

Hannah laughed, poured herself a cup of coffee, and motioned for her mom to follow her into the family room. Settling on the couch, Hannah told her mom the details of her job interviews and travel itinerary.

"What about Nathan?" Elizabeth asked when Hannah finished.

"What about him?"

"I sensed you were maybe getting more serious these past few weeks. No?"

"I wouldn't call it serious. I've made it very clear that I was leaving town when Molly and Ted got back."

"Too bad," her mother said. "I've enjoyed the lilt."

"The lilt?"

"Yeah, the lilt in your voice when you talk about him. I've never heard it before, not from you. Your enthusiasm for a man is refreshing."

"I didn't realize I was lilting." Hannah took a sip of coffee and paused, staring into the cup. "Nathan's great. I'm glad you got to meet him. I guess you'll see him whenever you visit." Hannah's eyes flashed wide as her words hung in the air. She placed her mug on the table. "I never considered it, but oh my god. You're going to see him whenever you come up here. Molly and Ted are going to be here all the time with Nathan right next door."

She bolted to a standing position and began to pace. Her speech quickened. "It never occurred to me. I just thought I'd leave, and Nathan and I would be over, and I'd become friends with him on Facebook and not see him again. I can't believe I didn't think about this. Molly will know everything. She'll know if he's dating someone, if he gets married, if he has kids. Oh my god, I can't believe I never even thought about that. Every time I come to visit, he will be right next door. I've been so busy with the treehouse and the kids and preoccupied with my job hunt, I didn't think about this."

"Are you having a panic attack?" Elizabeth rose and put her hand on Hannah's back. "Are you okay? Breathe."

"I'm fine. I'm just pissed at myself for not thinking about this. I've totally compartmentalized our relationship. I caught myself singing 'Summer Nights' from Grease recently thinking about us—*summer fling, don't mean a thing*," she sang, rocking her head back and forth. "But this is going to be impossible."

Elizabeth flopped on the couch and laughed. "Every single guy you have ever dated had an expiration date stamped on their forehead. They never see it coming, but I always do. Poor Nathan."

Hannah threw a pillow at her mother good-naturedly. "That isn't true."

"What's not true?" came a voice from the doorway. Molly, in her robe and slippers, appeared in the family room.

"Just that every guy Hannah ever dates has an expiration date stamped on their forehead," Elizabeth said.

"Oh, that's absolutely true," Molly said. She sat down on an overstuffed chair across from Hannah and Elizabeth. "Remember Jason, that guy she dated over the summer in college? She drove him all the way home to his house in Connecticut at the end of summer, and he wanted her to come in and meet his parents, and she said, 'No thank you' and drove off and never saw him again."

"He's married and has two kids now," said Hannah. "He got over it."

"Yeah, but not for a long time. Remember all those calls and letters and emails? We all felt bad for him," said Molly. "And don't forget all those poor Boston boys who never saw it coming."

"I'm good at not letting things go on longer than they should. I'm decisive. I refuse to slide; I decide. I don't think it's a bad thing. Rip off the Band-Aid. And you know, it's been done to me too, so I know how it feels. But I still think it's better than dragging things out with some dumb long-distance relationship."

"But then . . . there's the lilt to consider," Molly said. She shot a smile at her mother.

"Have you been talking to Mom behind my back?" asked Hannah, raising her voice. She looked at Molly with a furrowed brow.

"Of course. We've been talking about you and your giddy tone." Molly laughed. "It's never been witnessed before. It's exciting."

"I remember your voice when you met Ted," said Elizabeth. "It's kind of turned into a whine now, but I know you still love him."

"I have been whining more than I should these last few years, but I have to say this trip was great for us. We got along so well and didn't have arguments. It was like we were dating again. I'm so happy. We even kind of renewed our vows. We sort of had a wakeup call. We realized that if we could get through the tough days and years with kids, when they're gone, we like being alone together. I'm not sure that always happens."

"Very good epiphany," said her mother. "It's hard to see how long life is at your stage."

"But enough about me—we'll talk about that later," said Molly. She turned her gaze to her sister. "Let's get back to Hannah. She's out of here tonight. So, what are you going to do about Nathan? We've known him for less than twenty-four hours, but I, for one, think he's great. Plus, Nora thinks he's great, and she's the world's harshest critic."

"You guys, I've only known him for, like, two months. What do you expect me to do? I've got to get on with things. I'm going to get a kick-ass job in a kick-ass place and reboot my life." Hannah pulled a pillow across her chest. "I can't just stay in Molly's guest room and sleep with the guy next door. What kind of forward motion for me would that be? I wasted so much time in Boston, and now I want to do something I can get excited about. The job in Denver is amazing. If I had to write a job description for myself, that would be it. I'm sure Denver has a lot of guys like Nathan."

"Eww . . . harsh," said Molly. "Denver is so far away. Aren't you going to miss New England? It's so pretty here and not so crowded."

"That's the hard part. But Geez, I can fly back whenever I want."

"It won't be the same," said Molly. "Nora and Owen are

more in love with you than ever. It sucks you can't find something around here. Did you even try? I could put out some feelers. We know a lot of people."

"Molly!" Hannah threw her legs onto the floor and shifted to face her sister directly. "You aren't getting it. For the past three years, I've been doing something someone else made happen for me. Sara's brother hooked me up with that job. I don't want to fall into that trap again. I want to be in charge this time. I want to make the right decision, and I don't want so much pressure. Nathan. You. Mom. God, even Nora and Owen are making me feel guilty for trying to do what's right for me."

Hannah slumped back into the couch. Her blood pressure was rising. She could feel it, which was unusual for her. "You want me to do what works for you. I want to get back the feeling of overseeing my own life. I want to decide; I don't want to slide. I keep saying that to myself. I don't want to take the path of least resistance. I want to get out there and get messy and decide what makes sense for me."

"Yikes, okay, okay, I get it," said Molly. "I'm sorry to put pressure on you."

"Me too," said her mother. "But you're just so great to have around." She leaned in and squeezed her daughter's knee.

"But here's the thing," Molly said. "You have to promise not to make it like an escape—to Denver or anywhere else. If you do move away, it should be because the opportunity is the right one. It must be the whole package. I see the appeal, but I wouldn't want you to get out there and be lonely or hate your job again. You know, I've always imagined you'd do your own thing, own your own business instead of working for someone. You'd make a great entrepreneur."

"Yeah, I've imagined that too. I just can't think of anything

I'd want to 'entreprenew.'" Nora suddenly appeared in the doorway. "Hi, baby." Hannah rose and gathered the child into her arms. "Let's get some pancakes!"

THE PLAN FOR the day, Hannah's last in Vermont, had been the subject of much debate the night before. Molly wanted to be with her kids, but she also wanted to be with Hannah. Nathan wanted to be with Hannah. Bob and Elizabeth were staying for a few more days and had plans to go on a hike with some former work friends of Bob's who were visiting in the area. Nathan suggested they go on a float trip in his raft, and the idea garnered great enthusiasm. The four adults and two children would fit well in his craft. They would set out for a float along the Lamoille River for a couple of hours and bring a picnic lunch.

"He has ideas for things to do!" Molly whispered to Hannah as they passed each other in the kitchen. "Trait number one!" Molly was referencing their long list of ideal characteristics in men. One of their mutual teenaged pet peeves was how so many guys they liked depended on the girl to make plans for activities. The boys would always default to making out in the basement or playing video games. Both agreed it was exhausting to have to come up with ideas all the time.

Rafting could be a complicated logistical activity, but Nathan knew how to make it as efficient as possible. Two cars with the entire gang traveled to the put-in spot located off a dirt road near a lake. Everyone unloaded, and Nathan stayed with Molly and the kids to inflate and load the raft. Hannah and Ted drove the two cars to the take-out spot, leaving one of the cars there, and drove back together to the put-in place.

It was Hannah and Ted's first chance to talk alone. Ted expressed his appreciation to Hannah for all that she had done over the summer. He told her the kids thrived under her care.

"I'll never regret this summer and the chance to get to know them. But I had a lot of help. Lea and Chris were amazing. And I was pretty lucky to have Nathan willing to help me out."

"Indeed," said Ted. He looked at Hannah and smiled. "I like him. Easygoing, interesting, and smart. You could do worse."

"Not you, too!" Hannah said in mock frustration. "Mom and Molly are pretty smitten with him. C'mon, Ted, what am I supposed to do? I have to move on and get my life back on track. I just met him. I have some irons in the fire, and I've focused in on what I want to do next. It just dawned on me this morning that he's going to be in your lives as your next-door neighbor, and that could be awkward down the road. But don't worry, he's such a sweetheart of a guy. He'd never diss his next-door neighbors over a girl."

"Let's hope not." Ted put on his blinker and turned onto the main road. "So, what are these jobs you're going after?"

Hannah summarized her prospects, and Ted admitted that the Denver job was promising.

"We're never going to see you again," he said. He pulled the car into a space at the put-in spot.

"Stop it. You will too. Let's stop talking about it until things get settled."

The group set off in the raft along the winding river. The placid paddling was perfect for Nora and Owen's capabilities, and they enjoyed looking for fish and wildlife as they floated in the shallow river. Passing through the verdant landscape with views of the mountains and farmland off in the distance, Molly, Ted, Hannah, and Nathan talked effortlessly as they paddled. It was the perfect last day of her Vermont summer.

Thirty-Six

Still wanting to make the most of her last bit of time with everyone, Hannah split the difference for the evening between her family and Nathan. Dinner with the family; sleeping at Nathan's. She would leave the next morning. Everyone promised they would not spend her last evening expressing their sadness about her departure—although they did not keep that promise.

After dinner, Hannah said goodnight to her family and was starting to walk to Nathan's when her phone pinged. It was a text from Nathan asking her to meet him in the treehouse. She turned and walked to the back yard and climbed the steps. Nathan sat cross-legged on the floor of the tiny house. One of Owen's toys, a small plastic elephant, was placed in front of him.

"Can we talk about the elephant in the room?" Nathan asked.

Hannah laughed. "Can we talk about, literally, anything else?" She dropped her bag on the floor and slumped her shoulders. "Can't we just hang out and enjoy the evening?" She gave him an overly suggestive wink, nod, and gaping-mouth smile.

"We need to talk, Hannah. I thought this would be a good place to do it." He stood, took her head in his hands, and stared into her eyes. "I've been really good, really, really good, about not pressing you on this, but I've got, like, feelings for you. I don't want to scare you off, but they are big feelings."

Hannah laughed and grabbed his wrists gently. "Feelings are

nice. I have feelings." She paused, inhaling slowly. "But I don't want feelings to weigh in on my decision-making right now. I've learned a lot about myself this summer, and you've been a big part of that evolution, but I want to keep my feelings separate until I can put some space between this summer and determining what avenue I'll be taking next." Anticipating this conversation, she had carefully prepared this speech earlier in the week.

"That's stupid." Nathan dropped his hands from her face. "Let them out, for god's sake. Tell me what you're thinking."

"Why can't you understand I don't want to talk about it now?" Hannah turned her back to him, took a few steps toward the door, then turned around and faced him again. "If I let you —my feelings for you, your feelings for me—color my decision, then I won't own it. I want to mull things over without regard to a guy. I'm sorry, but we've only known each other for, like, a minute. I can't make a life-changing decision based on a minute. That's what I did last time, and I was miserable. Can't you see I can't do that again?" Hannah stopped. She was shouting at him. "My god, we're fighting. This is our first fight, and that's perfect. That's exactly what I'm talking about. How can you ask me to consider you in my life when we haven't even had a fight yet?"

"Point taken," said Nathan, exhaling sharply. "But I don't care. I've met a lot of people, a lot of women, and none of them are your equal in my regard. I think it's important you know that. Even though it's been a short time, sixty-four days since we first spoke, we've packed a lot of 'get to know you' into that time, especially in the last few weeks. Stop looking at it so objectively. Look at how you feel."

He counted the days.

"I don't know what you want me to do, Nathan. What are

you suggesting? What's your solution?" Hannah began pacing in a tiny circle.

"I think you need to go through the process of doing these interviews and checking out Boise and Denver, but I want you to consider how I might fit into your life."

"Are you saying you'd move to Boise or Denver with me? You'd do that? That's insane. You just bought a house. Your entire family is here. Your grandfather. You love it here. I'd never ask you to leave."

"And I'd never put pressure on you to stay if that's not what you want. But I'm just saying I'd be completely ecstatic if you stayed. I just want to be crystal clear that I want you in my life. I don't ever want you to have a doubt about it or think I'm ambivalent. Got it? Don't just jump in the car tomorrow and drive away forever. Please. Keep thinking. Keep talking to me. Don't cut off ties because of some self-imposed rules about how you think you should live your life. Keep your heart in it. Look at it from ten years out. What would you regret more, not moving out West or giving up on us?"

"Okay, yes, I got it. I hear you," said Hannah. "I was trying to avoid this conversation. I guess it was inevitable." She hung her head to her chest. "But it's a little like you breaking up with that girl on the train. We've had this big talk, and now we're supposed to spend the rest of the night together. She raised and cocked her head. "Awkkkwaard."

Nathan walked to her and rested his hands on her shoulders. "It doesn't have to be awkward. I'm fine now. I just needed to get that out. Nothing's resolved, but I wanted you to know where I stand. It's getting late anyway. How about we go cuddle up, and I'll finally tell you the story about my cosmetic surgery."

"Yes! That story will be the perfect finale."

"Really?" Nathan conjured up his best Eeyore posture, grabbing Hannah's hand and leading her down the steps of the tree-house. "Finale?"

"Sorry. Unfortunate choice of words."

Thirty-Seven

"I love you," Hannah said.

"I love you too. Please drive safe and let me know when you get there." Molly and Hannah embraced and held each other for a long time.

"I will, but I'm going to make a couple of stops, so don't worry." Hannah broke away and turned to close the hatch of her car.

She looked over at Nathan's house. Her last night with him had been sweet and tender and didn't include a lot of talk. They'd risen early, had coffee, and snuggled on the couch. When it was time for her to go, Hannah swung her body to lie atop Nathan.

"Hey, I gotta go," she had said. She looked directly at his face.

"I know." He took her face in his hands. "Will I ever see you again? Is this it? Is this what it feels like to have your heart broken and all your hopes and dreams die in one moment?"

"Stop being such a drama queen." She laughed and rolled off him. Standing, she pulled Nathan's arm so that he also rose. She pulled him into her body and wrapped him in a hug. "Thanks for a memorable summer, Nathan Wild." Hannah was both confused and contemplative. Nathan's body and hers felt so right together, and if she wasn't careful, she might just flop back on the couch and never leave.

"Keep in touch, Hannah Spencer," Nathan said quietly. "No pressure, but keep in touch."

Hannah had walked out the door, her overnight bag filled with all of her belongings that had migrated to Nathan's over the last few weeks. She slumped her shoulders as she walked back to Molly and Ted's. She was not looking forward to saying goodbye to the kids.

Nora had been inconsolable when she processed the fact that Hannah wouldn't be living there any longer, and was protesting by conducting a one-person sit-in atop the treehouse.

"But, Mommy, you don't make the special oatmeal, and you don't know how to braid my hair on the top of my head like a headband. Aunt Hannah can't leave; she just can't leave." Nora was sobbing. "I'm glad you're home, but I want her to stay."

"Aunt Hannah, I'm not speaking to you starting right now unless you promise to stay," said Owen, turning his back to her. Thankfully, his rejection was temporary, and he jumped off the porch and soon began speaking to her. Nora and her iron will, on the other hand, had refused to talk to her the entire morning. Hannah could do nothing to comfort her niece. What could she say? Her departure was hurting everyone, but the family needed to resume their nuclear routine, and Hannah knew the grief would be short-lived.

"Can you come down, please?" called Hannah to Nora. "I have something special for you."

Nora perked up at the mention of a gift but remained seated on the top step of the treehouse. "I don't want it."

"Yes, you do. You've wanted it all summer." Hannah held up a small gift bag.

Intrigued, Nora rose. "What is it?" she said with attitude.

"Come here and find out," said Hannah. "Or I can come up."

"Come up here."

"Okay," said Hannah. When she reached the top step, Nora got up and entered the treehouse and sat on the lower bunk bed. Hannah followed her and sat beside her. She handed her the bag. "I'm going to miss you so much, Nora. I hate to have to go, but I just do."

"No, you don't. You can stay," said Nora.

"No, honey, I have to go get a job and find a place to live."

"You can live here. You can marry Nathan and stay here."

Hannah laughed. "I can't do that. We just met."

"So what?" said Nora. "The grass isn't greener anywhere. It's greener here, Aunt Hannah."

Hannah silently chuckled. "I'm sorry, honey, but I have to go. I wanted you to have this to remember our summer together."

Nora took the gift out of the bag and quickly ripped off the paper and opened a small box. "It's a twin necklace." Hannah touched the identical necklace around her neck. "It's exactly like mine, and when we wear them, it'll remind us of our special connection. No matter where I am in this whole wide world, I'm always thinking of you, and I'll be back to see you before you know it." She removed the necklace from the box and clasped it around Nora's neck.

Nora silently stared at the silver earth charm, rubbing it between her thumb and forefinger. "Okay," she said quietly. "Thank you." She looked at Hannah and threw her arms around her neck.

Hannah wanted to burst into tears but instead said, "Okay, Norabean, I have to go." She took her niece's hand, and they climbed down the stairs of the treehouse. "And don't forget, we're going to video chat once a week. And I'll come back to visit just as soon as I can."

With all of the goodbyes completed and feeling as much closure as possible, Hannah got in her car, shut the door, and drove away.

Thirteen minutes later, Hannah arrived at her destination. She parked outside an adorable Victorian house just off Main Street in downtown Montpelier, the state capital. A few minutes early for her appointment, she peered into the visor mirror, adjusted her hair and lipstick, and then checked her phone for any new messages or email. At the appropriate time, she walked into the building.

"Hey there, Hannah. Thanks for coming down," said the man, appearing in the small waiting area of the former-house-turned-office-space. Hannah shook hands with Mark, Nathan's friend who had recently helped her obtain the solar panel for the treehouse. He led her through the hall, and they entered a sparsely furnished office.

"This is my partner, Shane. Shane Andersen. Shane, this is Hannah Spencer," said Mark. Hannah extended her hand.

"Very pleased to meet you, Shane."

"Likewise," Shane said, smiling. "Mark has told me so much about you. Have a seat, will you, and let's get started." He gestured to one of the two plastic guest chairs facing a desk that wasn't so much a desk as it was a plastic folding table.

Technically, this was Hannah's second interview with Mark, the first one having transpired over a cup of coffee the day she picked up the panel. She and Mark had hit it off immediately, and he explained his staffing needs for his new company, a solar panel installation and technology company, OneSun Solar. The company was specializing in electric car charging stations utilizing solar, as well as providing traditional panel installation. Because OneSun was a start-up in every sense of the word, their initial search was for people who were smart, ambitious, and willing to take a less-than-competitive salary.

"How's the treehouse coming?" Mark asked.

"It's all done!" Hannah said proudly. "I finished it before my sister got home, and the kids have been playing in it for a couple of weeks." Hannah pulled out her phone and pushed some keys until a photo appeared, and she handed the phone to Mark.

"Wow, that's impressive. My kids would love that," he exclaimed, handing the phone to Shane.

"Mark told me about a woman with a finance background building a treehouse with a solar panel, and I said that sounds like someone we need to work with us. This is great, Hannah. Love the detail on the door. How's the panel working out? Any trouble?" Shane asked, handing her back the phone.

"Works great. I got a little help from Keapers Electric with the connection, and it's been perfect," said Hannah.

"We should do a profile for our promotional campaign." Shane laughed and continued. "Let's get to it. Have you read over our prospectus and draft impact assessment?"

"Yes," said Hannah. "I've not personally worked on the establishment of a B Corp in my career, but I've done as much research as I can on their unique elements."

These two men were onto something innovative and exciting. A benefit corporation, or B Corp, was a corporate entity that provided a positive impact on society, the workforce, the community, and the environment. These were all the things she was looking for in her next job. The concept was to have a 'triple bottom line'—consideration given to society and the environment as well as financial performance.

"The role we're trying to fill is a great opportunity for someone with your skill set. It is a position that will grow with the company. As Mark must have told you, we can't offer a lot of perks at this time, such as an office with a window and assistants to make you coffee. Still, we can offer you a collaborative workplace where we emphasize a good work-life balance and employee-owned stock opportunities. Tell me, if we were to offer you the position, how would you feel about being a finance/communications/marketing jack of all trades?"

Hannah replied that she was up for the task. Shane and Mark spent the remainder of the interview peppering her with questions about her experience and life philosophy. She was over-qualified for portions of the position and underqualified for other parts. That was enticing. She liked the idea of learning on the job. However, such a small operation meant there would be no one to act as a mentor.

"It was a pleasure meeting you, Hannah," Shane said as the interview ended. "Would it be all right if we contact your references?"

"Yes, please do," said Hannah. "But please keep it confidential from anyone else." She shot a glance at Mark and smiled. "I haven't spoken to my family or friends, and I don't want anyone to hear anything before I have a chance to tell them."

"No problem. We have a couple of other candidates, but we want to decide soon. Expect to hear from us shortly," said Mark. He stood, and Hannah followed him back down the hall to the front door.

Driving to Boston, Hannah reflected seriously on the One-Sun Solar job. She weighed the pros and cons. It was the first of her four scheduled interviews; it was hard to compare the job responsibilities against the other three positions. One big unknown was the company's viability; the other was the salary. They had given her a salary range, but she wouldn't know the exact sum until they made an offer. The low end of the range was nearly half of what she made in Boston. Money wasn't everything, but it was hard to think about taking such a significant cut.

The interview had gone well, and she gave herself a silent high five for nailing it despite her range of emotions over the last twenty-four hours. With one meeting down, three to go, she felt back in the game. She would have her "safety" interview this week in Boston, see some old friends, and go to her cousin's baby shower on the weekend. Then she would fly to Boise, followed by a final interview in Denver. Things were getting real.

Thirty-Eight

"Yeah, I was shocked. I've not been paying attention to East Coast news over the past couple of weeks," said Hannah to her mother on the phone. Earlier that morning, while Hannah was still asleep on her high school friend Travis's couch in Denver, she received a robocall from the airline regarding her reservation. They suggested she rebook her flight from Denver to Boston, as a hurricane would affect the mid-Atlantic and New England coasts over the weekend. Hurricanes rarely came up north, so the entire northeast was on high alert. When she called the airline, they told her she could either take a flight the next day, Friday, or wait until the following Monday or Tuesday. The agent discouraged Hannah from waiting until after the storm, however, saying it was a much safer bet from a convenience standpoint to leave before the storm; the number of delays and cancellations would be much higher after the storm. Hannah was disappointed. Her stay in Denver was already brief, and now it would be cut by a day. Tomorrow she would have to take an evening flight to Boston that would not get her there until early Saturday morning.

"We're in high-prep mode," said Elizabeth. "Dad's outside bringing loose things into the garage in case there are high winds. They're even saying eastern Vermont might be affected. Molly and Ted and the kids are in Quebec with Ted's folks until next week, so they'll miss the excitement."

"I'm seriously bummed I have to leave Denver. It's beautiful here today, so I'll try and get outside. Two days isn't enough time to be here," said Hannah. "I can't stay on Travis's couch until next week, though. Oh, but guess what? He has chickens. They're so fun. Yesterday I helped him fix up his chicken coop, which was kind of falling apart."

"I just read an article about how urban chickens are all the rage. Too bad your time is getting cut short. But tell me, how was the interview?" asked Elizabeth. "What did you think?"

"It could not have gone better. They basically offered me the job but will confirm in writing. The salary is aaaamazing! More than what I was making in Boston. They're going to email me a written offer by tomorrow. So, it's good. I'm in love with Denver. It's similar in so many ways to Boston—cold, about the same number of people—but it feels younger, and it's newer except for some of the downtown parts. I like it. I didn't get to the mountains, but you can see them in the distance, and that's so cool. Travis drove me out to Golden, which was spectacularly pretty. There's a lot of sprawl, but the interstate seems decent. Denver has a different vibe—definitely more laid back than Boston."

"Okay. So, the Boise job was a bust and a waste of time. Denver went great, and Boston you're ambivalent about," said Elizabeth. "Now's the part where I'll try and keep my mouth shut about what I think you should do, my dear daughter."

Hannah knew if her mother were aware of the additional job opportunity in Vermont, she would have more trouble keeping her mouth shut. Hannah had told no one, except for her references, about the OneSun Solar gig. It was so unlike the other possibilities. While the Boston and Denver jobs offered stable, well-funded opportunities with promising longevity, the position at OneSun was vague and potentially risky. "I'll keep you posted, I promise," said Hannah. "I'm going to make the most out of my last few hours here. Travis is taking me out to his favorite bar tonight."

"Have fun, be careful. Call or text me tomorrow and let me know how things are going travel-wise."

"Will do. Love you. Bye."

TRAVIS WAS A great tour guide. After a few hours of hiking at Red Rocks, followed by a shower and nap, he took her to a trendy restaurant housed in a former auto garage. They met a couple of his friends, and after dinner, the four of them made their way to Travis's favorite bar—a pub boasting an eclectic array of beers and an attached brewery. After a brief brew tour and a flight of beers, it was off to a club for some loud—very loud—very bassy dancing. Electronic music was not Hannah's thing, but as an occasional departure from her usual routine, it was okay. She lost Travis in the crowd several times, got groped twice, and pondered whether she was past her prime for the dance club scene.

Hannah ended up taking an Uber back to his apartment since Travis wanted to stay out. She was asleep the second her head hit the pillow.

Thirty-Nine

An early morning rapping on the door startled Cooper, who jumped from his place beside Nathan but, as usual, did not bark. "Come on, Silent Bob, let's see who it is." Nathan rose from his chair, still dressed in his boxers and T-shirt after a restless night of sleep. Throwing on a pair of shorts, he opened the door to find his sister Grace.

"Surprise!" she said in a cheery voice. "I was in the neighborhood. Hope you don't mind a drop-in."

"Hey, sure, come on in," said Nathan.

"What's going on here?" she asked, walking into the kitchen, where dirty dishes cascaded over the lip of the sink. She picked up a "wood floor stain chart" resting on top of a pile of home improvement pamphlets, which were scattered over the kitchen table. "Doing some redecorating?"

"Trying to get going on some projects," said Nathan. He picked up one of the pamphlets and dropped it back on the table. "Been putting things off, and there's some stuff I want to get done before the winter."

"That's good," Grace said, thumbing through the stack of pamphlets. "But geez, this is a lot of projects. Floor finishing, paint samples, invisible fence, kitchen cabinets, lights, and what's this—solar panels?"

"I want to start picking away at things, so I'm looking at it all," said Nathan. "I think I'm going to do the outside stuff first.

I've already started with the roof. I'm getting one of those metal seam ones, and they're doing some insulation as well. The guys are coming today to start."

Hearing the informative yet listless response her brother provided, Grace looked at Nathan and rubbed his back. "How are you doing, Nathan? You hangin' in there?"

Nathan dropped his head to his chest, purposely melodramatic. "I don't know if I handled it right with Hannah. I know we were only together a few weeks, but now I might never see her again. I mean, I know I'll see her, but you know what I mean —be with her. She's going to take the job in Denver, I know it."

"What did you say to her?" asked Grace. "Did you tell her how you feel? Did you use the *L* word?"

"Not specifically, but she knows. It was clear that I wanted to continue our relationship, and I even hinted I'd follow her if she wanted me to," Nathan told his sister. "She knows I'm in love with her, but I didn't want to put the extra burden of saying so on her. She's so determined to make a perfect choice about her next job that she's throwing up all kinds of roadblocks. She doesn't want anyone else to influence her decision. She's adamant about not letting anything else matter, but *I* want to matter."

"I think it's good you told her how you feel. But would you move for her, Nathan? That's kind of drastic. You just got here. We all missed you so much when you were out of state. And you hated being so far away."

"True, but I'm now factoring Hannah into the calculations. Grace, she's awesome. She's all I want in a partner. She's the best thing that has ever happened to me, and it can't be over."

"Hang on, hang on," said Grace. She rubbed her brother's back.

Nathan could feel the tears welling in his eyes.

"I've never seen you this way. Frankly, I love it. You're emoting so openly. Go, Nathan!"

Before he could respond, the front door opened.

"Knock, knock," came a female voice from the front of the house. "Hellooo! Nathan? Oh! Grace! You're here." It was Kendall walking through the house with Adam, both dressed, as was Grace, in biking clothes.

"What? You guys were just in the neighborhood too?" asked Nathan. "What is this, an intervention?"

"Exactly," said his brother. "We figured you'd blow us off again if we asked you to hang out, so this way you don't have a choice." Adam dropped a brown paper bag on the counter and put some beer into Nathan's refrigerator. "This is for later. We are taking you for a bike ride before it gets too hot, and then we're going to come back and drink this beer and eat some lunch. Sound good?"

"Well, yeah, when you put it like that," said Nathan. He was grateful his siblings were here to save him from another cheerless day. "But don't you people have jobs? Isn't Friday still typically a workday?"

"I have today off, which is good because everyone is freaking out about this storm coming. And these two are kinda always available for fun," Grace said, nodding to Kendall and Adam.

"Work-life balance, man. It's time you got out of this house and got a good dose of Wild medicine. We're going to hit the trails hard and sweat out your blues," said Kendall.

"Okay." Nathan already felt better than he had ten minutes earlier. "I'll go get dressed. Let Cooper out, would ya?"

The four siblings spent a couple of hours doing what they all loved to do, riding mountain bikes through the woods. Pedaling through the forest, Nathan could feel the endorphins hit him, and his depressed mood lightened. His legs were more muscular than they'd been at the beginning of the summer, but he could still feel them burn on the last uphill.

"When was the last time we all did this together?" Adam asked once they had exhausted themselves and were walking their bikes back to the car. "I can't even remember."

"I think at Thanksgiving a few years ago, when we went to Pop's after he moved to Shelburne. We rode at Sleepy Hollow before dinner, right?" said Grace.

"That was, like, five years ago," said Nathan.

"Yeah, ridiculous. I'm so glad you're here now, Nathan. We should do this at least once a month," said Kendall, the family uber-planner. "We could alternate planning it and picking the route and arranging the lunch. It'd be so fun."

"I'm in. I need to up my game so I can kick some big brother ass," said Adam.

"Keep dreaming," countered Nathan. "I look forward to crushing you skiing this winter, too."

The four siblings attached their bikes to the bike rack, piled into Nathan's SUV, and headed back to Waterbury. When they arrived at his house, the roofers were at work, unloading sheets of metal that would soon become his new roof.

"I'm starving," said Nathan, opening the refrigerator. "What did you bring for lunch?"

"We've got this," responded Grace, handing her brother a beer and swatting him away from the refrigerator. "Looks like Cooper needs to go out. Let him out, and lunch will be ready in a second."

Nathan obediently left the kitchen and called for Cooper. He tied the dog on the rope and gave him a fresh bowl of water.

Nathan would take him for a walk later, but for now, he was enjoying the time with his family.

"It was a good idea to go early. It's getting hot out there," said Grace as the four sat at the kitchen table eating turkey sandwiches. The beer was consumed in big gulps, and their conversation got more amusing throughout the lunch, with Adam, the family comedian, recounting some escapades he and his friends carried out earlier in the summer.

When it was time for them to go, Nathan said, "You guys are the best." He hugged his little sister, lifting her off the ground, and gave Adam a man-hug with the requisite three quick pats on the back. "Thanks so much for showing up. See you tomorrow night at Pop's party."

Grace was at the kitchen sink cleaning the dishes, and Nathan hugged her, too. "You know, you're, like, the best sister ever," Nathan said. "I'm going to try and get out of this funk. Hannah isn't over necessarily. It isn't over till it's over. So, I'm going to go on with my life and hope for the best. What else can I do?"

"True that," said Grace. "Nick and I want to have you out to the house for dinner soon. Let me know what works in the next couple of weeks."

"That'd be great," said Nathan. "Hang here for a minute before you go. I'm going to go get Cooper."

Nathan went outside and saw the roofers were working on the side of the house. The foreman on the job had told him they were just going to do the staging and prep work and wait for the storm to pass before tearing off the existing roof. Nathan gave the crew a casual wave and turned to the back yard.

As he rounded the corner of the house, his heart stopped. Cooper was gone. Nathan ran to the long lead and found that the dog's collar was still attached to the rope. He must have pulled his head through the collar. Cooper had never done that before, and Nathan was dumbstruck as to why this happened today. Suddenly, a high-pitched sound came from the side of the yard. The roofers were sawing the metal roofing material. Nathan bolted to where they were set up with sawhorses and screamed at them to stop.

"Did you see my dog? Did you see him run off? Brown dog, about eighty pounds?" Nathan yelled at the two men, who were wearing over-the-head ear protection.

"Saw him when we got here," said one of the men, walking to investigate the back yard. "But no, didn't see him run off. Probably would have noticed if he'd come this way."

"Can you quit the sawing for a while? He gets freaked out by high-pitched noises, and he won't come back if it's still going on," said Nathan. He frantically scanned the perimeter for signs of the dog.

"Yeah, we're pretty much done for today, but you realize we have to cut every day, so you're going to have to make arrangements for the dog," said the foreman.

"Right now, I've got to find him," Nathan said. Thinking Cooper probably ran toward the creek, Nathan trotted to the embankment and began shouting. "COOPER, HERE, BOY. C'MON, COOPER." He did his usual whistle for the dog and followed it with more shouting. Nothing.

Panic began to rise in Nathan's body. Cooper had bolted without his collar. If anyone found him, they would not know who to call. Cooper had an implanted microchip, but if someone found him, they'd have to know to take him to a veterinarian or shelter to have him identified. Sometimes, though, the local police got calls about missing dogs and helped the owners find them. Nathan ran back to his house, where he found Grace.

"Is Cooper gone?" Grace asked. "I heard you yelling."

"Yeah, I have to go find him. He hasn't really taken off far since I moved here. I don't know which direction he may have gone. The noise is crazy from the saws. I can't believe I didn't think about it when we were having lunch. I'm so pissed at myself. I'm going to call the police and report him missing. He doesn't have his collar—it's still connected to the lead," said Nathan.

"No! That sucks. Make the call," said Grace. "I'll call Nick and tell him what's up—Kendall and Adam, too. And I'll make some signs and go put them up around town and call the local vets and shelters and ask them to be on the lookout. Oh, and I'll post something on Facebook. The quicker we get people aware he's missing, the better. And as soon as we find him, call the invisible fence people! There's a brochure on your table."

"Thanks, Grace, perfect," Nathan said, dialing the number of the local police. After reporting the missing dog, Nathan told Grace he would take the car and go start looking. He knew from prior experience what this could mean. Hours could be lost searching for the dog. He hoped Cooper had stayed on the roads instead of wandering into the forest. The enormous state forest was close by and would be impossible to search. And with the storm heading up the coast, time was not on his side. He grabbed the framed photo Hannah had given him as he left the house.

Nathan drove with the windows rolled down, calling for his dog. Whenever he saw a homeowner outside, he stopped to show them the picture of Cooper and give them his phone number. He figured Cooper could have run off at any time, but he had likely wiggled out of his collar when the sawing began, which couldn't have been more than two hours ago. *Two hours isn't very long. I'll find him.*

Forty

Hannah woke up midmorning on Friday with a fierce hangover. *Not worth it.* She dragged herself off the sofa and made some coffee. She had no idea if or when Travis had come home, but he was not in the apartment.

Hannah's flight, scheduled to leave late afternoon, was delayed, then delayed again. Once onboard, four hours late, Hannah settled in to sleep but found she could not. The plane finally landed at Boston's Logan Airport after one o'clock in the morning. She was exhausted from the past two weeks of travel and having to be "on" for so long. She would enjoy chilling for a few days at Sara's.

After disembarking, Hannah paused to watch the CNN news on a monitor in the terminal. Agitated reporters said the Massachusetts governor had declared a state of emergency and had activated the National Guard troops in preparation for the hurricane. Weather reports featuring "once in a century" storms usually struck Hannah as overly dramatic, but a state of emergency *was* a rather big deal.

Hannah proceeded to the baggage claim area and took a seat to check her phone until the bags came through. Her phone was dead, and she had absent-mindedly packed her charger in her checked suitcase. But soon enough the luggage carousel began to beep, and piles of luggage appeared. Hannah dragged her bag to the public transportation center but then, thoroughly beat, reversed her steps and entered the taxi stand.

By the time she reached Sara's apartment, it was nearly three o'clock in the morning. Dropping her bags in the hall, she flopped on the guest bed and passed out.

HANNAH SLEPT THE sleep of the dead and came to consciousness a little before noon. The first thing she did was search through her bag looking for her phone charger. As soon as it powered up, a flurry of *ping ping pings* began, and dozens of text message bubbles appeared. She hoped none of them were urgent. She hated that she and the rest of the world were so dependent on immediate communication. *I'll have to have some coffee before I deal with these.*

She made the coffee and sat at Sara's kitchen table. Scrolling through her phone, she saw that the first text was from her mom checking to see how she was doing. There were texts from Nathan, Molly, Sara (saying she was staying at Aaron's that night and would not be home when Hannah arrived), and some other friends. They were mostly about the storm. Everyone was semi-panicked. She froze when she read the one from Lea.

Today 9:16 AM

Lea: Hey, I wanted to let you know. Cooper is missing. He took off yesterday. Nathan's been looking for him night and day.

Oh god, Nathan must be a wreck. She reread his text. It mentioned nothing about Cooper, so he must have written it before the dog took off. She texted him.

me: I heard about Cooper. Any news?

She waited for a response, but none came. She phoned him, and it went straight to voice mail.

Hannah tried Lea, and her phone, too, went straight to voice mail. Chris answered on the first ring and told her he was meeting Lea at his in-laws, who, fortunately, owned a generator.

"There is no way I'm experiencing a possible multiday electrical outage with three kids," he said. He told Hannah he had seen Nathan just that morning, and Cooper still wasn't home. Nathan was searching for the dog obsessively.

"Why doesn't he answer my calls or texts?" Hannah asked.

"On top of everything else, he lost his phone in the creek last night," said Chris. "I'll keep you posted if I hear anything. We will be over in Moretown till the storm passes. I hope he finds Cooper . . . such a sweet dog. The kids are really upset about it."

Hannah said goodbye and hung up. Her brain was on fire. Cooper had been gone overnight. Nathan must be devastated. She opened her laptop and shot him an email asking him to call her. Hannah stood. Her heart was now racing along with her brain. God, she wanted a shower. Instead, Hannah hurriedly repacked her suitcase and headed out of the apartment.

Forty-One

The governor has declared a state of emergency on Saturday to ensure that Vermont is prepared as a strong hurricane moves up the East Coast. The storm is expected to hit the state with heavy rains, high winds, and a lot of power outages Sunday into Monday morning.

The governor's office said the National Guard is on state active duty and ready to help as needed. The state's emergency management operations center also is opening at 7 a.m. Sunday.

"The important thing is we want people to prepare themselves," said Juanita Morris, director of Vermont Emergency Management. "That includes stocking up on non-perishable food, water, flashlights and batteries, and knowing your escape routes. Just be ready —hunker down for the day, for the night, and just use common sense."

Nathan listened intently to the radio Saturday morning. Reports of the impending storm were all over the airwaves. He had barely slept, but when he did get out of bed, he received a tip-off on Facebook, thanks to Grace's post, that a dog fitting Cooper's description was found in Morrisville, about thirteen miles north of Waterbury. Nathan could not believe Cooper would roam that far, but he was anxious to check it out. Driving north on Route 100 to the house where he hoped to find his dog, he scanned the roadside, as he had been doing for the past twenty-four hours.

Before Nathan adopted Cooper, the dog had been brought to the shelter because he had been wandering the streets of sub-urban Chicago. The shelter permitted prospective pet adopters to bring home a pet on a trial basis to see if the animal was a good fit for their household. The staff at the shelter adored Cooper and provided Nathan with a touching letter that a previous would-be family had written when they were forced to return Cooper after a test weekend. The letter was written by a young boy who had cried hard when the family came to exchange Cooper for another dog. *I love Cooper so much*, said the boy, *but he keeps taking off trying to catch squirrels, and my dad doesn't want to go find him all the time.*

Nathan's experience had taught him to never, ever trust the dog. Between being frightened of certain sounds and loving chasing squirrels, deer, and rabbits, Cooper had developed a bad track record of bolting unexpectedly. But this was the longest he had ever been gone.

The previous evening, Nathan had driven, walked, and biked all over Waterbury. He had no idea where the dog could have gone but could not stop looking. He experienced a sinking sensation in the pit of his stomach every time he considered his buddy lost forever. At one point in the evening, while it was still light out, he had followed tracks near the creek for about a mile before they disappeared into the woods. The tracks could have belonged to any animal, and he knew they probably weren't Cooper's. While hiking up a steep embankment next to the creek, Nathan had dropped his phone into the rushing water. He could not believe his bad luck.

Being without a phone made him feel even more helpless in his search for his dog, so he had driven to the pharmacy in town as soon as it opened to purchase a burner phone. It took some time to get the phone working, and he made his first call to Grace, one of the few numbers he knew by heart. His next call was to the police department to inform them of his revised phone number. He wondered if the individual who took his call even took down the information. The whole state was in a frenzy because of the approaching storm.

Nathan arrived at the Morrisville house and jumped out of the car. As he approached the house, a man came out to greet him.

"You here about the dog?" he asked, continuing to walk by Nathan toward the side of the yard. "I have him out back here." Nathan followed the man into the back yard. There was a dog tied to the deck railing. Besides being brown, the dog did not resemble Cooper in the least.

"That's not him," said Nathan.

You know, come to think about it, this might be my neighbor's dog," said the man. "I just saw the flyer and saw the dog and thought he might be yours."

The guy was nice enough, but Nathan was livid. He managed to suppress his outrage at this person for wasting his time. He mumbled a "thank you" and jumped back in his car to continue his search.

Driving back to Waterbury, Nathan cursed himself for not keeping a record of Hannah's phone number—or anyone else's, for that matter. He figured she was still out West and presumed she was trying to at least text him. *Surely she knows about the storm. What could she do anyway?* He wished he could talk to her. She loved Cooper and would be the sympathetic ear he needed right now.

Hungry, Nathan stopped at Lexi's Diner for a quick lunch. The place was packed with patrons chattering about the coming storm.

"They're saying the ground is already so soaked it can't handle any more rain. There's definitely going to be flooding," said a man sitting at the counter.

"More damn water in my basement," said his companion. "We're going to lose power. There'll be downed trees for sure."

"Hey, everyone," hollered Nathan above the din of the crowd. "Can I have your attention for a minute. Sorry to bother, but I'm looking for my lost dog. He's a big, brown lab mix. Long hair. He's been gone for a day, and with the storm coming tomorrow, I'm worried about him. I put a flyer in the entry. If any of you see him, I sure would appreciate you getting in touch." He gestured to the front of the restaurant. "That's it. Thanks."

"Sure," shouted a waitress in reply. "We'll be on the lookout." A general roar of consensus followed, and the diners returned to their previous conversations.

"That's rough," said a woman standing next to Nathan, waiting for a table. "I'm sorry to hear that. I hope he turns up. Is that him?" The woman pointed to the flyer on the bulletin board.

"Yup, that's Cooper. He ran off yesterday without his collar. I've been looking all over town, but nothing."

"You poor thing," she said. "I'll keep my eyes peeled." She took out a paper and pen and wrote down Nathan's information.

Nathan exited the diner and saw Tom, the leader of his mountain rescue team, in the parking lot speaking to a woman.

"Hey, I've been looking for you." Tom ended his conversation and jogged to Nathan. "We're having a coordination meeting at four o'clock in front of the storm."

"Man, I forgot to call you. Sorry. I lost my phone and all of my contacts with it," said Nathan. "Also, lost Cooper, my dog. I've been looking for him since yesterday."

"Oh shit, sorry to hear that," said Tom. Nathan filled him in on the situation and assured Tom he would attend the afternoon meeting.

"With the expected flooding, we're going to need the swift water rescue equipment loaded and ready for dispatch," said Tom.

"Got it, no problem," said Nathan, for the first time seriously considering the approaching storm's impact on the town. He had been so concerned about Cooper, his participation as a rescue team member had completely slipped his mind. "I'll see you at the fire station at four."

NATHAN RETURNED HOME to find the bowl of dog food untouched in the humane trap that he had borrowed from Grace. Sighing, he opened his unlocked front door and proceeded straight to his computer. He needed to respond to some emails for work, which he'd completely neglected. Happy to see an email from Hannah, Nathan tapped out a response.

Hey Hannah, so good to hear from you. Cooper ran off yesterday afternoon . . . Around one o'clock—I think he got spooked by a loud noise and slipped out of his collar in my back yard. I've been searching for more than 24 hours. I called the police and put up signs and put a notice on Facebook, but nothing has panned out. I got a humane trap and set it up in my yard. I put in the toy you gave him and his food. Hoping he'll make his way home, and I'm scared I'll miss him if I'm not here. But can't be here as well as out searching for him.

Everybody's freaked out about the storm around here. To top it off I lost my phone—sorry I didn't call you, but I lost my contacts with my phone—I never wrote down your number. Or anyone else's. I got a Trac phone until I can get another real one so you can call me on it. The number is 802-555-5513.

This afternoon I've got a rescue meeting to get prepped for the storm, and then I'm going to my folks in Richmond for my grandfather's 80th birthday party tonight. I don't really feel like a party, but it's Pop and we've been planning it for months and the weather is fine tonight.

I miss you and hope you're doing well. How are things in Denver?

Forty-Two

Hannah waved at her mom's car from the platform of the Newton Highlands train station.

"Thanks so much for picking me up," Hannah said as she jumped into the car and leaned over to kiss her mother. "The Green Line was ridiculously slow today. And on a Saturday. Get your shit together, Boston." She glanced down at the phone in her hand. An obsession with the device started after she had read Nathan's email. Every buzz, every vibration, she needed to hold it, checking it constantly.

"Wow, you're wired. No problem picking you up, though I was surprised when you called."

"I need to get my car from your place. I'm going to Vermont. Lea told me Cooper is lost and Nathan is a wreck," Hannah said.

"No! Cooper! That's awful. Probably not a great idea to drive in this weather. Can't you wait until after the storm?"

"The forecast says it's not going to start raining until tomorrow. I want to help search for him."

"I bet. Poor guy. But I still think it's a bad idea to drive today; there could be high winds, trees in the road. Molly's not home. Her power could be out."

"Stop it, please." She looked at her mother in exasperation. "Nathan's right there. Lea and Chris. I'll be fine."

At the house, Hannah shot out of her mother's car, made a bathroom stop, lifted her keys from the hook by the door, yelled goodbye, and headed to her car.

"Back so soon?" asked Elizabeth when Hannah appeared moments later back in the kitchen.

"My battery's dead," she spat angrily. "I must have left an interior light on. I need a jump. Where's Daddy?"

"Dad ran to the store, but he should be back in about a half hour," said Elizabeth. "Maybe this is a sign you shouldn't go."

"MOM!" roared Hannah.

"YOU'RE LUCKY IT'S full of gas," Hannah's father said, gathering the jumper cables after the engine came to life. "Don't, under any circumstances, stop the engine unless you're somewhere you can get another jump."

"Thanks, Daddy," Hannah said, hugging her father. "I was extra mean to Mom this afternoon because she doesn't want me to drive with the storm coming. Maybe you can keep her calm till I get there?"

"You bet. She and your sister are worriers. You, my dear, are a warrior. Just be careful and call her when you get there. I'll keep her busy."

Hannah waved goodbye to her father, pulled out of the driveway, and made her way to the interstate.

"PIECE OF CAKE," Hannah said. Pulling into Molly's driveway as the sun was slipping over the mountains, she called her mom as promised. "Wasn't windy, wasn't raining. The literal calm before the storm."

"Great. Well, good luck, and keep us posted on poor Cooper," Elizabeth said.

"I will, and I'm sorry I was so mean to you before. I'm pretty stressed about Cooper. I love you." She tried to make the *I love you* sound as genuine as it felt.

"Love you too, honey."

Hannah walked right to Nathan's house. His car was not in the driveway or the garage. Near the front door was a most pitiful sight—the large humane trap with bowls of dog food and water but no Cooper. Hannah rapped on the front door, and when no one answered, she opened the door and went inside. She switched on the kitchen light and moved through the house, stunned by the disarray. "What the hell?" she whispered to herself.

Forty-Three

"Here's what we know," said Tom, bringing the rescue squad meeting to order in the Waterbury firehouse late Saturday afternoon. "This could be a total shitshow. Forecasters say there could be a boatload of rain causing extreme flooding. The ground is already saturated because of all the friggin' rain we've had this year. But the good news is, it's no longer a hurricane. As it headed up the coast, the winds have subsided, and it's been downgraded to a tropical storm."

The group of a dozen volunteers sat attentively as Tom reviewed the details of the storm and informed the group of the Incident Command System to be employed.

"We're going to be on standby starting this afternoon, so keep your phones close and your gear ready. I have no idea what we might be in for. Nathan, can you give everyone your new number—write it on the board," Tom said, directing him to the large whiteboard against the wall. "I'll dispatch teams as needed, but I'm going to be hesitant to send everyone out on a first call. I'll want to keep reserves ready. John, you will be my backup to dispatch if I'm out on a call. The National Guard is deployed, so who knows, we may not even be needed."

LEAVING THE FIREHOUSE an hour later, Nathan hurried to get to his parents in time to help with the last-minute preparations for his grandfather's party. The storm would not hit Vermont until the next day, so the family agreed the party would go on as scheduled. Most everyone attending was local, and a few relatives had already arrived from out of state.

The house was buzzing with activity when Nathan arrived, and his mom was barking out orders from her headquarters in the kitchen. Nathan helped Adam arrange tables and chairs while his sisters set the tables. The house was decorated with big poster pictures of James at various points in his life, and there was a cake iced with an edible photograph of him as a child.

Guests arrived, and soon the house was filled with much of the same gang recently seen at Grace's wedding. Besides congratulating James, all the guests could talk about was the hurricane-turned-tropical-storm headed to New England.

Nathan was chatting with his cousins when the chirp of his Trac phone rang out. He pulled the device from his pocket. "Hello," he said, eagerly knowing any call coming in on this phone would be important. "Hannah! Is that you?" Nathan walked to the front hallway of the house, where it was both quieter and the one spot where the cell service was slightly improved.

"Hi, Na . . . Han . . . . are you?"

"Hey, you're breaking up," said Nathan.

Hannah said, "It's Han . . . . ter? I'm . . . . drove . . . and . . . . . When . . . . ."

I'm at my folks. They have crappy cell service."

"Are . . . . over?" asked Hannah.

"Yeah, I'm going to stay over tonight."

"I'm . . . . . . and . . . . going to . . . . Okay?"

"Sorry, but I can't hear anything you're saying. I'll call you tomorrow morning when I have better service," Nathan said. "Sorry."

"Okay," Hannah said to no one.

"Was that Hannah?" asked Grace, walking toward her brother.

"Yes, but I couldn't hear her. The service here sucks," said Nathan.

"Duh, why don't you call her from the landline?"

"It was good to hear her voice. I'll call her back tomorrow. Besides, she's in Denver on a Saturday night. Probably going out with Traaavisss." They returned to the party in the living room. "Looks like Adam is getting ready to show the video."

Adam stood before the assembled family members next to the big-screen television. James was seated in a comfortable chair, front and center.

"Okay, quiet, everyone." Adam paused while the crowd grew silent. "Pop, for the last six months, I've been working with everyone present today to put together a special gift for your eightieth birthday. I know, I know, for the past thirty years, you've been insisting you don't want any damn presents, but I think you're going to like this one. Hey, Nathan, hit the lights, please."

Adam picked up the remote and turned on the big-screen TV. An instrumental jazz tune filled the room as a single picture of James as a toddler came into focus on the screen. What followed were video clips of his children, grandchildren, extended family, and friends, all telling stories and sharing their feelings about James. Interspersed with the video clips were both sweet and funny tributes.

The video concluded with a clip of James dancing with his wife, Anna, at Kristy and Connor's wedding about five years prior. As he watched, James held his handkerchief to his face. There wasn't a dry eye in the room.

"You're killing me," shouted James with a broad smile on his face. Rising, he walked to his grandson and wrapped Adam in a hug. "Thank you, son," he said. "That was the best present I could ever hope to receive. Such a wonderful reminder of how lucky I've been in my life." James turned to the rest of the guests and shouted out, "Time for cake!"

Forty-Four

The mild patter of raindrops against Molly's house woke Hannah early Sunday morning, and her eyes adjusted to the dull light streaming through the window. *It's beginning. Poor Cooper. Where are you?*

Still dressed in her pajamas, Hannah pulled on Molly's rain boots and raincoat and took an umbrella from the mudroom closet. She hurried across the driveway toward Nathan's house. The animal trap was empty but for the soggy bowl of dog food and saturated chew toy. Inside, there was no evidence of Nathan having been there since the last time she checked. He was probably still at his parents' house, continuing the visit with his cousins and family. Maybe he was out searching for Cooper? Although impatient to see him, she did not want to interrupt his family time by texting him that she was in Vermont. He would likely rush back. She would have to wait until he came back to his house. But what if he came back and left again without her seeing him? Finding a discarded manila envelope, she wrote on the back of it in bold print with a permanent marker: *Nathan, I'm here—over at Molly's. If I'm not there, I'm out looking for Cooper. Call me. Love, Hannah*

She looked around the house, wondering where the best place to leave the message was. Damn stainless refrigerators and their inability to hold a magnet. She placed the note on the kitchen table in plain sight.

Opening the kitchen door, she scanned the perimeter for the dog as a gust of wind and rain pelted her face. The rain drenched her as she ran back to Molly's house. Now all she could do was wait. Wait and worry. Worry and wait. She was, it turned out, a worrier after all.

She desperately wanted to go out in search of Cooper, but it was raining so hard she could barely see out the window. The faint outline of the treehouse in the back yard was visible. Would it survive the storm intact? It would be its first test of resiliency.

An hour later, Hannah still lay on the couch, hugging her pillow to her chest and looking out the window at the pouring rain and blowing trees. She listened absently to the news on the radio. State Police warned residents to stay off the roads. Thankfully, Molly, Ted, and the kids were safely tucked away in Canada and would not have to ride out the storm here. Still, she wanted to cry and wondered if a few minutes of all-out sobbing might break the tension gripping her mind and body. Pulling herself from the brink of weeping, she opened her laptop and began another Google search of how to find a lost dog. She had already read dozens of Humane Society tips and imagined Nathan had done his best, but perhaps more could be done.

Hannah's walks through the town of Waterbury all summer had given her the sense of a tight community. Surely someone from this town had saved Cooper and brought him into their home. But why hadn't they responded to the signs all over town, or called the police or one of the shelters? She read on one of the websites that some people did not like to take animals to shelters for fear they would be put to sleep. But everyone was connected to everyone in Waterbury in lots of different ways: schools, work, church, volunteering, sports. She knew if the dog was still in the town, eventually, someone would talk to someone else and figure out it was Nathan's lost dog. *If* Cooper was still in town. The panic returned with a gnawing in her stomach. What if someone picked him up and relocated him? Hannah switched her search to "lost dog finds its way home." The search engine announced, "About 3,346,000 results."

Hannah spent an hour reading the heart-wrenching stories about dogs lost in the woods on family camping trips, only to return two years later; dogs lost in storms that returned several months later; dogs that never came home; and dogs that got adopted by other families, which refused to return them to the original owners.

"That certainly didn't help," said Hannah to herself. She was now more worried than before she had started down the Google rabbit hole.

"MORNIN'," SAID NATHAN. His mother was seated at the kitchen table, reading the newspaper. He slowly and carefully took the last few steps of the stairs.

"Ha, good morning!" Kerri said cheerfully, looking at the clock. "Almost noon. You look a little rough. Coffee's ready." Kerri rose to pour Nathan a cup of coffee as he took a seat at the old farm table. Everyone under thirty-five had stayed up late drinking and talking. All the cousins were still sleeping in on the beds and floors of the second floor.

"Are you taking off soon?" she asked, taking the seat next to her son.

Nathan ran his hand through his hair and took a sip of coffee. "My plan for the day is to take a bunch of flyers and distribute them around town and wait to see if I get any alerts from mountain rescue. It's already raining though, which will dampen my efforts." He said the word "dampen" with a sarcastic tone and slumped back in the chair.

"What can I do? I've been so wrapped up in this party that I haven't done anything to help you find Cooper."

"There doesn't seem to be much to do. I've called all the shelters, I've hung flyers, we're all over social media. Maybe Cooper just wanted to return to a life on the streets. Somebody probably has him. Someone sees a lovable dog without a collar, and they presume he's unwanted."

"I don't know about that. Don't give up hope; it's only been a couple of days."

"Yup. Lost Hannah. Lost Cooper. Life back here sucks so far," he said, slamming his chair away from the table and heading upstairs.

"Nathan!" his mom said as her son trudged away.

Forty-Five

"Excuse me," a damp Hannah said as she approached the front desk of the municipal office building, which housed the Waterbury Police Department.

"Can I help you?" asked a uniformed officer gruffly, not looking in her direction. He was preoccupied with a radio transmitter he held in his hand.

"I'm sorry to bother," she said. "I'm looking for a lost dog and wondering if anyone reported finding one."

"Not our biggest priority right now," said the officer, still not looking at Hannah.

"Okay, again, sorry," she said, turning to leave.

"Hey, wait a sec. We did get a call a while ago," he said, pausing to look on the desk covered in documents. "Yeah, a guy called, found a dog." He scribbled on a Post-it Note and handed it to Hannah, looking at her for the first time. "Here's the number."

"Thank you. Thanks so much," she said, taking the scrap of paper.

"Be careful out there. You shouldn't be driving. Go home," said the officer, returning to the radio.

Hannah could not believe she finally had a lead. Standing in the vestibule of the town office, she punched in the number on her phone and anxiously waited. The phone rang. And rang. And rang. "Hey, this is Justin. Leave a message, or you know, text!" *BEEP*.

"Hi, um, hi, this is Hannah. My number is 617-555-0899. I'm looking for a dog, and the Waterbury police told me you might have him. Please give me a call back as soon as you can." Hannah then texted the same information to the number.

The rain assaulted her as she ran to her car. She sat with her arms wrapped around the steering wheel and her head resting on her arms. She felt her stomach swoop from hope to despair as she waited for an answer to her call and text. But there was nothing. No call back, no text back. *What the hell! ANSWER ME!* She lifted her head and beat the steering wheel with both hands. *Frickin' Justin.*

She drove slowly through the wet and puddling streets of Waterbury back to Molly's. Once again, she walked to Nathan's only to find no evidence of him or Cooper.

She considered trying to get in touch with Nathan but again hesitated. She wanted to find Cooper and bring him to Nathan. She fantasized about their reunion, envisioning him standing forlornly in his front yard as she ran to him with the dog and jumped into his arms. The fantasy stopped after their passionate kiss.

Returning to the couch, Hannah turned on the television and waited for Justin to call back.

About halfway through the first Lord of the Rings movie, Hannah's phone buzzed with an incoming text.

Justin: Sorry wrong number don't have a dog

Hannah's heart sank. *Wrong number.* How could that be? She rummaged through the pocket of Molly's raincoat and found the scrap of paper from the Waterbury officer. She compared it to the number she had entered in her phone for "Justin."

It was not a mistake; she had not misdialed. *Damn damn damn.*

Hannah studied the scrap of paper and thought maybe, just maybe, the number that looked like a 7 was actually a 1. She punched in the revised number, and once again, the call went unanswered. She left a message and then sent a text, hoping whoever it was would at least get back to her and let her know one way or the other if she had contacted the right home.

"HI, MOM, HOW'S it going?" Hannah asked as she continued to man her command post from Molly's couch.

"Lotta rain. Nothing too crazy, it just keeps coming. What are you doing?"

"Just waiting. I have a lead on Cooper. I got a number from the police of someone who found a dog, but when I called, it was the wrong number. The cops are pretty busy with the storm and weren't super helpful, but I'm hoping since someone found a dog in Waterbury, that the dog is Cooper and he's safe.

"Anyway, now I'm sitting here waiting and watching TV. I'm so frustrated. It's going to get dark soon, and it's so dismal out. Hey—I've got another call coming in. I'll call you back."

"Hello?" Her heart pounded with anticipation as she picked up the incoming call.

"Hi, I got your message about a lost dog?" said a man's voice. "Is he big and brown and super friendly?"

Forty-Six

Nathan drove slowly through the heavy rain south on the interstate, listening to the increasingly alarming weather reports. Obsession over his lost dog ruling his day, he stopped at the grocery store to hang a flyer on the community bulletin board. He desperately wanted to drive to Burlington to get a proper replacement phone but needed to stay close to town in case he got called up for an emergency.

Pulling into his garage, his Trac phone suddenly buzzed with an incoming text message. It was from Tom. Since his temporary phone did not have app capabilities, it was a screenshot of the emergency notification for a rescue call:

14:26:51 Sun Aug 28
Family of 4 trapped in car
Rising Water
Route 17 east of Cross Valley Rd
Waitsfield

Heart thumping, he tapped out the required response: *On my way to the scene.*

Before leaving, Nathan ran around the yard to see if Cooper was anywhere in sight. His last stop was the pathetic and empty humane trap and a soggy bowl of food. A despondent Nathan reversed his car out of the garage and headed to Waitsfield.

TOM AND THREE other responders—Sam, Mateo, and Gary—were at the site when Nathan exited his car a half hour later. The five squad members were briefed by state police as they huddled under a tree. Within view, the sedan rested in the middle of the road on a small rise, unable to go forward or back, as the rushing water was getting deeper and deeper every minute. A water rescue would be required, for which the police were unprepared. The parents of the two young children had a phone and were able to communicate with the first responders.

"We've got this," said Tom to the state police officer, both now standing in the pouring rain. Grateful for the rescue team's assistance, the officer left the scene to go to another storm-induced incident.

The team soon realized extracting the family from the car would be difficult. The driver of the vehicle had made a wise decision in stopping where he did. The car appeared to be stable as the rushing floodwaters surrounded the car.

"Under no circumstances leave the car or attempt to drive through the water," Tom said into his phone to the man at the wheel. "Doing so could cause the car to float and get you into a much more serious situation. Stay put, and we will get to you. Try and be patient a little while longer. We want to get you out as safely and quickly as we can."

The family was cold and uncomfortable, but not in any imminent danger for the time being. They had already been trapped in the car for more than two hours and were likely hungry and irritable.

"I can't imagine being trapped in a car for so long with kids," said Nathan. His mind flashed to Nora and Owen.

The first action the team took was to toss a throw bag attached to a rope to the car. They threaded personal flotation devices down the rope through an open car window and instructed the family to put them on. Nathan and Mateo, secured by ropes, then attempted to wade out to the car multiple times but were forced back due to the power of the water. While the team could likely make it to the car, they were not confident they would be able to get the group to safety walking through the roaring water. They determined the situation would require a rescue by boat.

The team set to work. They loaded the Zodiac boat, and Mateo and Nathan positioned themselves downstream with throw ropes. Gary and Tom would pilot the Zodiac to the car and get the family out and onto the boat. They would transport them to dry land, where Sam was waiting with an ATV, and Sam would shuttle them to the waiting emergency medical services vehicle.

Gary and Tom had to paddle against the current of the floodwaters to reach the car, but they expertly maneuvered the craft toward the vehicle in the pouring rain. Gary pulled the mother and little boy through the window first, and they paddled to Sam. The task was repeated to evacuate the father and little girl. Fortunately, although extremely time consuming, the rescue via boat and ATV worked out just as planned, and the entire family was safely in the medical vehicle before dark. The family, visibly shaken, was incredibly grateful to the rescue team members.

"I was so brave," said the four-year-old girl to Nathan. "Mama said I was so brave that I get to have candy for dinner." He smiled, thinking how much Nora and Owen were also obsessed with candy. He missed those kids.

With the rescue now behind them, Nathan was tired and anxious for some dry clothes and his warm bed. The rain had weakened by the time they arrived at the firehouse. Volunteers packed the large brick building—firefighters, police, paramedics, the spouses of the first responders—all busy setting things up. Another dozen town residents, who had fled their homes, stood around sharing stories of their individual flood experiences. Nathan led the family to the large open room outfitted with tables and chairs as well as cots and blankets. A paramedic appeared and escorted the family to the makeshift medical room.

A drenched Nathan made a beeline for the food. He was hungry, and a good meal trumped dry clothes at the moment. Gary joined him, and the two men gorged on the homemade pasta and salad provided by volunteers.

"That was intense," said Gary between mouthfuls. "But I'm surprised we haven't had more calls."

"Yeah. I wonder what's going on statewide. It can't be good. We should ask the chief," Nathan said, pointing to the fire chief. Nathan and Gary were just finishing up as Tom and Sam entered the room.

"Sorry, guys, I have some good news and bad news. Good news is we haven't had any more calls. The bad news is that the roads are flooded all the way to Waterbury. We don't think they are washed out, just unpassable at this point. It looks like we're bunking here tonight until the roads are open," Tom said. "Should be able to get out tomorrow."

"Shit," said Gary.

"Damn," said Nathan, throwing his napkin on the table and falling back into his chair. He pulled out his Trac phone to call Hannah. Without ringing, the call went straight to voice mail. He tossed the phone on the table and closed his eyes.

Forty-Seven

Hannah ran from her car in the pouring rain and banged on the door of the Randall Street home. Earsplitting barking came from behind the closed door. Her spirit collapsed. *Cooper doesn't bark. It's not him.*

A man, about her age, opened the door, holding the collar of a still barking yellow lab. "Hi. Come on in. What a mess out there," he said.

"Cooper!" Hannah cried as she entered the house. Nathan's dog stood calmly a few feet from the door, wagging his tail. "Oh, my god, I can't believe it. Where have you been? Nathan is going to be so happy. Where did you find him?" Hannah knelt on the floor, hugging the dog and rubbing him all over. Cooper jumped up and began chasing his tail, running in circles, and then plopped onto Hannah, who was still on the floor.

"He sure is happy to see you. My wife and I picked him up along Route 100 near the middle school this morning right after it started raining. He was just standing there looking around as if he had no idea which way to go. I called him, and he jumped right in my truck. He seemed to be happy to be out of the rain. He has no collar, so I figured I'd take him to the shelter, but they are closed on Sundays, so I called the police."

"Thank you so much for picking him up. I'm Hannah."

"Mike," he said, extending his hand, which Hannah shook.

"I was so afraid he might get hit by a car. He slipped out of his collar and took off on Friday, and we've been so worried. You're such a good boy, yes you are, such a sweet boy," she said, rubbing his belly as he lay on his back.

"You didn't have to come out in the storm," said Mike. "You could have waited till tomorrow. He's a good boy, and he's getting along great with Bubba here."

Hannah looked at the yellow dog, who wagged his tail at the sound of his name. She reached over and gave him a little pat.

"Thanks, Bubba," she said. "I haven't been able to sleep since he took off. It's not like I've been doing anything else in this rain but worrying about him. Things are insane out there. The roads are getting pretty flooded."

"Yeah, one of our neighbors told us we should move our cars to higher ground in case the street floods, so we did that a little while ago," said Mike. "Seemed like overkill, but we just moved in last fall, so we just did what he said."

"MIKE, MIKE, come here," shouted a woman's voice from a distance. The man turned and rushed toward a door that appeared to lead to the basement.

"Oh, hell," he yelled. "Shit."

Hannah looked down into the basement, where a woman stood up to her ankles in water. At the same time, a toddler sitting in a highchair in the kitchen began to wail. And, as if on cue, the yellow lab began to bark.

"Go help her. I'll . . . I'll watch the baby," said Hannah.

"Thank you." Mike vanished down the stairs.

Hannah went to the kitchen, Cooper at her heels, and introduced herself to the child, who was now calm and banging her spoon on the plate. "Hello there," Hannah said, using her most singsong happy voice. "What's that?" Hannah pointed to the food on the tray in front of the child, a girl about two years old.

"Is it mac and cheese?" The little girl promptly held out her spoon to offer Hannah a taste. "No, thank you. You show me how you eat it."

"Hi, I'm Ginny," a woman's voice said abruptly. "That's Annika. Do you mind watching her for a sec? Our basement is flooding. We have to get the stuff off the floor." Ginny's face was drawn and pale, and she kept looking behind her toward the basement. Hannah realized that she was—understandably—checking out the random stranger her husband had left with her child.

"Of course, go do what you need to do. We're good here," said Hannah. She was happy to do whatever she could to help these Cooper saviors.

When Annika finished her meal, Hannah lifted her out of the chair and washed her slimy hands in the sink. Thankfully, the child didn't fear this stranger, and she let Hannah hold her without complaint.

"Look, Annika, it's raining outside," she said, holding the girl up to peer out the kitchen window at the driving rain. Hannah was shocked to see that the entire back yard, lit by a floodlight, was a pool of water. She went to the front of the house and, although it was nearly dark, she could see the road filled with water. *This is getting real.*

Rushing to the basement door, she yelled to sound an alarm. "Hey, you guys, the back yard is full of water, and so is the road out front."

Mike walked up the basement stairs, carrying a large plastic bin. "I need to get as much as I can up to the second floor. Could you bring Annika upstairs and put her in her crib with some toys and give us a hand?" he asked, nodding his head to the staircase in the living room.

"Absolutely. You might want to bring this computer up there too," said Hannah. She pointed at the computer on a desk in the corner.

"There's no way it'll get this high," Ginny said, scanning the living room. "I don't think we need to move things from this level."

"Better safe than sorry," Mike said. He began to disconnect the computer and printer.

The three of them hurriedly made trips up and down the stairs, moving photo albums, papers, and mementos from the first floor and basement. They were all astonished by the suddenness of the rising water. Ginny was frantically pacing. Mike stayed silent as he took the stairs two at a time. Hannah used her best judgment, grabbing whatever she thought would be essential to save.

In the midst of ferrying items up and down, an urgent banging came from the front door. All three rushed to the front of the house to see a fireman already entering.

"Folks, I'm here to let you know we're experiencing some serious flooding from all this rain," he said, stepping farther into the house. "There is a car parked on the road out front, and we're recommending you go ahead and move it to higher ground."

"We already moved our cars, but our basement is flooding. This is ridiculous. Why is this happening?" an increasingly terrified Ginny asked.

Hannah, holding Annika, said, "That's my car. I should move it."

"Some people are evacuating, and you're in a very low area. The river is cresting, and it's happening pretty fast. You might want to consider getting yourselves out as well. You can go to the Congregational Church or to family or friends. It's going to get worse," warned the fireman.

"The water is up to my knees in the basement . . . Should we do something about the electricity? Water might get to the electric panel," said Mike.

"You'll want to switch off the main power to the house," yelled the fireman as he departed. Mike gave Hannah and Ginny flashlights and went to the basement and flipped the switch, putting the house in near total darkness. The women switched on their flashlights as Mike came up from the cellar with his headlamp illuminated.

"Shit. The water is about three feet deep down there now. What else should we bring upstairs?" he asked, looking around the first floor. "Your mom's paintings?"

"We should leave, Mike," said Ginny. "Let's do one more sweep, get Annika and Bubba, and get out of here. We can go to the church, then call Rachel."

"Okay, all right." He turned to Hannah. "I'm so sorry, what's your name?"

"Hannah."

"Would you mind taking the dogs and heading up to Main Street? We'll meet you at the church."

"MIKE, the yard is full of water!" screamed Ginny. Mike and Hannah sprang to the front door. There was now a foot of water in the yard, reaching to the house.

Hannah looked with horror into the street at her car, which was now in a foot of water. "Jesus," she whispered to herself, realizing that in her haste to find Cooper, she had left her wallet and phone on the car seat. She sighed a heavy sigh and grabbed the back of her head with her hands. "Of course," she said to Mike. "Better put your phones and chargers in Ziploc bags. Mine's toast. I left it in my car, and now I can't get it."

Mike handed a leash and collar to Hannah and secured

Bubba with another leash. Hannah took the dogs and left through the front door. The water had, in an alarmingly short time, reached over the steps of the front porch. It was dark and still raining, but Hannah could see some other displaced home-owners making their way down the street. She walked carefully through the thigh-high water, taking slow steps, following the person just ahead of her with a lit headlamp. The dogs were do-ing a sort of swim-hop, tugging the leashes, trying to free them-selves from the bizarre and frightening situation. "Calm down, guys, calm down, almost there," Hannah said.

Fortunately, as she walked up the slight incline to Main Street, the water became shallower. At the top of the street, it was only ankle deep. Other "refugees" headed to the church. The electricity was out throughout the town, and emergency vehicles with flashing lights lined the roadway. It was an eerie scene. Scared, cold, and a little bit in shock, she and the dogs climbed the steps of the church.

A state police officer was addressing the shivering people gathered inside the dark church. "We're going to be moving everyone to the elementary school. The school has electricity and volunteers, and you can stay overnight. If you came here in a car and parked on this side of town, go ahead and head out. If you came on foot, see if you can hitch a ride with someone. Drive slow. There are police out there who will direct you."

As they began to disperse, grouping up for carpooling, Hannah approached the officer. "Can I bring the dogs to the school?"

"Yes, of course, but keep them on the leashes at all times," he said, petting Cooper's and Bubba's heads.

Hannah turned to see Mike, Ginny, and a wailing Annika enter the church.

"So glad you got here. They're moving us to the elementary school."

"Thanks for your help," said Ginny, visibly crying. "This is so friggin' crazy. We just bought the house last year. I can't believe this could happen."

"I am so sorry," said Hannah. Ginny was shaking, and Hannah wanted to comfort her, but she agreed with the frightened woman. "It is crazy, and everything is happening so fast. But I think you guys did a great job in getting things upstairs, and you are going to get through this. It sucks, though. Do you have any family around? Do you have somewhere close to go?"

"I called my friend Rachel, but she can't leave her house because her husband's not home and her kids are sleeping. And she's afraid to go out. I guess we have to go to the school for the night. They've blocked the roads coming into the Village from the north anyway."

"Let's get to the school," said Hannah. "You go with Mike and Annika, and I'll find someone to take me and the dogs."

It's like a movie. Surreal. There was something about the way the now displaced people filed into the school's lobby that reminded Hannah of a film she had seen about immigrants landing in Ellis Island. Every woman looked stunned; every man confused. If the children were not whining or crying and hanging on their parents, they were running around hyperactively, laughing with each other.

A volunteer stood in the middle of the lobby and directed people to take any available classroom for the evening for their family or group. Hannah stood in the corner, looking for Ginny and Mike, and when they appeared, they immediately walked over to Hannah.

"Hey, thanks for taking him," said Ginny. She reached out

to take Bubba's leash. "Sorry I was such a basket case before."

"You weren't. You have every right to be upset. They're telling everyone to go into the gym or a classroom for the night. There are mats to sleep on for us. There're some blankets and some provisions, but not too much—snacks and water. Like we want any more water. I haven't seen any baby stuff. How's she doing?"

"She's fine now. She's been quiet, observing all of the commotion," said Mike. "But we need to get her some dry clothes."

The three adults, one toddler, and two dogs found a vacant room. Hannah stayed with Ginny and Annika while Mike left to get sleeping mats and hopefully find some diapers. The exhausted, wet dogs picked a spot near the teacher's desk and plopped down. Hannah did not remove the leash from Cooper, so he lay with his leash attached, curled up with his new friend Bubba.

They appeared to be in a preschool or kindergarten room. "Hey, check this out," said Hannah, holding up a couple of princess dresses she found in the dress-up corner. "They might be big on her, but they're dry. Annika, do you want to wear this pretty dress?"

Ginny peeled Annika out of the wet sleeper, and the three of them commenced a game of dress-up. There were two adult costumes as well. One was the Cat in the Hat, which Hannah donned, and Ginny squeezed into a red crayon shift but skipped the crayon hat. It was wonderful to be dry again, and they took their wet clothes and hung them on the little chairs around the room.

Mike soon returned with four mats, three of which he put together near the windows and one, for Hannah, nearer to the door. "And look what I scored," he said, showing them a handful of diapers.

They had picked the right room. The children who occupied this room must have still had a nap incorporated into their day because they found several blankets and additional mats in a small closet. They doubled up the mats to make their makeshift beds more comfortable. Mike turned down the lights so they could get Annika to sleep. The child ate a banana and passed out on a cozy mat covered in blankets in quick time.

It was nearing midnight, and Hannah wanted to take the dogs out to do their business before she settled in for the evening. The thought of going back into the rain was not appealing, and when Mike offered to do the chore, Hannah gratefully accepted. While he was gone, she took her turn at the communal bathroom and went to the main room for some granola bars, a couple of apples, and a bottle of Gatorade.

She walked through the halls of the school, her long black Cat-in-the-Hat tail dragging behind her. She felt humbled by every experience of her evening, the suddenness of the flooding, the way everyone played their part to keep the community safe. She had a new appreciation for victims of natural disasters.

It was painful not to have her phone. She had spoken with her mom, and Molly was in Quebec, so they probably were not concerned about her. Anyone else would figure she just was not picking up. She regretted leaving the note for Nathan. Was he now searching for her as well as Cooper? *What a shitshow.* She reentered the darkened classroom. *And my car is probably trashed.*

Hannah settled onto her mats with three little blankets rolled up for a pillow and three others covering her body. Cooper rose and stretched and then nuzzled in beside her.

"Good night, bud." She patted him gently and fell asleep with the leash wrapped around her wrist.

Forty-Eight

Hannah's eyes flashed open from an intense dream. She had been swimming in the dream, swimming in a street stinking of sewage and fuel. *Well, that's not very original.* Looking around the dim room and processing where she was, she sat up on her mat and stretched. Mike, Ginny, and Annika, situated across the room, were also stirring. The early morning light bathed the room in a soft glow, and Hannah looked at her shorts and T-shirt hanging on a chair and hoped they were now dry enough to wear. The clock on the wall said 6:56 a.m.

Cooper did not move as she rose quietly to get her still damp clothing. Despite his unwillingness to wake, she did not want to let him out of her sight. She snuck out the door, dragging the reluctant dog behind her, and headed to the girls' bathroom.

"Good morning," said an older woman who was washing at the sink.

"Good morning," said Hannah. "Were you able to sleep last night?"

"Not much," the woman said with a sigh. "The cot was extremely uncomfortable for me. I like my own bed." She reached for the paper towels and dried her hands vigorously. "I live in Burley House, and they made us come here as a precaution. It was just . . . just a nightmare last night. I was scared. I have lived in this town all my life—never seen anything like it. But we take care of each other. We'll be okay."

"I hope so, and I hope you can get back to your own bed soon," said Hannah. "I have to get back into some normal clothes. I feel a little ridiculous in this, but it was dry." Hannah went into one of the tiny stalls and changed into her nearly dry clothes, leaving the dog loose in the bathroom. She was anxious to find Nathan and reunite him with Cooper. But she was also in need of some coffee and something to eat.

Hannah and Cooper entered the school's multipurpose room, which was buzzing with activity. She poured herself some coffee and took a bagel while listening to snippets of disturbing conversations.

"The water is dropping, and they say folks will be able to get to their homes this morning."

"It's worse than anyone imagined."

"Electricity is going to be out for weeks."

"Climate change. This is the earth fighting back."

"FEMA's at the firehouse."

"The psychiatric hospital was flooded and all the state buildings too."

"The National Guard won't let people in their houses."

Mike, Ginny, Annika, and Bubba walked into the room. Ginny had changed into her clothes. Annika was all smiles, as if her entire world had not been upended overnight.

"They have bagels and coffee," Hannah told the couple. "Did you sleep okay?"

"I felt like I was up all night," said Mike. "But I think I did get some sleep. Annika slept through the night. I want to get to the house. Have you heard anything?"

"Mixed reports," Hannah said. "Grab something to eat, and I'll find out if we can go to your house."

Hannah, hanging on to the leash attached to her only possession, Cooper, walked outside. The sky was still overcast, but it was not raining. A police officer stood in the parking lot. He was the same officer who had given her Mike's phone number.

"I found my dog," she said, simplifying the ownership issue. "Thanks for your help yesterday." The officer did not recognize Hannah at first but gradually made the connection.

"That's good. Is this him? Did you stay at the school last night? Do you live in the Village?" he asked, in rapid-fire order.

Hannah explained her evening to him, noting that her car was still on Randall Street.

"I made a poor choice in not moving it off the street. Is it okay to go back there now?"

"Pretty soon," said the officer. "The water's receding, but I have to warn you, it's a mess on Randall. And whatever you do, do not attempt to start your car. That can cause problems. If it's waterlogged, get it towed, and maybe they can get it going again."

Disheartened, Hannah thanked the officer and trotted back into the school building to explain the situation to Mike and Ginny. They were changing Annika into an outfit provided to them by a better-prepared shelter parent. Another super-prepared shelter visitor gave dog food to Mike, and he handed Hannah a bag full of kibble for Cooper.

After tidying their "bedroom," the quartet and dogs set off for the half-mile walk to the Village.

As they walked toward the downtown, nothing was remotely as dramatic as the scene they had experienced the night before. The road was dry, the houses undamaged. There was no evidence of fire and rescue personnel. Turning the corner onto Main Street told a different story. A dozen cars with flashing lights blocked the entrances to the Village. Scores of people crowded the street, gazing at the partially flooded road. The big, dark National Guard trucks lined up in front of the Fire Department building made for an ominous scene.

"C'mon, let's keep going," said Mike, continuing down Main Street. No one stopped them, and they walked toward their street, encountering only a few areas of ankle-deep water.

"Oh my god," cried Ginny as they turned onto Randall Street. The devastation was overwhelming. Debris was everywhere. Downed trees and upended bushes dotted the neighborhood. Random items were strewn about: a bike, a basketball hoop, chairs, garbage cans. The most remarkable sight was the layer of gray sludge that covered the entire landscape.

"Damn," said Mike. "This is unbelievable. It looks like it filled up like a bowl between the river and Main Street."

"That's exactly what it did," said Hannah as she headed toward her car. But the car was not in front of the house where she had parked it. The floodwaters had transported it several yards down the road. It stood facing the wrong direction, completely covered with rippled mud. She yanked several times on the door, which finally opened, revealing a disgusting smell and horrible mud-covered seats and dashboard. Her wallet and phone were on the floor of the car, covered in mud. Always the optimist, Hannah picked up the phone and attempted to turn it on. Nothing. She looked in the back seat. Thankfully, she had unloaded her suitcase at Molly's. But there on the floor, sad and peeling and melted into a coagulated mess—her vision board. The irony was not lost on her. The hopes and dreams for her future, which she had plotted and planned all summer and depicted on the poster board, obliterated. It did not matter. Her future was finally clear to her, and she no longer needed a vision board to see it.

Hannah walked with Cooper to Mike and Ginny's home,

wondering what their house must look like if the flood had thoroughly trashed her car. The steps to the front porch were gone, relocated to the side yard. Tying the already mud-covered Cooper to a post out front, Hannah stepped inside the front door.

Holy shit. The living room was a sea of mud. Everything was wet, and the stain on the walls showed just how high the water had risen, about three feet. Scattered and overturned furniture filled the space. In the kitchen, the refrigerator was tipped over and open, still filled with river water. A heavy muddy sludge covered the entire place. Every loose item was covered in mud and strewn in completely random places. Hannah picked up a stuffed animal sticky with gray silt. Sobbing came from the far end of the house, and it was not Annika.

To give them some privacy, Hannah went outside and sat on the front porch, hanging her muddy feet off the ground where the front porch steps should have been. She petted the dog as she looked at the neighbors gathered in small groups along the street. They were hugging, talking, many crying. It was a dream-like scene. Apocalyptic. She watched a woman at the house across the street using a shovel to get the mud off her porch. And the smell—the neighborhood reeked like a stagnant pond.

Hannah stood. It was about a two-mile walk to Molly's, where she could reunite Cooper with Nathan. She needed to get to a phone and call her parents to let them know she was okay. She looked up and down the street as people arrived back home to assess the damage and start on the cleanup. It would be a Herculean task to clean up just one house, let alone dozens.

Mike appeared on the porch next to her, holding a bucket. "Our friend Rachel's going to pick up Ginny, Annika, and Bubba at the church, so they're heading back," he said.

"Well then, you and I can get to work," said Hannah, looking directly at Mike's beaten face.

Once again, she tied Cooper to the post out front using a harness and, as double security, a collar and two long leashes. Hannah went in search of some supplies and found a shovel. Following the lead of the woman across the street, she began clearing a path to the house. She pulled around a large tub and started shoveling mud out of the first floor. Mike was gathering suitcases and filling them with clothes, valuables, and important papers.

After a couple of hours of back-breaking work, Hannah received some much-appreciated news. "Hey, Mike, one of your neighbors said the firehouse has some food. I'm going to go get us some."

Cooper at her side, Hannah headed back to Main Street and the firehouse. People populated the streets, some talking to each other, some shoveling mud, some openly weeping. It was one of the saddest days she had ever experienced, but the community camaraderie was incredible. She stopped in the middle of the sidewalk and peeked into her favorite brewpub, where she had enjoyed happy times with Nathan, Nora, and Owen. The floodwaters had walloped it. Chairs and tables were overturned, dishes and cutlery scattered about. Hannah's heart sank at the loss of this thriving business.

RUFF RUFF RUFF. RUFF RUFF RUFF. RUFF RUFF. Cooper frantically began barking and pulling at his leash. He nearly knocked Hannah off her feet, tugging and lurching. Cooper never barked. That was his thing, not barking. *RUFF RUFF RUFF.* He went up on his hind legs, practically on point, and peered down the sidewalk, then pulled Hannah out of the pub's vestibule and into the empty road. *RUFF RUFF RUFF.* Hannah surveyed the street, expecting to see a dog or another animal that caught Cooper's attention.

Instead, it was Nathan.

Cooper broke free of Hannah's grasp and tore down the street toward Nathan, dragging the leash behind him. Nathan was standing in the middle of the closed-off street, eating an apple and talking with a man, oblivious to the barking, running dog. Nathan glanced up just as Cooper nearly bowled him over.

"Cooper!" Nathan cried out, hugging the dog to his chest. "Where did you come from? Cooper! Good boy, I missed you. I've been looking for you everywhere." Nathan knelt on the ground, hugging the dog with both arms. "You scared me, Coop. I thought I'd never see you again. Where were you?"

"I found your dog," Hannah said in a loud voice. She casually strode toward Nathan. "You really oughta get a fence."

"Hannah?" Nathan's eyes were wide. "What the hell? What are you doing here?" He stood up and stared at her, not moving.

Hannah did not speak either, just stared back at Nathan. A lot of information was transferred in that silence. She moved into Nathan, and he drew her to him and embraced her tightly, his hands clasping her head against his chest.

"Hannah," he whispered. "Hannah." After several moments he released her and, not letting go of the leash or her shoulders, pushed her back a foot and assessed her. She was covered in gray mud from head to foot. "You look like you might have a story to tell."

"Yeah, well, Vermont has some shitty weather."

"So, what you're saying is you love me." Nathan pulled her close to him again.

"You're all right," she said, smiling. He reached down to kiss her, and she could not imagine a better feeling. It had been her pride and adherence to a rigid plan that had held her back from this man. And now here they were. No doubts. No confusion. They stayed in place for a few minutes, petting the dog, hugging, and giving each other intermittent kisses.

"Where you headed?" he asked as he wrapped his arm around her shoulder, looking over the wreckage of the downtown area.

"First, I'm going to go get some food at that there firehouse and bring you to meet the guy I spent the night with."

"Okay, I think. Then what?" asked Nathan.

"I want to check on the treehouse and see if it survived the storm. And then I'm going to need a place for a shower and a nap."

"I know a place. Thinking about staying long?"

Hannah took a step away from him, staring at the town as if she had just entered Oz. Along Main Street, scores of people filed in and out of doorways carrying shovels and wearing mud boots. People, young and old, already working to clean up their town just hours after its carnage.

"I like this place. It's pretty and the people are scrappy. Plus, I have a fence to build so that our buddy here doesn't run off." She gave Cooper a scratch on his head and turned her gaze to Nathan. "Oh, I've been meaning to tell you. I'm accepting a job offer in Montpelier with your friend Mark at that solar place. And I'm going to start a side hustle building chicken coops and sheds and playhouses and stuff. I could probably even help with this town's rebuild. So, I'm pretty sure I live here now."

Nathan stepped forward, threw his arms around her, and lifted her off the ground, squeezing her tight. Hannah's heart soared. He pulled her to his chest and nestled his face into her muddied hair as Cooper moved in, leaning against both their legs. Nathan raised his head, letting out an enormous sigh, and pressed his forehead against Hannah's, staring into her eyes. "Excellent choice. Solid decision," he whispered.

Afterword

This story is based on events from Tropical Storm Irene in Vermont. The storm started out as a hurricane for a brief stretch over North Carolina, but its winds dwindled once it made landfall. What made this storm so destructive was the rain. Irene dumped as much as eleven inches of rain in parts of Vermont in August of 2011 and caused $733 million in damage. In all, it checked in at $14.3 billion, the eighth-costliest hurricane in American history at the time. In Vermont, more than 2,400 roads, 800 homes and businesses, 300 bridges (including historic covered bridges) and a half-dozen railroad lines were destroyed or significantly damaged, according to the National Oceanic Administration Agency (NOAA).

ACKNOWLEDGMENTS

Thank you to all the people in my life who never laughed when I told them I was writing a book. You made me think I could do it.

My family bore the most from my launching a second career as an author. Thank you to my husband, Rich, who I had the good sense to marry when I was just twenty years old. Father of daughters, builder of treehouses, best veterinarian in the world. The love, respect, and appreciation I have for you is immeasurable. Your daily encouragement as well as "construction oversight" made this possible. You are my eternal split-apart.

Thank you to my daughter Julia, the fiercest and most no-nonsense, get-it-done person I know. You spoke truth and circled all the words that millennials would never say or do. Your encouragement and enthusiasm for my writing means everything to me.

Thank you to my warrior daughter Bridget, for convincing your friends to sit in a hot tub with me and confide the realities of current dating norms, and thank you to Chelsea Pepi and Joanna Giharldi for your honest revealing. Bridget, your intellect and keen eye for detail improved this story. Your gentle steering and illumination of problem areas was priceless.

A special shout-out to Tom and Matt for enthusiastically reading your mother-in-law's book. Your thoughtful feedback and sincere interest were most buoying and helped me get to the finish line. And, Tom, thank you for sharing your expertise as a member of the Stowe Mountain Rescue team.

Thank you to Jess Rogers for your incredible notes at the end, which spun it around but made for a better landing. And to Rebecca Condit, Susan Donaldson James, Kerri Ratcliffe, Michal Saraf, Hailey Schaeffer and Martha Sullivan Sapp, who all had a role in making this project a reality. You women are all brilliant and so generous of spirit.

Three remarkable writers coached me along this journey. Thank you, Connie May Fowler, for showing me how to hone the craft and for seeing the potential of my storytelling. Thank you, Robin MacArthur, for declaring I was almost there. I may have quit if not for your encouraging words. Thank you, Miciah Bay Gault, for being my champion. Your guidance was invaluable and, if not for you, I would never have sought publication and missed out on all this fun.

Huge thanks to the team at She Writes Press, especially Brooke Warner and Shannon Green. This book would not be in the world without your steadfast enthusiasm and talent. And much gratitude to my wise and gifted sister authors: Isidra Mendos, Lindsey Salatka, Elisa Stancil, and Susan Speranza.

The first person to ever read a word of this book was my sister, Diane, who read the first chapter and said, "Keep going." Thank you, Diane, for a lifetime of laughter, support, and daily inspiration. I was days away from sending her the finished first draft when she had an aneurysm at work and died. I was shattered and am immensely grateful for my family and friends who saw me through the days, months, and now years following her passing. She is missed beyond measure. I am crushed that she did not get to read the entire book, because she would have helped me make it better.

And finally, thank you to the strong people of Vermont, who weather storms and pandemics and continually aim to do the right thing.

ABOUT THE AUTHOR

CATHERINE DRAKE enjoys life with her husband, dog, and family in Stowe, Vermont. *The Treehouse on Dog River Road* is her first novel. To learn more, visit CatherineDrake.com or follow her on Instagram @catherinedrakewrites.

SELECTED TITLES FROM SHE WRITES PRESS

She Writes Press is an independent publishing company
founded to serve women writers everywhere.
Visit us at www.shewritespress.com.

Fire & Water by Betsy Graziani Fasbinder. $16.95, 978-1-93831-414-8.
Kate Murphy has always played by the rules—but when she meets
charismatic artist Jake Bloom, she's forced to navigate the treacherous
territory of passionate love, friendship, and family devotion.

Keep Her by Leora Krygier. $16.95, 978-1-63152-143-0. When a water
main bursts in rain-starved Los Angeles, seventeen-year-old artist
Maddie and filmmaker Aiden's worlds collide in a whirlpool of love
and loss. Is it meant to be?

Playground Zero by Sarah Relyea. $16.95, 978-1-63152-889-7. When
the Rayson family leaves the East Coast for the gathering anarchy of
Berkeley, young Alice Rayson embraces the moment in a place that's
fast becoming a cultural ground zero—and for a girl, that's no Summer
of Love.

Size Matters by Cathryn Novak. $16.95, 978-1-63152-103-4. If you take
one very large, reclusive, and eccentric man who lives to eat, add one
young woman fresh out of culinary school who lives to cook, and then
stir in a love of musical comedy and fresh-brewed exotic tea, with just a
hint of magic, will the result be a soufflé—or a charred, inedible mess?

Swearing off Stars by Danielle Wong. $16.95, 978-1-63152-284-0. When
Lia Cole travels from New York to Oxford University to study abroad
in the 1920s, she quickly falls for another female student—sparking a
love story that spans decades and continents.

The House on the Forgotten Coast by Ruth Coe Chambers. $16.95,
978-1-63152-300-7. The spirit of Annelise Lovett Morgan, who
suffered a tragic death on her wedding day in 1897, returns in 1987 and
asks seventeen-year-old Elise Foster to help her clear the name of her
true love, Seth.